"I would never bat my lashes and cry on command, Mason.

"If I want something, I use the direct approach, not deception. It's just one of those things you'll learn about me over time."

Mason stepped closer and backed Gillian against the wooden door. The warmth from his body scalded her entire length. The silk robe felt like liquid fire pouring over her flesh.

He reached out a hand and tenderly stroked the exposed skin of her throat.

"There's something you'll learn about me, too, wife-to-be." The backs of his fingers slid down the lapels of her robe. "If this wedding takes place, I'll be claiming my husbandly rights."

Gillian secretly smiled. Two could play at this game. "I have a feeling it will be my pleasure."

Marcia Evanick is an award-winning author of numerous romance novels. She lives in rural Pennsylvania with her husband and five children. Her hobbies include attending all of her children's sporting events, reading and avoiding housework. Knowing her aversion to the kitchen, she married a man who can cook as well as seemingly enjoy anything she sets before him at the dinner table.

Her writing takes second place in her life, directly behind her family. She believes in happy endings, children's laughter, the magic of Christmas and romance. Marcia also believes that every book is another adventure waiting to be written and read. As long as the adventures beckon, Marcia will have no choice but to follow where they lead. She hopes you will join her for the journey.

HIS CHOSEN BRIDE

MARCIA
EVANICK

Published by Silhouette Books
America's Publisher of Contemporary Romance

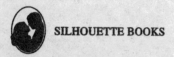

SILHOUETTE BOOKS

ISBN 0-373-51181-7

HIS CHOSEN BRIDE

Copyright © 1996 by Marcia Evanick.

Chapter 1

Gillian Barnett stood at the side of the room and watched as the party swirled, glided and mingled around her. How the society loved to throw parties. How she hated to attend them. The mandatory age of attendance was twenty. Gillian had been attending parties for over four years, and they hadn't gotten easier.

Her gaze roamed the room until it landed on the reason for her anxiety, the man she had pledged to marry within the next couple of months, Mason Blacksword. No one could accuse him of being a doting bridegroom. Since she had entered the room an hour ago he hadn't done more than raise an eyebrow at the amount of cleavage she was showing and nod his head in a greeting.

All the work she had gone through to stuff herself into the glittering spandex contraption that the saleslady had assured her would heat a man's blood was for naught. She wondered if she should demand a full refund. Mason didn't drool, stammer or break out in a sweat. He barely acknowledged her existence.

Strike up a loveless match by the Council. Although they were few and far between, for some reason their matches usually seemed to work out wonderfully, but not this one. Mason acted as if he would rather donate a major organ than even strike up a normal conversation with her. Well, the major organ she wanted was his heart and she was prepared to fight for it.

This ice blue sequin number squeezing the air out of her lungs had been her first offense. She might have lost this battle, but she was determined to win the war.

She had met Mason when she was twelve and scared to death, not only to be standing before the Council for the first time in her life, but because she was meeting the man she would marry one day. Mason had been sixteen and more a boy than the man he was today. At first she had cursed and cried against the powers of her birth. But she matured, and with age came wisdom. She learned to appreciate and accept the fact that she was a witch. Her mother was a witch, her grandmother, and even her baby sister, Raine, was a witch. Her father was a warlock, as were her twin brothers, Cullen and Kent. It stood to reason her husband would be a warlock, too. She was just having a hard time adjusting to the fact that her husband had been picked by the Council because of his sperm count, and not by her heart.

Ever since the witch-hunts in Salem, Massachusetts, in 1692, a strange and frightening thing had been occurring to the witches and warlocks around the world. They were becoming sterile. On her twelfth birthday she had been taken to a doctor and pronounced fertile. She understood the reasoning behind the Council's decision that she must marry a fertile warlock, in the hopes of

producing strong, fertile offspring. But she wished they
had gone about it in a different way. A nice list containing all the names and addresses of fertile warlocks
within a three-state radius would have been nice. Maybe
the Council would consider starting a video dating center for all fertile members of the society.

She was positive she could have picked someone
suitable to be her husband. A nice, safe man who loved
children and had a sense of humor wouldn't have been
that hard to find. *But no*... The Council had to hook her
up with Mason Blacksword, the complete opposite of
everything she would have looked for in a mate. Mason
was a control freak and she had never seen him smile,
let alone actually laugh. To top it all off, considering
his lack of response to the cut of her dress, she could
now add cold-blooded to his list of appalling qualities.

It had taken her fifteen minutes to secure the top of
her dress without having her breasts falling out every
time she took a deep breath and exhaled. She was now
positive the only thing keeping the bodice up was the
fact that it was cold in the room.

For years she had allowed Mason to set the pace and
faded into the background, but not any longer. She
wasn't that skinny little twelve-year-old who was all
arms, legs and tears, standing before the Council and
being ignored by her chosen mate. She was a woman,
all grown up. Her arms and legs were in proportion to
the rest of her five-foot-seven-inch body. Plus she had
put on quite a few pounds, all in the right areas. An
orthodontist had done wonders with her overbite, and
the short cap of blond, stringy hair had grown halfway
down her back, and with the help of miracle shampoos
it was thick and silky. Men always complimented her
on her hair or the unique color of her eyes. She thought

the color of her eyes was lifeless and dull. Whoever heard of pale blue eyes being romantic or fiery? A person couldn't drown in light blue pools. They had no spark, no soul. Every time she looked into a mirror they reminded her of pale, cold ice. How was Mason supposed to gaze deeply into them and fall madly and passionately in love with her?

Other men had gazed into them and professed love while meaning lust. A lot of men. At the age of seventeen she had naively waited for Mason to ask her to her junior prom. The thought of going out with anyone besides Mason was appalling to her romantic seventeen-year-old mind. She had waited in vain. By the time she was eighteen she had her choice of boys for her senior prom and had a wonderful time. Over the years she dated frequently, but never allowed herself to become too involved with any one man. If Mason objected to his future bride dating other men, he never voiced it.

Gillian thought of her dating as a learning experience. Since her future husband refused to court her, she needed to learn some of the ropes for when she made her move on Mason.

In two months she would be turning twenty-five, and the wedding was set for the week after her birthday. The one thing she wanted most from the marriage was happiness. She wanted to be as happy as her mother and father were in their marriage. She wanted a house full of laughing children. But most of all she wanted to love and to be loved in return. If Mason was truly the man who was destined to walk beside her for the rest of her days, she had a lot of work to do. It was time to begin the courtship.

Gillian fortified herself with another sip of ginger ale and placed her empty glass on the tray the waiter was carrying. She glanced down to make sure she was still decently covered and headed to where Mason was holding court with three elderly members of the Council. She would rather confront Mason without the Council present, but he had probably guessed that and was using them as a shield. The Council members, especially the elders, struck awe and fear into most members. But not Mason; he wasn't like most members. So why did she keep on thinking he would respond like most men? The least he could do was be curious as to what kind of wife he would be acquiring in two months. She was damned curious about her future husband.

He wasn't getting away with ignoring her from now on. The Council had gone through a lot of trouble to secure Senator Targett's formal gardens for the wedding ceremony. Of course, it hadn't hurt that the senator was one of the head elders and loved using his gardens for "arranged marriages." Her mother had dragged her to over a half-dozen bridal shops before they agreed upon a dress. The Council was handling the reception and her best friend, Tabitha, was supplying all the flowers from her shop. All she had to do was show up wearing the simple white gown and repeat her vows. Her sister, Raine, was more excited at the prospect of being in the wedding than she was. At sixteen, Raine was still looking at the world through rose-colored glasses, seeing Mason as the dashing silent hero.

Raine was one of the lucky ones—or unlucky ones, depending on your point of view. It was determined four years ago that Raine was sterile. She now had the opportunity to marry the man she loved, instead of getting married and then worrying about falling in love with her mate. She was half-envious of Raine, but her other half felt sorry for her baby sister. Raine would never be a mother, at least not naturally. Gillian was offered the chance to conceive a child, have it grow within her womb and give it life. She wanted that child, and many more. If she had to marry and bed Mason Blacksword to achieve her wish, so be it.

Gillian skirted around another waiter and avoided her mother, who appeared to be trying to get her attention. She didn't want to discuss another detail about the wedding. Every time her mother tried to talk to her lately, it was about the wedding. What kind of centerpieces did she want? Had she gone for the second fitting of the gown? Did she make a hair appointment for the morning of the wedding? Did Raine talk to her about the floppy hats Tabitha, she and her niece, Celeste, the flower girl, were supposed to wear? Raine hated the hats. The questions were endless and she was sick to death of talking about the wedding. She'd rather be spending her time talking about the groom.

She came up on the far side of the room and studied the man in question. Mason appeared to be in some debate with the elders. By the look of apprehension darkening the elders' faces, she guessed Mason was winning the argument.

She inspected her future husband. He was just a little bit over six feet, on the lean side, without being too thin and bony. His shoulders were broad and he filled the black suit he was wearing to perfection. His clothes, as always, were black as midnight and matched his conservatively cut hair. The brilliant white of his shirt set off his tanned complexion, and the gray design in his tie suited the lack of color. His preference for black would be considered grim, if not morbid, but for one fact. Mason Blacksword looked devastatingly handsome in black.

On silent feet she snuck around behind Mason and closed the distance between them. She didn't want to give him a chance to beat a hasty retreat. If he thought the elders could protect him, he had better think again. Two could play this game, and it appeared to be her turn.

Dr. Robert Lang, a noted psychologist at a famous institution on the outskirts of Philadelphia, gave her a friendly smile as she joined their group. "Gillian, so nice of you to join us."

Gillian stepped right next to Mason and tenderly laid her hand onto his arm, as if she had done it a hundred times before. She ignored the tightening of his muscles and smiled sweetly at the three elders. "Nice to see you again, Dr. Lang." She nodded at the other two men. "Dr. Lyons. Mr. Clement."

"Gillian," acknowledged Mr. Clement.

"So how's our bride-to-be? Getting nervous?" asked Dr. Lyons.

"I'm fine, Dr. Lyons." She forced her smile not to slip. "Why should I be nervous when I'm about to marry the catch of the society?" She turned her smile up a notch and faced Mason for the first time. "Right, darling?"

Her fingers, clutching his arm, trembled slightly as the muscle beneath the expensive material of his jacket turned to stone. She had a feeling she had just stepped on dangerous ground, but it was too late to turn back. How was she ever going to make something of their marriage if she ran every time Mason glared?

"Right—" Mason glanced at the low cut of her dress and growled the word "—darling."

To her ears it didn't sound like an endearment. More

like a threat. But it had fooled the elders. All three glanced at each other and grinned.

"So, Gillian, how are the wedding plans proceeding? We can't get a thing out of Mason."

Gillian batted her eyes up at Mason, not to be coy but because she feared if she met his gaze she would be turned to stone. She turned to Dr. Lang, who had asked the question. "Mamma always said if I caught the strong, silent type, I should appreciate him." She gave Mason's arm a playful squeeze that didn't dent his arm. "No one could possibly know how much I appreciate him." Laughing softly with the elders, she glanced beneath her lashes at Mason. He wasn't laughing. In fact, his face had turned more emotionless. "I've been so busy with all the plans, I barely have time to get my work done. Just today I had to run into Bloomingdale's in center city Philadelphia to register our china pattern."

"Good, good," nodded Edward Clement, the CEO of a computer software company in center city Philadelphia. "It's the little things that make a marriage."

Gillian couldn't imagine how a china pattern was going to make her marriage. When her mother and grandmother demanded she pick a pattern, she had shocked them both by picking a simple pattern of all white with three black pinstripes around the edge of the plate. When they had started to argue, she said it was either that or she was going to the novelty department to purchase the Halloween set with orange pumpkins and black bats and cats printed all over them. She even threatened to invite the Council over for dinner one night to show off her new dishes. Her mother and grandmother quickly agreed that the white china with the black stripes was perfect.

Witches and warlocks everywhere hated the commercialization of Allhallowmas and what it had done to their reputation. Never once in her twenty-four years had she whipped up a potion in a black caldron or ridden a broom across the night sky. She never cackled and there wasn't a wart anywhere on her body. If someone handed her an eye of newt she would probably faint dead away. To top it all off, she was allergic as hell to cats. She'd like to find the person or persons who started all this ridiculous talk about black, pointy hats and flying hags and teach them a thing or two.

The modern society of witches and warlocks was contributing so much to mankind, yet they received no recognition for their deeds. Fear had kept the society "underground" throughout its existence. The Salem witch-hunt back in 1692 had graphically reminded the society what could, and probably would, happen if the society went public. The Puritans had brought back devices of torture from centuries past. Who was to say these devices wouldn't be brought back, with dozens or possibly hundreds or thousands of innocent people being put to death once again. The society wasn't about to take that chance. The sad, if not ironic, truth was that not one real witch was put to death in Salem.

But she was here tonight to entice her future husband, or at least put a couple of cracks in his iron control. She wasn't going to do that if she stood around talking about china patterns and thinking about torture devices.

Gillian smiled charmingly at the elders. "Would you gentlemen mind if I stole Mason away for a few moments?" She winked at Dr. Lang. "I have this incredible urge to dance."

Dr. Lang glanced at the shadowy far end of the room, where a small band was set up and couples were entwined with each other, and grinned. "By all means, my dear." He nudged Dr. Lyons. "We might be old now, but we were all young at one time." He waved his hand toward the small dance floor. "Go on now."

Mason nodded to the elders before clasping her hand. "Come along, Ms. Barnett."

Gillian felt herself being dragged away. She glanced over her shoulder at the elders and grinned. "I just love it when he gets all formal."

The growl that rumbled in Mason's throat caused her grin to slip a notch. She glanced over her shoulder one more time before Mason stopped at the edge of the dance floor and hauled her into his arms. The three elders had their heads together and appeared to be chuckling over some private joke. She had a disturbing feeling in the pit of her stomach that she was the butt of the joke.

Mason's arms felt like a vise as he expertly stepped into a slow dance step. She concentrated on following his smooth steps and not tripping over her own two feet. The scent of his after-shave, up close and personal, flooded her senses. She had always picked up small snatches of his cologne before, but she had never been this close. It overwhelmed her reason, together with the feel of his arms. Mason Blacksword, her future husband, had finally taken her into his arms.

The fact that she had needed to trick him into dancing wasn't lost on her. But the old cliché about the end justifying the means mollified her guilty feelings. She snuggled a few inches closer and toyed with the collar of his suit with her fingertips. This was a nice beginning, being in Mason's arms. The only thing better would be if he wasn't so stiff and unyielding. She was amazed he could dance smoothly and effortlessly, but

Frankenstein on speed would have been more relaxed. It was time to up the ante.

"Relax, Mason, I'm not going to bite." Her gaze was level with his clenched jaw. She could practically hear his teeth grind. "At least not yet." That time she could hear the enamel grinding.

"Gillian…" Mason growled with deadly intent.

"Yes, darling?" She inched her fingers up higher and played with the ends of his hair against his neck. The wisps of hair felt soft and silky against the tips of her fingers.

"Stop calling me that."

"Why? We *are* about to be married. What do you want me to call you? Your Honor?" She spotted Dr. Lyons in conversation with one of the other elders, Bruce Wilson, the former gold-medal holder in three different Olympic swimming events who currently operated six recreation centers in the Philadelphia area for underprivileged children. Dr. Lyons and Bruce Wilson both looked up at her and Mason. She flashed them a grin and waved.

"Who are you waving at?"

"Our audience." She gave a lock of his hair a gentle tug. "Smile once in a while and at least pretend you're having a good time."

"I would be having a much better time if my future wife wasn't dressed like a streetwalker." He glared down at the portion of her breasts overflowing the gown. "Who in the hell picked out that outfit? You usually have better taste."

"How would you know what my taste is?" Mason never paid any attention to her, let alone her clothes. Maybe she should have listened to her grandmother. Virginia Kenwood might be seventy, but she claimed to know men. One afternoon a couple years ago Gillian had confessed how scared she was about marrying Mason, saying she wanted to find love in her marriage bed. Grandmom Ginny advised that the way to a man's heart isn't through his stomach, but a good twelve inches lower. Gillian had blushed and was extremely thankful her mother hadn't been around to hear that lascivious piece of advice. Grandmom Ginny had howled with laughter.

"That is not the kind of dress you usually wear to these events."

"Oh, hush, Mason. You never once noticed what kind of dress I wore." Gillian came to a stop the same instant the music halted.

"I..."

"Don't bother to deny it, Mason." She stepped away from the warmth of his body. "Now behave. The person who not only picked out this dress, but paid for it, is coming this way."

Mason turned around and came face-to-face with Virginia Kenwood. He nodded his head in formal greeting, "Mrs. Kenwood." He glanced over Gillian's grandmother's white chiffon hair as if searching for someone else.

"When are you going to call me Ginny? We're about to become family and I hate to stand on formalities, especially with my newest grandson."

"Very well—" he seemed to hesitate for a moment before saying the name "—Virginia." He gave her a ghost of a smile. "I must say you look stunning tonight."

Gillian glared at Mason. "That's more of a compliment than I got." Granted, her grandmother looked to be sixty instead of seventy. Her hair was neatly styled and the black dress she was wearing was made to conceal *and* highlight her figure. No one looking at Virginia Kenwood would have guessed she had conceived, carried and given life to nine babies. The shame of it was, only two proved to be fertile, and Gillian was her first grandchild to be betrothed by the Council. Her grandmother understood her anxiety and was trying to help her.

Mason glared at Gillian.

Virginia chuckled and pulled Gillian closer. "I can imagine Mason's reaction." She gave her granddaughter a loving smile and then turned to Mason. "I bet you nearly had heart failure when she first walked into the party."

"Something like that."

Virginia beamed. "Gillian, I told you it would knock his socks off."

Gillian glanced at Mason's feet. They were both still encased in expensive black leather shoes and black socks. So much for knocking his socks off.

Mason shifted his feet and asked curiously, "You told Gillian?"

"Well, of course. Who do you think dragged her into the store and made her try it on?"

Gillian grinned at Mason. The man looked as if he had swallowed a mouthful of castor oil.

"I knew it was perfect for her the moment I spotted it in the window," Ginny went on. "It matches her eyes perfectly, don't you agree?"

Mason glanced at Gillian, and she had the absurd notion he was actually comparing the light blue sequins to her pale blue eyes. In reality she knew he probably hadn't any idea what color her eyes really were.

"I bought it for her to take along on your honey-

moon, but she tells me you aren't going on one." Ginny
frowned up at her newest grandson. "Why?"

Mason jerked his gaze away from Gillian's eyes and
looked at the elderly woman. "Why what?"

"Why aren't you taking my granddaughter on a honeymoon? Every young girl wants a honeymoon."

"Grandmother," Gillian said, sighing, "I'm not a
young girl."

Mason glanced at the length of Gillian's legs before
answering Ginny's question. "I can't get away from
work right now. Things are really backed up and my
calendar is completely jammed. Maybe after everything
has calmed down at the courthouse we can take a short
vacation someplace."

"The Council might buy that excuse. I won't."
Ginny matched him stare for stare. "The date for this
wedding was set four years ago. Surely that was plenty
of time to arrange even your busy schedule."

Gillian groaned and was tempted to leave them both
facing off. Her grandmother was trying to force a dead
issue. What good would a romantic honeymoon do either one of them, if there was no romance involved?
Tropical beaches, swaying palms and quiet, starry
nights couldn't ignite a fire of passion if the spark of
desire wasn't there to begin with. She could forgive her
grandmother for trying, but Mason was a different story.

Not only wasn't there going to be a honeymoon, he
had made sure the Council knew the reasons behind his
refusal. She had picked up through the society's grape-
vine that Mason told the Council there wouldn't be a
honeymoon because he considered the marriage a nui-
sance and he wouldn't miss his work for some stupid
romantic notion that had nothing to do with him or his

marriage. Mason's words had cut deeper than she cared to admit.

If she could, she would call this entire marriage off, but she couldn't. She had sworn an oath before the Council when she was twelve to marry this man. The Council was depending upon her. The bloodline of the society was depending upon her. Generations of women had married on command, and amazingly most had found happiness and love. Her grandmother and mother before her had found both.

The odds were in her favor that she would find love. But every time she looked at Mason's emotionless face or into his dark eyes that revealed nothing, she felt the odds slip a little. Tonight the odds seemed overwhelmingly against her. She didn't know if she had the strength to fight for Mason's love and to combat her own fears.

All she wanted now was peace. If anyone was going to argue with Mason about a honeymoon, or lack of one, it was going to be her. "Grandmom, why don't you go find Mom. I'm sure she has a dozen details about the wedding she would love to run by you."

"A bride, not her mother, should be discussing the details."

"This bride has a full-time job and a very busy schedule. Picking out flowers for centerpieces I probably won't even notice doesn't excite me." She gave her grandmother a kiss on the cheek. "I trust Mom's and your judgment at this sort of thing." She gave her grandmother a wink. "Besides, I heard Gladys Bomberger bragging that no one could outdo her granddaughter's wedding last year."

"That old witch said that?" demanded Ginny.

Gillian chuckled. "Grandmom, you know how the society frowns on that kind of talk."

"Poppycock and balderdash," Ginny snapped. "I've produced more children for the society than three Gladys Bombergers combined. Her granddaughter married a mere mortal, for goodness' sake. My granddaughter's marriage is blessed by the Council and no one, and I mean no one, will attend a finer wedding this century."

Ginny turned to go, then stopped and turned back around. "Mason, I need to ask a favor from you. Could you drive Gillian home this evening? I promised her I would take her home, but I think my time would be better spent discussing the wedding."

"It's okay, Grandmom." Gillian quickly jumped in before Mason could answer. "I can call a cab. No sense taking Mason out of his way."

"Nonsense, dear," Ginny said.

"It's all right, Virginia." He gave Gillian a stern look. "I will see she gets home safely."

"Thank you, Mason. I worry about her constantly. As you must know, her 'gift' is love and compassion. I live in fear someone will try to mug her in that neighborhood she lives in and she will invite them back to her apartment, fix them dinner, then give them her television as a parting gift."

Mason raised one eyebrow in Gillian's direction but didn't comment. "You won't have to worry tonight. I'll see she gets into her apartment without the benefit of a mugging."

Ginny reached up and brushed a kiss across Mason's cheek. "Thank you, young man. I always knew those stories about you were false." She turned and threaded her way through the crowd.

Gillian watched and grinned as her grandmother made a beeline for Gladys Bomberger. The tournament of the weddings was about to begin. She should never have told her grandmother about Gladys's comment, but she had spoken before thinking. All she wanted to do was hurry her grandmother on her way, not create a society rivalry, a challenge that involved her own wedding.

She turned to Mason and stifled a laugh. The look on his face was priceless. She didn't know what flustered him more, the kiss her grandmother had given him or the comment about what people said about him.

She had heard the stories concerning Mason, but had paid little attention to them. The society was riddled with gossip and petty jealousies. Someone was always envious of someone else's gift. A gift was bestowed on every member of the society at birth by the creator of life. Every witch and warlock had a special talent. These gifts were all human qualities, only intensified. Gillian had been blessed with the gift of love and compassion. Her grandmother was partly right in her assessment of Gillian's response to a mugging.

Three months ago a kid, high on drugs, tried to steal her purse. Between her witch powers and her gift, she had talked the kid into seeking help. Last week she had spotted the boy working with a bunch of other teenagers and adults fixing up one of the local playgrounds for the kids. Gillian cherished her gift.

Mason's gift, as far as she could tell, was his control, his inner strength. He had done amazingly well for himself in such a short period of time. He graduated from law school with honors and he was one of the most respected, and youngest, judges in the county. Many members were jealous of his achievements, especially since Mason made sure everyone knew he never relied on his powers to achieve his goals.

Mason was a loner and the gossips of the society hated loners. How were they ever going to get more fuel for their tongue-lashing fires if Mason never confided in anyone? The fact that he ignored his chosen bride only fed the gossip fires. Speculation was rampant throughout the society. Was he in love with someone else? Could it be he didn't like women at all? Maybe he wasn't fertile and was afraid to admit it. Everyone knew he had his eye on a seat on the Council, but only warlocks who proved their worth by producing children could be elders. The stories were endless, and as far as Gillian was concerned, nothing but sour grapes and speculation.

The problem was that their gifts clashed. Mason demanded control, and he had none where his choice of a bride was concerned. She demanded love.

Chapter 2

Mason shifted the car into third as soon as he had turned off the country club's driveway and shot off into the night. He glanced at the woman silently sitting beside him in the dark. He thanked whatever lucky star was shining down on him that she had finally quieted down. Gillian Barnett had tempted, teased and almost single-handedly broken down his iron control. Damned if his future bride didn't have a mouth made for sin.

All evening long she had latched on to him and refused to be shaken. Tenacious didn't even begin to describe Gillian tonight. What had gotten into her? And that dress! Lord help him, but he had spent half the night trying to figure out what was holding it up, and the other half praying that it would slip.

He expertly exited the highway leading to his home in one of the better neighborhoods, then headed east toward the river and the seedier side of town, where

Gillian lived. Why would she rent an apartment in the section of town known as "The Blades"?

The newspaper's headlines almost always took place in The Blades, and none of it was good news. The gang that had taken over the once-prestigious neighborhood known as Garden Heights had destroyed it beyond recognition. The massive parks overflowing with gardens that had dotted the neighborhood had been bulldozed under to make way for housing projects. Luxury brownstone town houses had been converted into apartments, many of which were now burnt out, unlived-in or were headquarters for the drug dealers and gangs.

The brownstone where Gillian lived had been turned into six apartments. She rented a one-bedroom apartment on the ground floor. Her neighbor across the hall was an elderly gentlemen who at one time owned the old house and lived in splendor. Now he was the landlord, the maintenance department and in charge of security. The four apartments above her were rented by senior citizens—three lone widows and an elderly couple. Mason had quietly checked up on the residents and the neighborhood when he found his future wife had moved there after graduating from college. He was not pleased with her choice, but he kept his opinion to himself, knowing full well Gillian could take care of herself. Gillian's powers were undeniably strong.

"When you get to Washington Boulevard, take a right," Gillian said.

"I know where you live." He didn't want to admit he had known from the beginning, but it was beyond him to play stupid. Three months ago he had been working late in his den when an urgent feeling of danger had overcome him concerning Gillian. He had rushed to her apartment, only to spend half the night sitting in his car outside her building watching her windows. A soft, welcoming glow shone from the two massive windows that overlooked the street, and occasionally he had spotted her silhouette as she walked around the room. Bemused by the intensity of the fear he had felt for Gillian, he had watched as light after light was extinguished as she headed for bed. Whatever the danger had been, it passed. Gillian had handled the problem.

Gillian turned her head and looked at him. "You do?"

"Don't sound so surprised."

"Why shouldn't I be surprised? You've never been there before."

He wasn't about to enlighten her regarding his actions. Hell, even he didn't understand them where she was involved. He wanted nothing to do with her. He didn't want to get married, and the last thing he would ever want was a child. Yet, after all his proclamations of not wanting Gillian Barnett, he felt, in some ways, responsible for her.

"The Council notified me when you moved there."

"Why?"

He didn't like the way her fingers clutched the silver beaded purse sitting in her lap. She looked ready to chuck it, and it would undoubtedly be headed in his direction. "They felt I should know the current address of my future bride."

"Why? It wasn't as if you were planning to come a-calling, was it?"

Mason cringed inwardly at the sarcasm dripping on her words. Gillian had obviously been very upset about the lack of attention he had focused on his future bride. Curious, in spite of himself, he asked, "Did you want me to?"

Her hard glare should have turned him to stone. Without saying a word, she turned away and stared out the side window into the night.

Mason silently sighed and turned right at Washington Boulevard. The quiet setting of the country club and expensive suburban homes fell away to tall buildings, congestion and noise. It was after midnight and still the streets were crowded with cars, blaring horns and the distant sounds of sirens. People, huddling in groups, occupied nearly every stoop, taking advantage of the warm spring night.

He glanced over at Gillian as he turned off Washington and headed into The Blades. Her face was turned away, so her features were hidden from his view, but not from his memory. Gillian had the most unusual eyes. They were the color of a summer sky—piercing light blue. A man, if he was fool enough to try, could surely fall into them and float away to heaven. Her cheekbones were high, and her nose was classical. The overbite he remembered from his youth was gone. Gillian's straight teeth gleamed white in a mouth which was slightly on the generous size. Twice tonight he had caught himself staring at that mouth, wondering what it would taste like. Dangerous thoughts for a man who professed not to want anything to do with Gillian.

Her blond hair was swept up into some tousled style that looked sexy as hell. It bared the smooth skin of her neck, and the occasional disobedient wisp of hair that escaped the half-dozen pins he had spotted softened the style. Tiny blue-stoned earrings pierced her ears, and the long expanse of throat was bare of any jewelry. He didn't know what he would rather wrap around her throat—a string of diamonds to complement her beauty, or his hands for the way she caused a reaction he couldn't control. He didn't want to respond in any way to Gillian. He forced his gaze back to the road.

A moment later his glance slid off the road once again. This time it slid over her shoulders and the lush curves of her breasts. The blue sequined dress hugged every curve, leaving him a good idea of what his future bride would look like naked. The maddening thing was, it also allowed every man who saw her in that dress the same vivid picture.

When she was standing, the dress ended very demurely just above her knees. It was the only modest characteristic the garment displayed. Problem was, when she sat down, the hem slid up her thighs, which now gave him a very generous view of her legs. Gillian had legs that could make a grown man cry. He was a grown man, but he refused to cry, or even acknowledge the heat that invaded his gut every time his gaze accidentally landed on those splendid limbs.

He pulled his gaze away and silently cursed his over-imaginative hormones. This wasn't about Gillian, the woman he would be marrying in a little over two months. Gillian and his hormones never encountered each other on such a level before. Hell, as far as he knew, they had never been in the same room together. It had to be the dress that was causing this unusual reaction. The sooner she was out of it the better off he'd be.

Mason groaned a curse at the mental image that thought caused.

"Did you say something?"

His fingers gripped the wheel so hard they turned white, but he didn't look at her. He expertly maneuvered the car into a parking spot directly in front of her building. "I asked if it's safe for me to park here."

"You don't need to get out. I'm perfectly capable of seeing myself in." She reached for the door handle.

"I promised your grandmother I would see you safely inside." He turned off the ignition and pocketed the keys, glancing up and down her street. The building next to hers had a group of six men sitting on the steps. Six very big men. He raised one brow and said, "Nice neighborhood."

"I happen to like it," Gillian snapped.

Catcalls, hoots and whistles filled the air as Gillian opened the door, got out and started toward the building.

"Lord save me!" cried one of the men. "I've gone to heaven and I'm seeing angels."

"Mamma, check out the babe!" came from another.

A third called something that made Gillian cringe.

Gillian stopped before reaching the double doors to her building. Her spiked heel tapped out a deadly little tune on the concrete walk before she turned her attention to the group of men making lewd and suggestive remarks. "Chico, does your wife know you're out here making rude comments to the neighbors?"

"Oh, Gillian, you're the best thing that's happened to us tonight. We're just having a little fun."

Gillian felt Mason come up and stand beside her, but she didn't look in his direction. This was her neighborhood, and the day she would need his or anyone else's help was the day they should strip her of her Witch Society membership card.

Chico stood up and glared at Mason. "Who's the *man?*"

She felt Mason stiffen and take a protective step closer to her. Lord, save her from macho men. Mason, after all his indifference tonight, was now acting the role of a concerned date, and Chico had no right to hassle one of her escorts. "The man's my date." She shook her head at the group and walked to the door and began unlocking it.

"You holler real loud if he tries anything funny, Gilly," Chico said. "We'll teach him some manners."

Gillian gave Mason a hard look, daring him to say something. The last thing she needed tonight was Mason and some of the locals getting into it. This evening was a disaster and all she wanted to do was to see it end. Mason looked mad enough to take on the group for their comments. The man had hardly spoken to her over the years, yet he could tell her she was dressed like a streetwalker. But let her neighbors, whom she saw every day, make a few remarks, and he got indignant. She flashed Chico a smile. "I'll do that." It was an empty threat, and Mason knew it, but it felt good saying it, anyway.

The laughter of Chico and his companions followed them into the building.

Gillian unlocked her apartment door, took a step in and flipped on the lights. "There, I'm in and safe. Your duty is done."

Mason stepped into the apartment and closed the door behind him. He glanced idly around the room before saying, "Nice place."

"As in 'nice neighborhood'?" Gillian tossed her keys and purse on the counter separating the kitchen from the living room. She really didn't like Mason's condescending tone when he referred to her neighborhood. She liked living in the Garden Heights district. She especially liked living in this building. People here needed her.

"Your neighborhood has the worst reputation in the city, but your apartment is nice."

Gillian glanced around and tried to figure out what feature had caught Mason's attention so much that he would label it "nice." She thought the apartment was nice, but her nice and Mason's nice were at different ends of the spectrum.

The tiny kitchen was an ordinary one with oak cabinets and white-tiled countertops. The living room was large, and the ten-foot-high ceilings gave it an even more spacious feeling. All of her furniture had been purchased used, and the Oriental rug covering most of the wooden floor was threadbare in spots. The bedroom and bath were out of view at the rear of the apartment.

Decorating wasn't one of her passions, but she did manage to give the place a homey, lived-in feel. She purchased things because she liked them, not because they coordinated with anything else. Her couch was a green-and-white check that would have looked right at home in the country, but the green matched the green in the oriental rug. The two red wing chairs also matched the rug, and the glass coffee and end tables somehow managed to go with the group. A huge marble fireplace that took up nearly an entire wall was no longer working. She had filled the hearth with huge Boston ferns and set a porcelain three-foot-high dragon to guard the bushy forest.

All in all, the entire room looked relaxed. Just the way she wanted it. It was disconcerting to hear Mason regard her home as nice. She would have expected him to turn up his nose at such a simple abode. "Thanks for the compliment about the apartment, but I like the neighborhood, too."

Mason walked over to the porcelain dragon and

stared down at the silver-and-purple beast. "What ever possessed you to move to this neighborhood after you graduated from college?"

"It was where I was needed the most. Garden Heights was, and still is, extremely short on social workers."

"Maybe that's because one of them turned up dead last year."

Gillian shrugged her shoulders. She didn't want to think about poor Maureen O'Hare and the way she had died. Guilt assaulted her every time she did. Maureen was too young, naive and innocent to have been sent out into the neighborhood a couple of blocks over from where Gillian lived. Maureen had been hired to replace Gillian after she left the agency over a year ago to start her own business. The case should have been Gillian's.

"I like living here."

"You like coming home every night to whistles and lewd suggestions from the neighborhood thugs?"

"Chico and his buddies are harmless." Chico and his pals put on a good act at being tough. They had to. It was that, or let the neighborhood be overrun by some gang who would snatch their children and bring in drugs. Chico had a beautiful young wife named Maria and two gorgeous daughters to protect.

"They sure didn't act harmless!" Mason glanced at the array of silver-framed photos scattered across the mantel.

"Listen to their hearts, Mason, not their words." Gillian wasn't in the mood to defend Chico and his friends or to entertain Mason. She wanted to get out of this torture contraption called fashion and put her feet up and enjoy a cup of tea. Who in the hell invented high heels, anyway? She kicked the offending shoes under the coffee table and wiggled her toes.

She frowned as Mason picked up a framed photo of her and her siblings, Raine, Cullen and Kent. She knew that photo by heart. It had been taken at an amusement park the week before she was pledged to Mason. She had been twelve when the photo was taken and looked exactly as she had the first time Mason had seen her. By the way Mason kept glancing at the photo and then back at her, she knew he was trying to compare the then and now versions of Gillian Barnett.

Mason replaced the picture on the mantel without a comment. "The Council thinks you listen too much with your heart and not your mind."

"The Council knows my gift." She cautiously sat in one of the wing chairs and fumed. What right did Mason have to tell her how to think? He might be her husband soon, but he wasn't her keeper. No man was ever going to tell her how to think. If she preferred to look for the good inside every person she ran across, that was her choice. Every heart had a story to tell, and she was curious as hell about what kind of story Mason's heart could tell.

Annoyed at his pacing and with the fact that he just didn't leave, she snapped, "Sit down! You remind me of a tiger I once saw in a cage."

Mason stopped pacing at the side of the other wing chair but didn't sit. "I think we need to talk."

Gillian glanced heavenward and sighed. She couldn't stand another minute in this dress, feeling vulnerable with half her bosom hanging out. She had made an utter fool of herself showing up at the society's party dressed for seduction. Mason never so much as batted an eyelash. "If it's going to be a lengthy conversation I want to get changed first."

Mason waved his hand toward her bedroom door. "Please do."

She rose and slowly walked toward the bedroom. "There's coffee in the cabinet above the maker. I could use the caffeine."

Mason watched the enticing view of her sequin-covered bottom sway across the room before disappearing behind the door. The last thing in the world he needed was any more stimulation. He forced himself to look away from the closed door and not think about Gillian changing out of that dress. When she had mentioned getting changed, he had nearly shouted with joy. He couldn't think straight while she stood before him wearing that dress.

He turned toward the kitchen and the coffee. Anything she put on would be better than that dress. He was praying for a ratty old bathrobe and fuzzy slippers. Something disgustingly big and bulky. Something that would hide the lushness of her breasts and the curve of her hips. He didn't want to be thinking about Gillian and sex, especially when he asked her what he wanted to ask her.

He wanted Gillian to go to the Council and call off the wedding.

Five minutes later he sat at the counter drinking a cup of coffee and trying to decide what was the best way to approach Gillian with his request. He couldn't go before the Council and make such a plea. They had put him through college and law school and allowed him to achieve his chosen career. They were helping him put his younger sister, Kara, through med school, and they had granted his mother permission to remarry outside of the society. His mother deserved the happiness she had finally found with Walt Martin. How could he possibly refuse to do the one thing the Council had asked of him, to marry Gillian Barnett?

Gillian would have to be the one to plead with the Council. There was no way around it. Surely with her gifts of love and compassion the Council wouldn't sentence her to a loveless marriage. The Council had to be stern and insistent in their dealings and laws governing the society, but they weren't heartless.

Mason heard the bedroom door open and made the mistake of glancing up. The coffee he was in the midst of swallowing went down the wrong pipe as he spotted Gillian. She was indeed dressed in a robe, but it wasn't bulky or ratty. The Oriental-style garment was made of pure silk and was brilliant red. It covered her from neck to ankle, but it was anything but discreet. Red silk wrapped around her body like a pair of lover's hands.

He regained his breath as she entered the kitchen, gave him a strange look and poured herself a cup of coffee.

"Are you all right?"

"Yeah." He frowned at his cup and silently dared the dark brew to defy him again before taking another sip. This time the liquid went down the right pipe and he risked taking another look at Gillian. The robe was indeed Oriental. The red silk was shot through with gold and black threads, making intricate patterns around the wrists, hem and lapels. Across the entire back was a delicately embroidered, fierce-looking dragon half-obscured by the flowing length of her blond hair, which she had let down.

The way the silk clung to her every curve as she made her way into the living room and sat back down made him wonder what exactly she had on under the robe. Mason's gut told him the change into the robe hadn't helped one bit. His concentration was still shot to hell.

He poured himself some more coffee and followed her into the living room. For the first time in his life he wished he wasn't a warlock and banned from all alcohol. A witch or warlock could do unforeseen damage while intoxicated, hence the banning. He could surely use something a lot stronger than coffee right about now.

"What did you want to talk about?" Gillian took another sip of coffee and set the cup down on the table.

Mason placed his full cup next to hers and cleared his throat. "The wedding."

Gillian sighed. Now he wants to talk about the wedding? Where was he four months ago when all the plans were being discussed? Where was he when the Council wanted approval for the catered menu? Where was he when her mother dumped six monstrous books of invitations in front of her and told her to pick one? She knew exactly where he had been—at work or at home enjoying his solitude. Her one and only phone call to him had netted her nothing but a pat "You handle it, Gillian. I have work to do."

"What about the wedding? Most of the decisions have been made, Mason. It's a little late to make any major changes."

"I don't want to make any changes. I'm sure whatever you've decided will be perfect."

Gillian raised an eyebrow at that one. Her tastes usually didn't follow tradition, a fact her mother and grandmother had repeatedly pointed out to her over the past couple of months. "What did you want to discuss then?"

"I want you to do me and yourself a favor."

"What type of favor?" The intensity of his dark gaze was making her nervous. Whatever he was about to ask had to be important. From what she knew about Mason, he wasn't the kind of guy who asked favors.

"I want you to go to the Council and ask them to release you from your pledge."

The only outward sign of the shock that rocked her body was her eyes. She blinked twice. "Are you referring to my pledge to marry you?" No one had ever requested to be released from their marriage pledge before. It just wasn't done.

"Yes."

Gillian felt her heart skip a beat. Mason didn't want to marry her! Well, that shouldn't have surprised her. He had made it very clear more than twelve years ago that he didn't want to marry her. And nothing he had done since then had given her any hope that he had changed his mind. "Why do you want me to approach the Council? If you don't want to marry me, you should be the one requesting the release from your pledge."

"I can't."

She could see by his expression that he was fighting some internal monster. "Why not?" She refused to allow her overzealous compassion to rule her head. Everyone had monsters to slay, including herself.

Mason lowered his gaze to his hands before raising it back to her. "Honor."

Gillian felt as if she had just been slapped. Mason wouldn't request the release because he felt honor-bound to the society, yet he thought it was okay for her to make such a plea. Her voice shook with anger. "You think I have no honor?"

"I didn't say that, Gillian." He stood up and paced to the windows overlooking the street. "You misinterpreted my words." He pulled back the heavy curtain and stared out into the night.

"Then explain to me why you can't go before the Council because of honor, yet I can."

Seconds ticked by before he asked, "Who paid for your education, Gillian?"

She would have preferred that he at least turn around and face her when talking to her, but if he chose the darkness of the night, so be it. "My parents."

"The Council paid for mine. My mother couldn't afford to send me across town, let alone through law school. My father died when I was twelve."

She knew all about Mason's father. There wasn't a member of the society who didn't. Mason's father was one of the rare warlocks who had been shunned by the society, not only because he broke the ban concerning alcohol, but because he deserted his wife and three children. Gillian didn't know how the Council stripped Mason's father of his powers, only that they had. Clint Blacksword had died a vagrant's death, alone and drunk, in some back alley two years after he had deserted his family. Mason's mom had raised him and his two younger sisters on her own without the help of the society, until Mason graduated from high school. Then they insisted on helping with his education.

"The Council never would have put you through school if they hadn't thought you were worthy of it." What did his education have to do with their upcoming marriage?

Mason glanced over his shoulder at her for a moment. "Thanks."

"Only stating the truth, Mason. You are a wonderful judge and this city is very grateful for your services." The city might be grateful, but the criminals weren't. Mason had a reputation in the courtroom for being notoriously tough on the criminals.

"Last year the Council granted my mother permission to remarry outside of the society."

"I've met Walt Martin. He's a very nice man and appears to be deeply in love with your mother. Why wouldn't the Council grant such a request?"

"It means a lot to me that my mother has found some happiness."

"That's nice, Mason. But I don't see the connection between who paid for your education, your mother remarrying and calling off our wedding."

Mason's grip turned white as he clutched a handful of curtain. "I can't go back on my word to the Council, Gillian. It has to be you who requests the release."

Gillian stood and carried her empty cup to the counter at the opposite end of the room. Her fingers trembled so badly the cup clattered against the saucer the entire length of the living room. She turned around and faced Mason. "We have a problem then, don't we?"

"What problem?"

"I can't break my word to the Council, either, Mason. They might not have paid for my education or granted my mother a special request, but they are our ruling elders who govern the society as a whole. When I was twelve, I gave them my word to marry you. I won't go back on that pledge now." She clasped her hands together and raised her chin a notch. "I, too, have something called honor."

"Is your honor strong enough to see you through a loveless marriage?" Mason snapped.

Gillian's teeth sank into her lower lip to still its trembling. No, her honor wasn't strong enough to see her through a loveless marriage. She was determined to move heaven or hell to make this marriage work, one way or another. There was only one thing that could derail the entire situation. "Do you love someone else?" If Mason's heart was already spoken for, their marriage didn't stand a chance.

He seemed to take a long time before he spoke. "No." His hot gaze scorched her from head to toe with one long look. "I don't believe in love, Gillian. Can you give your body to a man, night after night, who doesn't love you?"

She tried to listen to his heart, but he wouldn't let her in. He had thrown up shields at every angle. Mentally he was like stone, cold and hard. The emotional shields were made of solid ice, burning her gentle probing at the slightest touch.

Could she give herself to Mason, night after night? Good question, and one she didn't have an answer for. He certainly was a handsome man, and physically he could hold his own with what the latest Hollywood heartthrob had to offer. But would his touch be as cold as his shields were now? Could she stand it if it was? So many questions without answers.

She knew he was a caring man by the way he talked about his family. He was concerned for his mother's happiness, and she knew he was helping to finance his sister Kara's education through med school. His other sister, Amy, was married to a nice warlock named Brandon. They had just adopted four-year-old twin boys from Russia, and if rumors were correct, Uncle Mason had helped out with the adoption fees and footed the bill for the remodeling and furnishing of the boys' bedroom. Mason Blacksword didn't strike her as a man without a heart.

As long as he possessed a heart, he was capable of loving. It was that slim hope that held her future. "I'm sorry, Mason. If you want to break the pledge, you'll have to speak to the Council."

"You would marry me knowing that I would never love you?"

The hard edge in his voice plunged into her heart. He would never love her. Never was an awfully long time. If she was honest with herself, she had to admit she didn't love Mason now. It was very doubtful she would fall madly in love with him before the wedding. She didn't know Mason. She doubted if anyone really knew him. He wouldn't allow anyone, except his family, to get that close to him. Well, in a little over two months she would be family. It would be hard for him to hide when she was living with him, especially if he was forbidden to erect any shields against her.

Of course the same held true for her. She couldn't erect any to keep Mason out. He would have an open view to her soul, if he chose to look. This whole issue of marriage was becoming much more complicated than she ever dreamed possible. She wanted a marriage like her parents', filled with love, happiness and children. Why did her dream seem so terribly out of reach?

She was tired, bone tired. Between work and the upcoming wedding, her days weren't long enough to fit everything in. To top it off, her sleep had been fitful at best. She didn't need this now. What she did need was eight hours of uninterrupted sleep—with no fears snatching away that precious, sleep-filled bliss.

With a weary sigh she pushed away from the counter and walked to the door. Her left hand gripped the knob. "Listen, Mason, this isn't getting us anywhere." She turned the knob and opened the door. "There's only one way for the wedding to be called off, and that's if the Council calls it off. If you want out, go talk to the Council. I'm not the one forcing you into this."

Mason slowly walked across the room without taking his gaze off her. "But you're the one who could put an end to it."

"What makes you think I have the power to sway the Council into making a momentous decision and releasing us from our pledge?" The idea was crazy. No one had ever been released from a marriage contract, and as far as she knew, no one had ever asked. She wasn't going to be the first.

Mason stopped in front of her. "You have the power. Bat those baby blues and pour on some tears. You'll have them granting you any request within minutes."

"I never bat my lashes and cry on command, Mason. If I want something, I use the direct approach, not deception. It's just one of those little things you will learn about me over time."

Mason stepped closer and backed Gillian against the wooden door. The warmth from his body scalded her entire length. The silk of her robe felt like liquid fire pouring over her flesh, over skin that had never before felt so alive.

He reached out a hand and tenderly stroked the exposed skin of her throat. "There's something you'll learn about me, too, wife-to-be." The back of his fingers slid down the lapels of her robe and brushed across a breast. "If this wedding takes place, I'll be claiming my husbandly rights."

Gillian felt the fire from his touch through the robe. Her nipples hardened into twin points of pleasure, begging to be touched. She held his heated gaze with every ounce of strength left inside her. He was trying to scare her away. What was he, crazy? Did he actually believe his touch would repulse her?

She allowed her glance to caress his body slowly and seductively. She secretly smiled as his body grew taut. He wasn't as immune to her as he wanted her to think. Two could play this game. "I have a feeling you claiming your husbandly rights will be my pleasure."

Mason dropped his hand as if she burnt him and uttered a curse that made Gillian chuckle. She had heard worse on the streets of The Blades, but never once suspected Mason would use the word. "Shame on you, Mason. What would the Council think if they heard you say that word, in front of a lady, no less?"

Mason turned and stormed out of the apartment and into the night without saying another word. She closed and locked the door. Wearily, she leaned against it and closed her eyes. What was the matter with her, baiting Mason like that? He had clearly been upset about the upcoming wedding. Where was all this compassion she was so privileged to receive as one of her gifts? She should have been comforting him and easing the strain between them instead of escalating it.

She opened her eyes, stared down at the front of her robe and groaned in humiliation. Two berry-size nipples were pushing against the silk of her robe, still begging for Mason's touch. Desire still burned deep within her belly. He had felt her reaction. There was no way she could have hidden that response from his gaze. Mason Blacksword had left tonight knowing that his wife-to-be wanted him.

Chapter 3

Gillian unlocked her office door and bent down to retrieve the scattered mail lying across the threadbare carpet. Two days' worth of advertisements, junk mail, bills and hopefully some checks had been shoved through the tiny mail slot with a vengeance. She dropped the mail on the corner of her desk and headed for the small coffeepot she kept in the corner of the room. The office she had rented was a twelve-by-twelve room, with a cubby-size closet and an even smaller powder room. The rent was cheap because it was located in the center of the worst area in the entire city, but she had a nice chrome plaque on the door with her name and occupation: Gillian Barnett, Child Support Recovery Investigator.

As the coffee dripped through the filter she watered the half-dozen plants scattered about the bland off-white office. The day she opened her office she had bought herself a nice low-maintenance philodendron to sit on the corner of her desk, just to brighten up the place. She had five different plant deliveries her first day. Most were from her family, one was from her best friend, Tabitha, and one was from the Council; all wished her well. None had been from Mason. Her office was beginning to feel like a jungle, as the greenery grew and overtook anything within its path.

The two side windows, overlooking an alley and the scarred brick of another building, were heavily barred. The sun streaking through the thick bars cast a sinister shadow across the room. She didn't like the bars—they made her feel trapped—but she understood their purpose. Hidden in an old locked cabinet, behind her desk, was the heart of her business, a computer. At first glance, her office appeared to hold nothing of value, just as she had planned. The thought of replacing the computer had been enough to make her go through the inconvenience of having the cabinet custom-made to appear worthless. So far her trick had worked. In the eighteen months she had been in business the worst thing that had happened was someone had swiped the chrome plaque on her door twice. She could live with that.

She poured a cup of coffee and carried it to her desk. She had two hours to kill before she was due in court. Her fingers trembled slightly as she set the cup down and smoothed a wrinkle from her navy linen skirt. The suit she had put on this morning was modest, respectable and downright boring. It was one of three suits she wore to court. The honorable Judge Blacksword's court, to be more precise. Mason's court.

With a heavy sigh she sat down and took a sip of coffee. She wondered how he was going to react to seeing her in his court. They hadn't seen each other in over a week—since the night he asked her to call off the wedding and stormed out of her apartment. Knowing Mason, he would look right through her as he always did and pretend she was just another lawyer.

She wasn't a lawyer, and never wanted to be one. Her clients had the right to represent themselves, but they weren't sure of themselves or the law. They also couldn't afford a lawyer, so they hired her to handle all the paperwork and to make sure the judge would issue a court order. It was all pretty simple and straightforward, once you waded through the paperwork and located the culprit who was refusing to pay child support.

This was to be the last court appearance she would have in front of Mason. The wedding was now less than two months away, and sooner or later they were going to have to make the announcement to the general public. Mason would no longer be able to grant her any court orders without someone crying "conflict of interest." He would never grant her or anyone else a special favor within his court. It just wasn't in his character. But there were only a few in the current judicial system who would believe in such honesty. Fewer still practiced it.

Gillian picked up the pile of mail and started to sort through it. The top three pieces landed in the circular file without even being opened. The next two were small weekly payments from two of her previous clients. The note from Clair Addams brought a smile to her mouth. Clair wanted to let her know that the children were so grateful for everything she had done that they named their new kitten after her. Gillian was a six-week-old orange tabby who loved getting scratched behind her ears, drinking warm milk and playing with spools of thread.

Another advertisement joined those in the wastebasket. Gillian reached for the next envelope and froze.

Fear pulsated throughout her body as her fingers stopped an inch from the plain white envelope. It was happening again!

Gillian closed her eyes and tried to concentrate on the sender. A lot of the time her powers would enable her to visualize the person. Not this time. All she could pick up was the sender's dark, deep and twisted hatred. He—and she was positive it was a he—was one sick individual.

She slowly backed away from the letter. She wanted to throw the thing away, but knew she couldn't. She had to open it and find out what was so important that he mailed her another letter.

Cautiously she picked up a letter opener and slit the envelope. Using the opener and a pen, she pulled the single sheet of paper from the envelope and anchored it open. Six short words were neatly cut from different magazine articles and pasted onto the paper: Your Time To Pay Is Coming.

Gillian felt shivers slip their way down her spine and cursed her moment of weakness. She shouldn't have been scared. Whoever was sending her the notes couldn't harm her. A mere mortal could never hurt someone with her powers. Yet, for some reason, she felt terror quake in her belly.

As carefully as possible, and making sure she didn't touch the paper, she slid the note back into the envelope. She studied the typed envelope. No return address and it was postmarked within the city. Whoever was sending the threats was close by. This was the third letter she received in the past two months.

The first one she wrote off as someone's joke. The second had given her pause. This one terrified her. The hatred poured from the paper as if it was a tangible thing. She hadn't the first clue as to what to do with the notes. There were a couple of members of the society who were in the police department, and she was positive they would run a fingerprint test on the note if she asked them. That was the problem. If she asked them, they would feel duty-bound to mention it to the Council, and they would feel duty-bound to tell Mason.

She didn't want Mason learning about the threats. He wasn't too happy with her choice of careers as it was. The last thing she needed was for him to start harping on her about going to work every day. She didn't understand Mason's dislike of social workers and he hadn't bothered to explain himself. That was one of the things he would have to do once they were married.

The first important step to a good marriage was communication. As long as they communicated with each other, they might be able to make the marriage work. She might never agree with a lot he had to say, but she was willing to listen. Problem was, he wasn't talking. Mason rarely talked and never explained himself.

The road to a happy marriage was littered with boulders, rock slides and mile-deep potholes. She wasn't looking forward to traveling down that particular road, but there wasn't a detour sign anywhere.

With a heavy sigh she opened the bottom drawer of the desk and pulled out a manila folder. Very carefully she placed the envelope containing the note in the folder. It joined the first two notes. This was no longer someone's idea of a joke, and it surely wasn't a coincidence. Whoever was sending the notes was serious. Dead serious.

She placed the folder in the center of her desk and stared at it while finishing her coffee. Whoever had sent the threats was obviously a deadbeat father she had caught up with and filed a court order against to have mandatory income withheld from his paycheck. The warning that it would soon be her time to pay was too telling.

A quick, rough estimate of how many court orders she had filed since starting the business was thirty-five to forty. Two more appearances were already scheduled, including the one this morning. Filing for a court order was the easy part of her business; all it required was paperwork. The hard part, and the part she enjoyed the most, was tracking down the unsupportive fathers. She liked pitting her mind against a person bent not only on breaking the law but on being irresponsible where his own children were concerned.

Any one of the thirty-five to forty men could be responsible for the threats. None of them had wanted to be found in the first place and every one of them could be harboring a hatred for her. This afternoon, as soon as she was done in court, she would boot up the computer and compile a list of all the deadbeat fathers she had found.

She placed the folder back in the bottom drawer and finished going through the remaining mail. She wanted to arrive at court early to observe Mason while he was in his element.

Forty-five minutes later Gillian quietly slid into an empty seat in the back of the courtroom and silently contemplated the man beneath the black robe. With the lift of one black brow he had silenced a cluster of squawking lawyers, plunging the room into an eerie hush. No one dared to breathe loudly for fear of provoking further retaliation from the judge. Gillian grinned.

The Honorable Judge Blacksword was magnificent, but then, she knew he would be. He always was, and it would take more than a bunch of whiny, demanding lawyers dressed in expensive suits to throw him off his stride. This was his court and he wasn't afraid of letting everyone know it.

Desire ignited throughout Gillian's body as Blacksword's dark and intense gaze landed on her. She mustered a cocky grin that belied the riot of emotions storming her body, then stared back. Her treacherous body remembered the heat of his touch. It was as if he was touching her again. Her breasts swelled slightly and her nipples hardened into twin points of desire against the lace of her bra. Her heart picked up its pace and her mouth went dry. How could he do all this to her with only a look?

A small victory was hers when he looked away first. She glanced down at the briefcase sitting on her lap and sighed. If only all the victories were that easy.

Mason Blacksword's dark and dangerous looks kept most people at arm's length. He was devastatingly handsome with his dark hair, long, flowing black robes and his preference for dark clothes. Mason Blacksword was the personification of a modern-day warlock and, in her eyes, sexy as sin. He was also her chosen groom. In less than two months she was going to become the warlock's bride!

Ten minutes later Gillian met her nervous client, Rosa Gonzalez, outside the courtroom doors and tried to reassure her. "Listen, Rosa, everything is going to be okay. Juan isn't here. In fact, he knows nothing about this court order. He won't find out until he receives his first paycheck minus child support."

Gillian reached out and squeezed Rosa's hand. "It'll be over with in five minutes."

Rosa gave her a fleeting smile before returning her attention to her young sons. Four-year-old Juan Jr. was lifting two-year-old Jésus up to get a drink from the water fountain. "They haven't seen their father in over a year."

"That's his decision, not theirs, Rosa. Your ex-husband has visiting rights, and if he wishes not to use them, that's his choice. But it doesn't mean he shouldn't be financially responsible for the children he helped to create." Gillian glanced at her watch and frowned. "We better head in just in case they're ahead of schedule. Judge Blacksword doesn't like to be kept waiting." It was the understatement of the year, but she didn't want to make Rosa more nervous.

She turned to open the courtroom door for Rosa and her sons when it was snatched out of her hands and she was forced back. A small fortune in suits came hustling out of the doors, each one containing a grumbling lawyer. Gillian's smile grew as she caught snatches of their complaints.

A few young lawyers, who had obviously never appeared in front of Mason before, seemed awestruck. A couple of the older lawyers cursed his black heart and their rotten luck to have him presiding over their appeal. Their client, a young son of a famous suspected Mafia leader, had been busted with a couple of kilos of cocaine, and they had unsuccessfully tried to get him off with just a slap on the wrist and a fine for possession of a narcotic for recreational use. Judge Blacksword had laughed them out of his court.

Gillian hustled Rosa and the boys in just as the bailiff

called their case. Gillian gave Rosa a reassuring smile and led her to the front of the room.

Ten minutes later the court order was approved. The court would make sure it was promptly served, and Rosa would be receiving a child-support check directly from the courts, starting with her ex-husband's next paycheck.

Gillian's only disappointment was that Rosa's ex-husband didn't have any assets the court could order him to sell to make up for the back support he hadn't paid. She was pleased with the outcome, even if it was predictable. She had never been denied a court order, thanks to her expertise and how meticulously precise she was with her paperwork.

She wasn't disappointed that Mason seemed to look right through her and treated her with the same professional, if reluctant, courtesy he normally displayed toward everyone in his courtroom.

Gillian grinned at Rosa. "See, I told you it would only take a few minutes."

Rosa glanced around the courtroom looking a little bemused. "That's all there is to it?"

"He was already ordered once by the court to pay support when you filed for divorce. The amount had been set previously, so all we needed to do this time was prove he left his former employer and stopped paying support. Now that we located his new employer, the court order will see to it that child support will be taken out of his paychecks once again."

Rosa grabbed Jésus's arm as he tried to climb over the back of one of the benches. "How can I thank you?"

Gillian grinned at Jésus and Juan. They were charming little boys with mischievous eyes and killer smiles.

"Take good care of your sons, Rosa. They're a very precious gift."

Rosa beamed proudly.

"Ms. Barnett?"

Gillian turned and smiled at Bill Grayman, the court's bailiff. "Hello, Bill. What can I do for you?" She had known Bill for over a year. He was a permanent fixture in Mason's court.

"His Honor would like to see you in his chambers when you are finished."

Gillian glanced around the courtroom and noticed everyone was leaving for the lunch break. Mason must have called a recess, and she had been so busy talking to Rosa she hadn't even noticed. She kept her smile friendly. "Thanks, Bill."

Rosa wrung her hands together. "Is something wrong?"

"No, Rosa, I know the judge. We go back pretty far. He probably wants to give me a message from my grandmother."

Bill gave her a strange look. "Do you need me to stick around?"

"No, Bill, you go ahead to lunch. I know my way." She gave Rosa a nod as she snapped her briefcase closed. "Why don't you treat the boys to lunch and celebrate before you drop them off at the sitter's? Things should be getting easier for you once the checks start coming back in."

Rosa reached for Gillian's hand. "Thanks, Gillian, for all you've done. I'll start sending you your fee as soon as the checks start arriving."

"Take care, Rosa, and let me know if you have any more problems getting the child support. You shouldn't, but sometimes ex-husbands don't stay where they should.''

"You think Juan will run again?''

"It's possible, but he'll be notified that if we have to get another court order to attach his wages, the court won't be too happy with him." Gillian gave Rosa's hand a gentle squeeze before releasing it. "Don't worry about what might happen, Rosa.''

Gillian watched as Rosa and the boys left the courtroom. Bill, who was standing by the door, gave her another strange look, before following Rosa and the noisy boys out the door. What did Mason want that was so important that he summoned her to his chambers? Never once had he acknowledged her as anything other than a guest in his court. Now, at her last appearance in front of him, he wished to see her in his chambers.

She smoothed down her jacket, picked up her briefcase and headed for the door that led to his chambers. All he probably wanted was to ask her to call off the wedding again. She wondered if he visualized a noose being slipped around his neck and the Council tightening it. If he was going to fight against the marriage at this late stage, it served him right. He should be suffering nightmares about nooses and balls and chains. She might not be one hundred percent for this marriage, but she'd be damned if she would be left standing at the altar.

Taking a deep breath, she knocked lightly on his door. A moment later his deep voice responded, "Come in.''

Gillian opened the door and stepped into his chambers. She watched as he hung up his robe on an old-fashioned coatrack behind his desk. "You wanted to see me?'' Curiously, she glanced around the room. So this was where her future husband spent all his time. It was impressive looking, she'd grant him that. Two entire walls were nothing but bookshelves crammed with an entire forest of legal volumes. A massive desk sat in the center of the room. It looked both expensive and old.

"Close the door, Gillian." He walked around the desk and nodded toward a burgundy leather sofa. "I think we need to talk."

She closed the door and placed her briefcase near the sofa before taking a seat. "About what? The court order you just granted?"

"No. I granted the order because once again you had done your homework and everything was in order. If it wasn't, I would never have approved it."

"I know." Somewhere in his statement, she was positive, there was a compliment. She crossed her legs and tugged the hem of her skirt over her knees. She should have worn high heels instead of the navy flats. But this morning she had been dressing for comfort and hadn't given one thought to the way high heels enhanced her legs. "So if this isn't a business call, what's it about? Pleasure?"

Mason lowered himself onto the other end of the couch. "I want you to tell me why you were afraid this morning when you first entered the room."

Gillian silently groaned and studied her fingers twisting themselves into knots on her lap. She should have known Mason would have picked up on her fear the minute she walked into the courtroom. The incident with the letter was too recent to hide her fears. Mason was too perceptive, and she was too open. Lying to Mason never crossed her mind. She gave a casual shrug of her shoulders. "It's a business matter. Don't worry, I'm handling the problem."

He continued to stare at her for a long moment. "Need any help?"

"No thanks." It shouldn't have surprised her that he had offered to help. Although Mason didn't seem like the kind of guy who went around rescuing damsels in distress, she was about to become his wife. She knew it would seem tacky if she landed on the front page of a newspaper knee-deep in trouble.

She didn't like the way Mason kept staring at her as if trying to decide what to say next. She had thrown up her shields as soon as she realized Mason had picked up on her fear. The last thing she wanted him to sense was her desire for him.

"Was that what you wanted to discuss?" Gillian asked. "A little business problem I'm having at the moment?"

"No." He gave the knot in his tie a tug and undid the top button of his shirt. He shot her a peculiar look and said, "I wanted to apologize."

Gillian was so startled that her shields dropped for a moment. She quickly put them back up and stammered, "Apologize for what?"

"For my behavior the other night."

It was a good thing the door was closed. The slightest draft would have knocked her off the couch. Mason was apologizing for his behavior the other night! What was next, the earth falling off its axis and spinning wildly throughout the galaxy? "What part of your behavior are you apologizing for?" She could count quite a few things he should be apologizing for, starting with telling her she looked like a streetwalker and ending with asking her to call off the wedding.

"There are a couple things I need to apologize for."

Gillian narrowed her gaze. Mason had his shields up, too, so she couldn't read him, but she was getting a strange feeling in the pit of her stomach. Mason initiating the conversation was weird enough to begin with. His acting friendly and cordial was bizarre. But having Mason apologize to her was downright frightening. She should run, not walk, from the room. Curious, she stayed seated and met his gaze. "I can't accept your apology until I know what you're apologizing for."

"First, my comment concerning your dress was both uncalled-for and insulting."

She blinked and rapidly closed her mouth, which had fallen open.

"You looked quite attractive and stunning in that dress." He continued to stare at her. "If I'm going to be totally honest with you, I have to say you were the most beautiful woman at the party."

No amount of trying could convince her mouth to close this time. Mason thought she was beautiful? A fiery flush of pleasure swept up her cheeks. Lord, she was in trouble now. He really must be desperate to get out of the marriage if he was resorting to compliments. She gazed down at her hands and mumbled a polite "Thank you."

"I also want to apologize for asking you to ask the Council to call off the wedding and for my behavior when you refused."

Her gaze jerked to his face. He was serious. Dead serious.

"I won't give an excuse for my discourteous conduct—there is none. But I would like to say that the stress of our upcoming wedding has been playing on my mind lately." He gave a slight shrug of his shoulders and relaxed back into the corner of the couch. "I would like to consider the whole incident as a case of 'cold feet.'"

Cold feet! There was a big difference between second thoughts and opposition. Mason had always been opposed to the wedding. He was playing at something, and she hadn't the first clue as to what. For now, her only option was to play along until she learned what the game was. "Apology accepted."

Mason's mouth gave a ghost of a smile. "Thank you."

She looked away from the seductive fullness of his lower lip. The last thing she needed was to be fantasizing about what his kisses would taste like or what he would look like when he smiled. *Devastating* was her gut reaction on both counts. Why was her body having such a hard time remembering this was the man who didn't want to marry her? "So you decided to speak to the Council yourself?"

"No."

"No?"

"I've decided the marriage might not be such a bad idea after all."

"You're kidding?"

"I never kid, Gillian."

She knew that. Everyone knew that. Mason never kidded around. Never joked. Hell, he never even smiled. "What changed your mind?"

"I figured the Council will never give me a moment's peace until I do marry." He gave a casual shrug of his shoulders. "Might as well be you."

"Jeez, Mason. You say the sweetest things." The sarcasm in her voice was thick enough to choke a pig.

"I figured you for a person who would rather have honesty than pretty words."

"When have you ever used pretty words, Mason?" He was right about the honesty, but a few pretty words wouldn't have gone unnoticed. In several weeks, everyone, including him, would expect her to share his bed. "Might as well be you" wasn't her idea of foreplay.

"With my busy schedule, I don't have time for flowery speeches and unnecessary words."

"Three minutes ago you called me beautiful." She wasn't going to let him forget that.

"You are a beautiful woman." His glance wandered over her body for a quick moment. "I was only stating the truth."

Sweet fire burned throughout her body wherever his gaze landed. How could he sit there so calm and collected when she felt like a tumbleweed blowing through a blazing town? Sooner or later she was going to be blown directly into the flames. "So the wedding is still on?"

"It was never off."

She raised an eyebrow. "Only in your dreams."

"I don't dream."

"Ever?" She had never heard of someone who didn't dream. Was it even possible or did he control his mind so tightly that he refused to allow it such nonsense?

"Never."

"Maybe you just don't remember them. I heard that a person has three to five dreams a night, but they're lucky to remember just one."

"I don't dream, Gillian, therefore there is nothing to remember." He stood up. "I have to grab something to eat before court resumes. Would you care to join me?"

Gillian stood up and reached for her briefcase.

"Uh...no, thank you." Normally she would have grabbed the chance to have lunch with Mason. "I don't think it would look too proper if we're seen together enjoying a meal right after you ruled on my court order."

"That reminds me—" he picked up his suit jacket and put it on "—I don't think it's a good idea for me to be hearing any more of your cases."

"I already thought of that. My next appearance is before Judge Cronan." Why hadn't she noticed before how wide his shoulders were? She watched, fascinated, as they slipped inside the black jacket.

"He's a good, fair judge." He walked her to the door.

"I know." She stopped before the door. "Can you do me one favor?" She glanced at his mouth. Either she was very brave, or very foolish. At this point she didn't know which, but her curiosity was killing her.

"What?"

The childish proverb thundered across her brain: *Curiosity killed the cat!* She ignored the thunder and asked, "Kiss me?"

Mason went utterly still, his hand gripping the knob. He stared at her for a long, hard moment. His gaze seemed permanently locked on to her mouth. "You want me to kiss you?"

Gillian noticed the rough edge to his voice and couldn't decide if it was from horror or desire. "We'll be doing more than that in seven weeks."

One black brow rose high on his forehead and a glint of something that might have been laughter gleamed in his eyes. "True." He released the doorknob and stepped closer.

She forgot to breathe as his head lowered and his

mouth claimed hers. The sweet pressure of his lips drew her in closer. She wanted to taste more, to feel more. The warmth of his suit jacket heated her fingers as they roamed up the lapels, over the shoulders, to toy with the ends of his hair caressing his neck.

Mason hauled her closer and deepened the kiss. A groan of desire rumbled up his throat and into her mouth. The heat of the kiss turned into an inferno of need.

Her breasts were crushed against his chest and the door pressed against her back. And still she wanted to be closer. How was it possible to want a man so badly it ached and burned at the same time? She met the thrust of his tongue with a soft, seductive sweep of her own.

Hands roamed over her hips. Strong, capable hands caressed her body with feverish intent. She arched her hips forward and felt the full length of his arousal press against her abdomen.

Liquid fire pooled at the junction of her thighs. Her nipples tightened and ached for his touch. Emptiness filled her soul as he released her mouth and trailed a moist path of kisses down her throat.

The modest neckline of her blouse stopped his descent miles away from where she wanted him. She thrust her breasts outward and silently cursed their clothes and their surroundings. "Mason?"

His fingers flexed against the curve of her bottom and his hips arched forward. His tongue drew an enticing circle around the indentation at the base of her throat. "Hmm…"

Her head leaned against the door and she focused on the white plaster ceiling above, not on the delicious sensations Mason was causing. She had to call a halt to this before it got any more out of control. They were in his chambers, for crying of loud. Anyone could come by; this was a public building. She was surprised that Bill Grayman hadn't come to check up on her yet. He had given her enough strange looks moments before. Mason's reputation as a judge could be in jeopardy if he was caught in such a position. She knew Mason well enough to realize their upcoming marriage would never survive if she jeopardized his career.

She had the answer she had been seeking. Mason did desire her. The second line to the children's proverb brought a smile to her lips. *And satisfaction brought it back.* She wasn't satisfied, not by a long shot, but she would be. The physical aspect of their marriage was definitely not a concern.

Her fingers softly caressed the silkiness of his hair. "Mason, we have to stop." Her heart was pounding like a racehorse, and her body was still plastered to his, contradicting her plea.

Mason froze at her words. He slowly raised his head and stared at her.

Gillian colored, but held his gaze. The flush of desire darkened his face, and his breath was anything but steady. A lock of black hair had fallen across his forehead, and her fingers itched to brush it back into place. Mason Blacksword had the look of a man who had just been thoroughly kissed.

He took a step back, straightened his jacket and forcefully brushed the wayward lock of hair back into place. "I'm sorry. That shouldn't have happened."

Gillian tugged at her jacket and straightened her blouse. That and a lot more should have happened. She was about to become his wife and he apologizes for kissing her. Damn his warlock heart!

He knew what he had done to her. There was no way

he could have missed her response. A dead man could have seen how turned on she had gotten with just one kiss. Furious with him, and with herself for starting the whole thing, she picked up her briefcase, which had slipped from her fingers during the kiss, and opened the door. "It works both ways, Mason."

"What does?"

"The Council won't give me a moment of peace until I marry. So it might as well be you." She stepped into the hall and closed the door behind her.

Chapter 4

Mason sat in his car staring at the windows of Gillian's apartment. She was home. He had seen movement in the windows about twenty minutes ago while he had been debating with himself if he should ring her bell or just go home. He still hadn't made up his mind.

Today was her twenty-fifth birthday and she had spent the majority of the night dining with her family in celebration. Her grandmother had called him earlier in the week to invite him along, but he told her he had to work late. Virginia Kenwood hadn't been too thrilled with his excuse. She had given him the name of the restaurant and what time everyone was going to meet there. He had spent most of his night sitting in his office preparing for tomorrow's cases and feeling guilty. He should have gone.

Gillian was going to be his wife in five days and he hadn't even bothered to attend her birthday celebration. He glanced down at the small, brightly colored package sitting in the passenger seat. At least he had bought her a present. His glance landed on two small gray-velvet jeweler's boxes next to the birthday present. One contained matching gold wedding bands, the other an engagement ring. Gillian knew he had ordered the wedding bands because he had called her two weeks ago and asked her ring size. Buying her an engagement ring hadn't even occurred to him until he entered the jeweler's to purchase the wedding bands.

He had stood there silently, staring at row after row of gold bands, trying to decide if Gillian would prefer a fancy band, or a plain band, which he preferred. An elderly gentleman had been browsing through watches at the front of the store. But what really caught his eye was a young couple examining diamond engagement rings. It had struck him then that he and Gillian had never been formally engaged, only betrothed by the Council. The happiness and love that had shone on the young woman's face as she stared at the diamond ring glittering on her finger had touched something deep within him.

He and Gillian might not love each other, but for the sake of the Council, the society and their families, they were getting married. He wanted to have their marriage appear as normal as possible. No one within the society called attention to themselves, and all gossip was frowned upon. Gillian should have an engagement ring—if not for appearance' sake, then because she deserved it. She was forfeiting the rest of her life for the Council.

While staring through the glass cases containing gold bands, he realized how hard this must be for Gillian. He had no expectations of love, happiness or wedded bliss. Not with Gillian. Not with any woman. Love was an illusion. Happiness was a momentary feeling that was impossible to hold. And wedded bliss was great for selling greeting cards but had absolutely nothing to do with real life. To his way of thinking it was more important to be content with life. He was content with his life just the way it was. He didn't need or want a wife.

Gillian, on the other hand, had been *gifted* with love and compassion. It was going to be a lot harder on her being married to a man who not only didn't love her, but whom she didn't love in return.

The fancy glittering diamonds didn't capture his attention. They were too ordinary and customary, and there was nothing common about this marriage. The rubies at the other end of the counter drew his eye. Gillian, with her inner fire and pale hair, seemed tailor-made for the fiery gem. Within an hour he had not only purchased two plain gold wedding bands and an impressive ruby engagement ring, but he had bought a pair of ruby earrings as a birthday present and a matching necklace for a wedding present.

Tonight on his way home from work he had stopped at the jeweler's and picked up everything. The jeweler had wrapped the earrings in brightly colored paper and bow, and the necklace was tastefully done in white and gold. He had been two blocks away from the restaurant where Gillian and her family were dining. Instead of walking the two blocks, he had returned to the parking garage for his car and headed home. He didn't want to give Gillian the ring or her present in front of a crowd of curious onlookers.

He didn't want to face Gillian at all after what happened in his chambers a few weeks ago. He had avoided any society gathering and pleaded an especially heavy workload to his mother so she would handle anything

that came up concerning the wedding. It was a rotten
and unfair thing to do, both to Gillian and his mother,
but he was stalling for time. He needed time to understand what had happened when he kissed Gillian. He
had kissed other women before, but never with that kind
of response. He wanted time to understand or at least
accept his reaction before he saw her again.

Tonight time had run out. He couldn't very well give
Gillian an engagement ring after the wedding ceremony.
She needed the wedding bands so that they could be
attached to the ring bearer's pillow before he walked
down the aisle on Saturday. And today was her birthday. With those three strikes against him, he might as
well admit he was out. Out of time.

He picked up the three small boxes, got out and
locked his car. Night had fallen on the city, but the heat
of day still baked any citizens who were unlucky
enough not to have air-conditioning. July was an un-
godly time to live in the city. Stoops were crowded with
people trying to catch a breeze. The sounds of distant
sirens, horns and traffic blended with the persistent
humming of air conditioners and the crying of fussy
babies. Gillian's neighborhood was a virtual smorgasbord of sights, sounds and smells. He wondered how
she was going to adjust to living in his house in a quiet,
stately suburb. More important, he wondered how he
was going to adjust to having her live there.

He noticed that the group of men sitting on the neigh-
boring stoop was the same one that had been there the
night he had driven Gillian home from the party. The
man she had called Chico tilted his baseball hat and
grinned at Mason as he pressed the buzzer to Gillian's
apartment. He ignored Chico and his stoop-sitting buddies as she responded to his buzz.

Gillian's voice came through the call box accompanied by ear splitting static. "Yes?"

"It's me, Gillian."

The buzzing of the door was his signal to come in. He stepped into the hallway and made sure the door was firmly closed behind him. He slipped the rings into one pants pocket and her birthday present into the other. All of a sudden he felt rather stupid standing in the hall holding the box containing their wedding rings. Was this how other couples the Council had betrothed did it? Somehow he doubted it. As her apartment door opened, he plastered on what he hoped was a friendly smile.

"Hello, Mason."

"Hello." He noticed the way she stood in the middle of the doorway, blocking his way, and frowned. What was he expecting, warm greetings and hot kisses? "May I come in?"

She shrugged, moved back and opened the door farther.

"Why not?"

He stepped into the apartment and glanced around. Not one item had been packed up to be moved to his house. Granted, there wasn't a lot he expected her do. The movers he hired would be here in two days to move everything over to his place. But he thought there would be a few personal or cherished items she would want to pack herself. "Are you ready to have everything moved Thursday?"

"I canceled the movers you hired."

"Why?" He shot her a quick glance. Maybe she wanted to call off the wedding. She wouldn't be the first bride ever to get cold feet, just the first witch to defy the Council. From what little he knew about Gillian, he wouldn't put it past her. Maybe instead of spending years ignoring his future bride, he should have been getting to know her better. He was going to look awfully stupid standing alone at the altar on Saturday.

"I hired Chico and some of his buddies to move the stuff for me."

"Why did you do that?" Chico and his friends looked like they wouldn't know honest work if they tripped over it.

"They could use the money." She gave Mason a quarrelsome look. "Besides that, they're my friends and neighbors."

He hadn't come here to argue with her. By the stubborn tilt of her chin he was afraid that was what she had on her mind. Gillian looked awfully upset about something. It would be a lot better if they got away from the subject of Chico and his friends. "I take it the wedding is still on?"

She gave him a peculiar look before answering. "With no help from you." She walked over to the coffee table, where a pile of folders and papers were spread out, and started to gather them up.

Mason gave a slight nod to acknowledge her words as the truth. He hadn't helped to plan the wedding. His gaze slowly roamed the length of her bare, lightly tanned legs. Gillian obviously had changed after coming home from dinner. She was wearing a pair of denim cutoff shorts and a man's white T-shirt. If it wasn't for the shorts' soft white fringe teasing the tops of her thighs, her outfit might have been indecent. Her feet were bare and each toenail gleamed with pink polish. All traces of makeup and jewelry had been removed, and her long blond hair was pulled up high off her neck and into a ponytail.

He had spoken the truth when he said she was the most beautiful woman at the society's party. Gillian Barnett was a very desirable woman and he, after all, was human. He still had his doubts about their upcoming wedding but not about the physical aspects of their marriage. Getting Gillian into his bed was becoming more appealing to him with each passing day.

Gillian finished picking up all the papers and carefully put them into a folder, which she placed on the kitchen counter. She joined Mason by the couch and sat down. "Any particular reason why you didn't bother to show up at the restaurant?"

So that's what had her in such a bad mood. Here he had thought she was still ticked about the day in his chambers when he told her he might as well marry her as anyone else. He hadn't realized how bad his words had sounded until she turned the tables around on him and said it back. He really should apologize for that remark, but he wasn't going to. He had apologized more to her already than to any other person he had ever known. This marriage had been a bad idea from the start, but he wasn't going to make the whole affair worse by playing the submissive, apologetic partner.

"I told your grandmother I wasn't going to be there when she issued the invitation."

"We held dinner for almost an hour waiting for you."

Damn the guilt he felt and damn her sweet blue eyes. "Talk to Virginia about that, not me." He sat down on the far end of the couch and tossed her the small gray box. "Here's the wedding bands I told you I'd pick up."

She caught the box with one hand. Slowly she opened the box and stared at the rings for a moment before softly closing the lid and carefully placing the box on the coffee table. "Was that all you wanted?"

Mason cringed. Her lack of a thank-you was never more obvious or more deserved. She had been working on their wedding for months, making all the decisions while he sat back like a sulking child hoping the whole thing would go away. Well, it wasn't going to go away and five nights from now he would be a married man. "No, that wasn't all I wanted."

She shot him a quick glance before sinking farther back into the couch and putting her bare feet up on the coffee table. "Well, what else do you want?"

Gillian looked as if she didn't have a care in the world. He was about to knock that nonchalant look off her face. "I want you."

He lowered his shields and allowed her to feel the heated desire pumping through his veins. There was no way he would be able to hide the physical need he felt for her after the ceremony. Gillian might as well get used to the idea that he wanted her.

"Oh?"

She gave him a guarded look but continued to look calm and cool. She hadn't even tried to read him. He wondered if she naturally assumed he had his shields up or if she was afraid of what she might discover. "What do you suggest we do about that?"

Gillian raised one brow and grinned. "Get married?"

Mason couldn't help it. He gave a rusty bark of a laugh and sputtered, "Get married!" Why hadn't he noticed the spark of humor in his future wife before? "All right. What are you doing Saturday around five o'clock?"

"Nothing much."

Mason shook his head and pulled the box containing

the engagement ring out of his pocket. This time, instead of tossing the box, he held it out toward her. She presented him with the perfect opportunity to give her the ring without making a big deal about it. There was no way he was getting down on bended knee and asking for her hand in marriage.

Gillian took the box with a bemused expression on her face. She glanced between the box and Mason several times before opening the box and gasping. "Good Lord Almighty, Mason. Is it real?" She gingerly took the ruby-and-diamond ring out of its velvet bed and held it to the light next to her.

Mason didn't know if he should be insulted or flattered. Did she honestly think he would buy her a fake engagement ring? "I had to eat twenty-seven boxes of Cracker Jacks before I found that."

She held the ring closer to the light. "My Lord, it's real!"

"Of course it's real. What were you expecting, cubic zirconia?"

"I wasn't expecting anything. Why would you buy me something like this?" She turned the ring this way and that way, seemingly entranced by the way the light lit the gem.

"Isn't it traditional for the man to buy an engagement ring?"

"There's nothing traditional about this marriage, Mason."

"I know. That's why I bought a ruby instead of a diamond. Diamonds seem so cold, like little pieces of ice. Somehow I don't picture you as a cold person."

"You picture me as a bloodred ruby?"

"No. If you hold the ring just right, there seems to

be an inner fire burning within the gem. The inner fire reminded me of you.''

''Oh.'' She stared harder at the ring for a minute, as if looking for the inner fire. ''How would you know what I'm like on the inside?''

''I have a few ideas, which I'm sure will be either confirmed or proven wrong over the coming years.'' His gut instinct told him Gillian was all wrong for an arranged marriage. She was probably looking for love and a house full of babies. The first thing he couldn't give her and the second was something he didn't want. Not only was he going to make a lousy husband, but as a father he would be deplorable. He was his father's son, after all.

Children should be cherished and wanted by both parents, not forced upon people by the Council. He understood the need to keep the sacred bloodline flowing, but why did it have to be him? The day it was determined he was fertile was one of the darkest in his life. Not only was the Council thrusting a wife upon him, they were forcing parenthood upon him, too. Just because both he and Gillian were deemed fertile didn't automatically mean there would be children. There were other supposedly fertile couples in their society that had never produced any children.

Gillian's voice pulled him away from his dismal thoughts. ''I'm sorry, what did you say?''

''I was just remarking on your comment about the 'coming years.'''

Mason noticed the way her fingers trembled as they toyed with the ring. She hadn't put it on yet. ''What about the 'coming years'?''

''It just sounded like a long time.''

''It will be a long time, Gillian.'' He gave a heavy

sigh and wearily leaned his head against the back of the couch. There was no way she would call off the wedding, and he knew he wouldn't approach the Council. So they were getting married this coming Saturday. "I see only two options, Gillian."

"What's that?"

"First we could try to get along and make this marriage appear normal, or we could fight each other on every little thing and make both of our lives a living hell."

"Gee," Gillian said on a chuckle, "do I really have a choice?"

Mason felt a muscle jerk at the corner of his mouth but suppressed the smile. He had absolutely nothing to smile about. He felt like a condemned man, despite looking forward to the reward of having Gillian in his bed. Her tempting body had been depriving him of sleep for weeks now.

"How about if we try to get along?" he suggested.

"I don't know, Mason. With the current divorce rate, we might be bucking tradition."

He glanced at the ruby ring. "You already know my opinion regarding tradition."

She twirled the ring between two fingers and gave a ghost of a smile. "Are you politely trying to tell me that you won't be getting down on bended knee to declare your undying love for me?"

"Is that the kind of husband you want?"

"What I want and what I'm getting appear to be entirely different things."

"But it will work—" he raised an eyebrow "—won't it?" He studied the emotions flitting across her face. Gillian looked half resigned, half unsure. Who could blame her? He felt the same way, too.

She gave a soft sigh and slipped the ring onto the third finger of her left hand. "One way or another, Mason, it will work."

"I'm sure it will," he lied. He wasn't sure about anything concerning Gillian or the wedding. He stared at her hand and the ring she had slipped onto her finger. The gem caught the light and burned a fiery red. He'd been right about his choice. The ring looked perfect on Gillian's finger.

"What time Thursday are Chico and his buddies moving your stuff?" Maybe he would make the first gesture and try to be home when they arrived. Gillian had never been inside his home.

"Around dinnertime, I guess. You don't have to be there—they won't make off with your family silver."

"I wasn't worried about that. Besides, I don't have any silver." Gillian was still defensive about her neighbors. "I emptied a spare bedroom for some of your stuff. The rest of the furniture can go in the empty apartment above the garage."

"You have an apartment above the garage?"

"It came with the house. The garage at one time housed the housekeeper and her gardener husband. The original owner believed in servants."

"You don't?"

"I have a cleaning lady who comes in twice a week. She also prepares a couple of meals and freezes them for me. I also employ an outside lawn-maintenance man who sees to it that the lawn gets mowed and the bushes get trimmed. You won't have to worry about keeping up with the domestic end of the house."

"I don't mind cooking or cleaning." She shot him an amused look. "Unless you're one of those slobs wives are always complaining about. Do you pick up your dirty socks, clean the sink after you shave and consider a bowl of cereal a nutritious breakfast?''

''I know what a hamper is for, the sink is always clean when I leave the room and I don't eat cereal.''

''Two out of three isn't bad. I'll have you munching down those little O's within a month.''

''I usually prefer two eggs over easy and two slices of lightly buttered toast with my morning coffee and paper.''

She gave him a disgusted look. ''You expect me to cook eggs over easy every morning?''

''No. I expect you to eat your Cheerios while I cook my own breakfast. I'm not marrying you to gain a cook.''

''Well, that's good. My cooking skills are there, but I only have about a dozen dishes in my repertoire.''

''I'm sure we'll manage not to starve to death.'' He stood up and stretched. ''See, that wasn't too bad. We discussed the wedding, and the domestic and physical aspects of our upcoming marriage.''

''What about financial?''

''There's nothing to discuss. I'm more than able to support a wife. You don't even have to work if you don't want to.'' He had quite a few problems with her career, but he wasn't about to forbid her to work. Maybe he could encourage her to better spend her time rather than chasing down deadbeat fathers.

''What am I supposed to do all day while you work?''

''You could volunteer at the local hospital.''

''That would be interesting, considering I faint at the sight of blood.''

''Your mother is a surgeon.''

Gillian shrugged her shoulders. ''So sue me.'' She

stood up and walked Mason toward the door. "I happen to love my job."

"The world would be a nicer place if everyone loved their job." He was afraid of that. What was a man supposed to do now? This was the nineties and he couldn't very well tell her to quit. He would have to wait until they were married to figure out another approach. How was it going to look having a judge's wife running around the sleazier side of the city tracking down deadbeat fathers?

He leaned against the door before Gillian could open it. For weeks he had been wondering if her kisses were as powerful as he remembered. His gaze caressed her mouth, and heat rolled into his groin. There was no way he was waiting till Saturday night to find out. He reached out and gently touched her cheek. "You don't look any older than when you were a teenager."

"Jeez, Mason. There you go sweet-talking me again."

He pulled her closer. "Are you putty in my hands yet?"

She gave an unladylike snort. "There you go dreaming again."

"I told you, I don't dream." He brushed a soft strand of pale hair away from her cheek and lowered his mouth.

Gillian raised her face and met his kiss. Her arms wrapped around his neck and she pressed herself to his body. A primitive moan of desire erupted between them. Neither knew who made the sound. Neither cared.

Mason deepened the kiss with a forceful sweep of his tongue. Gillian responded with a playful nip of her teeth. His hands roamed the soft cotton of her shirt and the seductive flair of her hip. Heat pounded through his veins and pooled at his groin. Urgent need hardened his shaft to a painful column that tugged at his underwear and bulged the zipper of his pants. He wanted Gillian more than he wanted to breathe. He wanted to sink himself so far into her warmth that he would never want to come out.

His strong masculine hands cupped her bottom and pressed her against his arousal. He wanted her to feel exactly what she was doing to him.

Gillian arched her hips forward before jerking backward and moaning in pain.

Mason immediately broke the kiss. "What's the matter?"

"What the hell do you have in your pants?"

Mason fought the flush stealing up his face. "I... Um..." He glared at the grin spreading across her face. "What the hell kind of question is that?"

"I wasn't referring to *that!*" Gillian made a valiant effort to control her laughter but failed. "You have something hard in your pocket." She glanced down at the front of his bulging pants and chuckled again. "That wasn't right, either."

He finally understood what she was referring to. "Keep laughing and maybe I won't give it to you."

She bit her lip. "Come Saturday I'll have the right to take it."

"I have a feeling we're talking about two different things." The prospect of Gillian taking him Saturday night only made his situation harder.

She glanced down again. "I don't know. What are you talking about?"

He pulled the brightly wrapped box from his pocket and handed it to her. "Happy birthday, Gillian." He brushed a soft kiss over her moist mouth and opened the door. She looked like she'd been thoroughly kissed and had enjoyed it. "I better leave while I can still walk."

The small package fit neatly into the palm of her hand. "Aren't you going to stay while I open it?"

"If I stay any longer the only thing that will get opened is the snap on your shorts." He kissed her mouth before stepping out into the hall. "I'll see you at my place on Thursday around dinnertime."

He gently pulled the door closed behind him.

Gillian stood in the middle of Mason's driveway Thursday night and smiled. "Well, we made it." Three pickup trucks overflowing with furniture and Chico's car, crammed with cardboard boxes, sat behind her loaded car. The small motorcade had made it from her apartment with only one stop—at the local Golden Arches for burgers and fries.

"So I see." Mason glanced at each vehicle and its driver before turning his attention on Gillian.

"Anywhere in particular you want us to start?" His massive brick house stood to her left, and the garage was directly in front of her. She was feeling a little edgy. There was something so intimate about putting all of her belongings next to his. They'd be sharing closets, mixing furniture and hanging their toothbrushes side by side.

"Why don't I give you a walk-through of the house so you can decide what you want in the house and what you want stored in the garage for now?"

"Sounds like a plan to me." She joined Mason on the brick walk that led to the side door and his kitchen.

Mason glanced at Chico and his buddies as they unpiled from the vehicles. "Why don't you guys come on in. There's plenty of cold sodas in the fridge."

Gillian stood in the driveway three hours later and waved goodbye to the moving crew and their empty trucks. For better or worse, she was moved into Mason's house. Until the wedding, she would be staying at her parents. Her bedroom furniture was in the spare bedroom along with boxes containing personal items and clothes. Her living room furniture and kitchen set was stored above the garage, along with boxes of dishes and pots and pans. Mason's kitchen had been totally equipped, and all her mismatched dishes would have looked ridiculous sitting in his glass-front cabinets.

She walked over to her car and took out the last item sitting on the back seat. The purple dragon weighed a ton but she managed to close the door and carry him toward the house. She didn't mind too much about condemning her dishes to the garage, but never her dragon. Mason could object all he wanted, but she wanted to see something of hers when she walked into this house Saturday night after she became Mrs. Mason Blacksword.

Mason took the dragon from her arms as soon as she stepped into the house. "Here, give me that before you pull a hernia."

"Can't have that, now can we? Think of the delay that would cause in the wedding." She walked through the kitchen and hall and stood in the front foyer glancing around.

"What are you looking for?"

"A perfect place for Simon."

"Who's Simon?"

"You're holding him." She glanced into the formal

dining room and scrunched her nose. The room looked as if it had never been used. Pale gold carpet matched the shiny wallpaper and seat cushions. The gold was the perfect background for the dark, massive table, chairs and buffet table. A crystal chandelier hung directly above the table. Simon would never be comfortable in such a haughty setting.

"You named your, um, statue?"

"I name everything." She walked around the bottom of the stairs and entered the living room. It was just as pretentious as the dining room. She kept on walking right out of the room. She gave Mason's office behind the living room a scornful glance. The room was too dark and gloomy and filled with nothing but boring law volumes. Her last hope was the family room at the back of the house. She had casually glanced at it during his nickel tour and wasn't overly impressed. But considering the state of the other rooms, it had to do. She didn't want to tuck Simon away somewhere upstairs.

She walked into what should have been a family room. There was no evidence of a family anywhere. The room was just as immaculate as the rest of the house, but it had possibilities. Two sets of French doors led to a patio outside, and one wall was a massive fireplace. The burgundy leather sofa and chairs looked inviting and comfortable. The rest of the room looked sterile enough to perform open-heart surgery in.

She pointed to a set of French doors. "You can put him down there." Sunlight should flood the room during the morning, but for now the soft glow of an outside light didn't penetrate the doors. The patio was huge and empty but held endless possibilities. A white table and chairs, a couple of chaise lounges with bright-colored cushions should liven up the patio. That and about half a dozen massive tubs filled with flowers.

Mason set down the dragon and followed her gaze out the doors. "So what do you think of your new home?"

She looked away from the backyard. *Dismal* came to mind. The house looked like it was decorated by a professional. Beautiful to look at, but don't you dare touch. How could he stand to live in this place all by himself? She shrugged her shoulders and politely said, "It could use some color."

He glanced around the room. "You think so?"

Gillian shook her head. Mortuaries boasted a brighter color scheme. "I'm sure a couple of plants here and there will lighten the place up." Along with a couple of coats of paint, some dazzling artwork and new curtains, she added silently.

He gave Simon a condescending look. "Plants will be fine."

Gillian ignored Mason's obvious displeasure at having Simon invade his home and mentally added a cheery fire, new lamps and a big hairy dog sleeping by the fire. Now that she was moving out of the apartment, she could finally get a dog. Her landlord frowned on pets. Lord knew, Mason's house was big enough to handle a large dog, and there was plenty of property. A herd of cows could graze in his backyard. Maybe this marriage wouldn't be so bad after all. Not only was she about to gain a husband, but a dog, too.

Chapter 5

Gillian glanced around the noisy guest bedroom in Senator Targett's home and grimaced. What in the hell was she doing? In fifteen minutes she was scheduled to walk down an aisle set up in the senator's formal gardens and become Mrs. Mason Blacksword. She was about to marry a man she didn't love and who didn't love her. She wasn't even positive that she liked Mason.

He had a reputation for being fair and just in court, which she hoped carried over into his private life. The only thing she knew about his personal life was that he played golf, which she had discovered by accident when she opened a closet at his house and found three different sets of golf clubs. Mason never talked about himself, and his house had revealed very little about him. There had been only one personal photo in the entire house, and that had been an eight-by-ten of his mother and two sisters sitting on an end table in his sterile living room. How could she like a man she knew so little about?

She wasn't fearful of Mason. He had a quiet, refined essence that surrounded him. In a way he reminded her of what elegant lords of old England must have been like. But who wanted to be married to a stuffy old lord? They had reputations for keeping mistresses. Mason didn't strike her as a man who was keeping a mistress on the side, and his response to her when they kissed left no doubt about his desire. If he had a woman tucked neatly away in some corner of the city, then she was doing a lousy job of satisfying him.

A fiery blush swept up her cheeks as she thought about what was going to happen tonight, long after the wedding guests departed and they returned to Mason's house. Her nights of sleepless frustration were about to come to an end. The fire his kisses had started threatened to become an inferno whenever she thought about them. Tonight she wanted to burn. Tonight she wanted to experience what it meant to be a woman.

She might not love Mason, but she wanted him. She only prayed it was enough to build a marriage on.

"Nervous?" Tabitha asked.

Gillian jumped at her friend's voice. She had been so busy daydreaming she hadn't noticed her maid of honor had finished getting the crown of pink flowers pinned onto her hair and had joined her. The floppy bridesmaids' hats were history. "I'm sorry, Tab, what did you say?"

"I asked if you're nervous." Tabitha held Gillian's bridal veil in one hand.

"Not really. I've been preparing for this day since I was twelve."

Gillian carefully moved the train of her dress out of

the way and gingerly sat down on the vanity bench. The excited chattering in the room was giving her a headache. There were eight women in the room, along with Celeste, her flower girl, and the photographer snapping picture after picture of the final preparations.

Tabitha positioned the veil on top of her hair and started to pin it down. "You look a little pale."

Gillian glanced at herself in the mirror in front of her. She looked whiter than her gown except for the two patches of blush staining her cheeks. "It's all this white that I'm wearing, that's all."

"You sure?" Tabitha studied her friend with a critical eye. "It's not too late, you know."

"Too late for what?" She helped Tabitha hold down the headpiece so she could secure it better.

"To call off the wedding." Tabitha stuck in the last pin and adjusted the lace. "I think it's barbaric the way the Council is treating you."

"They aren't treating me any differently than any other fertile member."

"They can't make you marry a man you don't love."

"Who knows, maybe love will grow, Tab." She gave her friend a wishful smile. "I agreed to this marriage years ago. I wouldn't back out now." She tucked a stray lock of hair behind her ear and checked the mirror one last time. "Mason's not that bad, Tab. He's handsome, has a good job and doesn't seem to have any abnormalities."

Tabitha always had a hard time adjusting to the fact that her best friend was being forced to marry a virtual stranger. They had been arguing about it for years.

"Maybe he's into kinky sex," Tabitha whispered.

Gillian's laughter overflowed the room and caused every head to turn in their direction. The photographer snapped a picture as tears of mirth filled her eyes. "Oh, Tab, you're priceless." She dabbed at the corners of her eyes before the moisture had a chance to damage her makeup. "You always know just the right thing to cheer me up."

Tabitha's dark brows rose in mock horror. She leaned in closer so no one bustling around the room could overhear. "What if he pulls out black leather and chains tonight?"

Gillian bit her lip to stifle another fit of laughter. If Mason wore leather, it would definitely be black. Mason had a preference for black in all his clothing. She couldn't even picture straight-as-an-arrow Mason thinking about the S and M scene, let alone acting on it. "Oh, Tab, stop it before I have an accident. This gown wasn't designed for Mother Nature calls."

Tabitha grinned as Gillian's mother finished securing a crown of flowers onto a bouncing Celeste and made her way in their direction. Tabitha bent down and whispered, "What if he wants to smear your body with whipped cream and pretend he's a cat?"

Gillian stood up, forcibly controlled another bout of laughter and smoothed down her gown. She gave her mother a warm smile before leaning closer to Tabitha's ear and whispering back, "I'll remind him that turnabout is only fair and that I've been having fantasies about chocolate sauce and sprinkles lately."

Both women looked at each for a long moment before busting out laughing. Leave it to Tabitha to make everything seem so easy.

Tabitha had been more involved with her wedding plans than Gillian herself had been. She had made the flowered headpieces for her attendants and herself. She had also seen to the white lattice arch and the hundred

white roses decorating it. Dozens of huge palms and
ferns had been brought into the senator's garden to add
more background, and the forty-odd tables set up for
the reception held centerpieces designed by Tabitha and
her staff. Flowers from her shop and from the senator's
garden were everywhere throughout the house. Tabitha
had also designed each bouquet being carried down the
aisle. Tabitha's flower shop on the outskirts of the city
had a wonderful and growing reputation as being the
best.

Gillian reached for Tabitha's hand. "How can I ever
thank you for all you've done?"

"Make me a godmother to one of your dozen or so
babies."

She squeezed her hand. "The very first. I promise."

Tabitha gave a ghost of a smile before looking away.
"Here she is, Mrs. Barnett," she said to Gillian's
mother. "All ready to walk down the aisle, and I didn't
have to resort to my grandmother's soothing tea recipe."

Gillian grimaced. Every grandmother had a "soothing tea" recipe. "I still don't see why a stiff drink now
and again is against the rules." From everything she
had seen and heard about brandy, she could sure go for
a snifter right about now.

"Now, dear," purred her mother, "you mustn't talk
so. The rules are for our protection, not to punish us."
Her mother reached up and straightened the already-
perfect veil. "It's time."

"Go ahead down, Mom. We'll be coming."

Her mother seemed to hesitate for a moment.
"There's so much I should have told you."

Gillian noticed Tabitha silently slipping away to give
her and her mother a moment of privacy. She gave her

mother an amused grin. "I already know about the birds and the bees, Mom."

"Birds and bees have nothing to do with it." Her smile matched her daughter's. "Are you sure you want to go through with this?"

"It's a little late to change my mind now."

"If you want to, your father and I will stand beside you."

Gillian wasn't shocked. She knew her parents loved her and would never force her to do something she didn't want to do. Council or no Council, her parents would honor her decision. "Thanks, Mom, but it's okay."

"Are you sure?"

"Mom, you and dad had an arranged marriage and it worked out beautifully."

"But you don't know Mason that well. Your father and I fell in love from the moment we first saw each other. I was fourteen and scared to death to be in the Council's chambers when your father walked into the room. I took one look at him and knew everything was going to be all right."

"People are different." She took her mother's elbow and started for the door. She didn't want to discuss her feelings for Mason. "Some of us take a little longer to take the plunge."

"Do you love him, Gillian?"

Ah, the million-dollar question! She couldn't tell her mother that she didn't love Mason, but only wanted his body and what his kisses promised. Tabitha, yes, her mother, never. "Mom, you better get going. You don't want to keep your new son-in-law waiting, do you?" She opened the door and handed over her mother to her father, who had been patiently waiting in the hall with his grandson, Turner, the ring bearer. "Tell her to go on down, Dad."

"Patricia, they're waiting for you downstairs."

Her mother turned toward Gillian. "But..."

Gillian reached out and gently kissed her mother's cheek. "Everything is fine, Mom. The longer it takes you to take your seat, the longer it will be before your next grandchild is conceived."

"Gillian!" cried her mother.

Luther Barnett's boisterous laugh filled the hallway.

"Come on, Pat, don't you know yet when Gilly's teasing?" He took his wife's arm and gently led her to the top of the stairs.

Gillian watched them as they walked away arm in arm. Her father had been wrong. She hadn't been teasing.

She gave her nephew a wide grin. He looked adorable in his black tux, complete with a pink carnation boutonniere, and slicked-down hair. "Ready, Turner?"

"Okeydokey."

Everything was "okeydokey" in Turner's life. No matter if it was good, bad or ugly, he always answered with the same response. Maybe he had something there. He just described how she felt about this wedding. It wasn't real good, but it wasn't real bad. It definitely wasn't ugly. It was okeydokey.

Gillian turned back into the room and managed a smile for everyone. "Well, ladies, I believe it's time to get this show on the road."

Five hours later Mrs. Mason Blacksword took the last sip from her champagne glass and wiggled her nose. The bubbles from the ginger ale tickled her nose. Well, the deed was done. She was now officially a married woman. The bouquet had been thrown, the cake cut and the garter had been flung. Her feet were killing her from all the dancing. Her scalp ached from the pins anchoring what now felt like a twenty-pound veil. And her shoulders and back were screaming under the weight of her wedding dress. Who would have guessed that the simple white dress would feel like sixty pounds after hours of dancing, socializing and eating?

Under the cover of her lashes she snuck a peek at her husband standing beside her saying his farewells to their families. Mason looked devastating in his black tux. He still looked as neat and pressed as he had when she had caught a glimpse of him standing by the arch, waiting for her as she walked down the aisle on her father's arm. Her breath had caught and something akin to hope had flared within her heart. He had looked magnificent. When she joined him, and the veil had been raised, she had tried to read the expression burning in his dark eyes, but she couldn't. His emotions seemed to be shifting like sand during a squall. The instant the justice of the peace proclaimed them man and wife, she felt his shields drop as she lowered hers. She refused to read him. It would be like cheating on a final exam.

If she was going to pass the test, she wanted to do it on her own merits and not take the easy way out. She wanted a normal marriage and that meant no hocus-pocus. Mason must have agreed with her because she hadn't felt the slightest probing.

There was something very rewarding about doing a job well, and doing it with no special help. She never used her powers while doing her job. Tracking down men who didn't want to be found by using her brain, skills and know-how was a challenge—one she enjoyed immensely. She wasn't about to deprive herself of that joy in her marriage by cheating. The same rules applied now. If her marriage worked, it would be because she cared.

"Gillian, are you listening to a word I'm saying?" her grandmother questioned.

"Of course, Grandmother. You said I'm to wear the white negligee tonight and the black one tomorrow." She smiled with amusement and love at her grandmother. "I won't repeat your other advice." Who could possibly take offense at such a well-meaning gesture? Her grandmother had given her not one, but two peignoir sets for a bridal-shower present. She glanced at Mason, hoping he hadn't overheard her grandmother's unsubtle hints on how to seduce one's husband. Mason was shaking her father's hand goodbye.

Mason turned to her and asked, "Are you ready?"

"Yes." *No! I could use some more time here. Can't you see how nervous I am?* She reached up and gave her father a kiss on his cheek. "I'll call you and Mom in a couple of days."

"You better, young lady, or we'll come looking for you two."

Mason took hold of Gillian's arm and led her out the front door of the senator's house and toward his car parked in the circular driveway. The front entrance and path was lit by concealed lights. "Watch your step here."

Gillian allowed Mason to escort her to the car. She had both hands full trying to hold up the hem of her gown and maneuver the train that had been hooked into a huge bustle of satin. Someone—and her guess would be her sister, Raine, and her boyfriend, Jason—had painted the words *Just Married* on the back window of

Mason's car in white. Gillian prayed it wasn't paint and that whatever it was could be easily removed.

Mason scowled at the artwork and the three strings of tin cans tied to his bumper, but didn't comment. He opened the door and helped her and her twenty-seven yards of satin and lace get in. "Can I ask a question?"

"What?"

"Are you comfortable in that dress?"

"What do you think?" It took her three tries before she could get all the dress into the car so he could shut the door.

"I think beauty has its price." Mason closed the door and walked around the car to the driver's side.

Gillian watched as he slipped in behind the wheel and started the car. "I think there was a compliment in there somewhere."

"There was."

She waved to her parents and Mason's mother, who were still standing in the open doorway seeing them off. The sound of tin cans clanging against the senator's cobblestone driveway filled the night. She suppressed her laughter and watched beneath lowered lashes as Mason expertly drove down the drive and onto the main road. He drove about a quarter mile before pulling over to the side of the road and stopping the car.

"Thank you for keeping them on this long. I'm sure whoever decorated the car appreciated it."

It astounded her that he had allowed the cans to stay on. Mason wasn't the type of man who liked to call attention to himself. Driving a car pulling enough tin to make a roof out of was indeed calling attention to himself. The racket they made as they drove down the street had every dog within two miles barking its head off.

"Do you know who did it?"

Did she detect a streak of mischief in his voice? "I have my ideas." She couldn't very well accuse Raine when she wasn't totally sure. It could very well have been one of his sisters. Both Amy and Kara seemed to have taken great pleasure in watching Mason tie the knot earlier.

"Let me know when you plan your revenge." He got out of the car and walked toward the back bumper.

Gillian twisted as far as her dress would allow. Three minutes later the trunk was open and the clanging of cans echoed throughout the car as he dumped them all in. The car shook momentarily as the trunk was slammed shut. She watched as he slid behind the wheel, and they once again headed off into the night toward his house and their wedding night.

Mason paced the floor of the master bedroom while waiting for his wife. They had arrived over an hour ago and his bride still hadn't seen fit to leave the guest bedroom, where she had retreated as soon as they entered the house. The most he had seen of her was when she turned her back and asked if he would undo the pearl buttons. He had counted twenty-eight buttons. Each one slipping through its hole had weakened his control. By the time he finished with the last button he had been so hard that he feared for the brass zipper on his pants. He had almost dragged her down onto the hallway carpet and satisfied his lust. The look of desire mixed with confusion gleaming in her pale blue eyes had stopped him before he could do more than whisper her name.

It made sense when she fled to the guest bedroom. Most of her belongings were there. Thursday night she hadn't had the time to put away most of her clothes or toiletries. Her bed had been set up in the room and it was piled with a small mountain of presents from her bridal shower. Whatever she needed to do before she came to him had to be done in that room.

He had heard the shower start about thirty minutes ago and had done the same. The penetrating cold water had done nothing for his desire. Within minutes of toweling himself off and slipping into a pair of black silk pajama bottoms he was hard as a rock once again. Even his fingers trembled slightly as he shaved for the second time today. The small nick under his chin was a silent testimony to how tense he was.

He paced to the other end of the room and stared out into the night. What was taking her so long? The shower in the other room had been shut off before he was even done with his. So where was his bride? He wondered if she was expecting him to come to her. That didn't make any sense. She was the one in the guest bedroom with a bed piled halfway to the ceiling with boxes. The door to the master bedroom was open, all she had to do was walk twenty paces and hang a right.

Maybe she was reluctant. That made more sense than her pacing the room like a virgin bride waiting for him to make the first move. He could understand. He felt the same way. But it was too late now to change a thing. As soon as she showed up, he was planning to consummate the marriage and fulfill his vow to the Council.

He glanced at the tray he had carried up from the kitchen. A bucket holding a chilled bottle of sparkling water and two glasses sat in the center along with a couple of small dishes containing things to munch on. He was unsure of Gillian's tastes, so he selected an assortment of different goodies. There were fancy cookies, nuts, mints and chips.

Okay, he thought, so I'm not going to jump her bones

the second she waltzes through the door. I'll give her a glass of water and a mint to suck on first.

His fist balled the curtain into a wrinkled mess as he thought about that lucky mint.

He wasn't going to survive this. He barely got through the reception in one piece. For some absurd reason he couldn't stand to have Gillian out of his sight. It was as if the instant the vows were spoken he became responsible for her. He was to provide, protect and cherish her. Providing and protecting were no problem. What was his he always took care of. Gillian was now his. But the cherishing end of the deal was iffy. It sounded too close to love for his comfort. He didn't want Gillian getting any ideas into her pretty little head.

Love had no place in his life and in this marriage. He married Gillian because she was his chosen bride. Chosen by the Council, not him. He wouldn't have chosen Gillian out of a pool of a hundred different witches. She didn't possess any of the skills he deemed necessary in a wife.

With his job he needed a wife who would be comfortable entertaining in a multitude of settings. Gillian appeared to be a backyard-barbecue or call-for-a-pizza kind of hostess. He had ambitions of one day becoming an elder within the society, and to achieve that goal it was essential that he had the cooperation of his wife. Gillian didn't seem to be in awe of the elders or their powers. How could he expect her to climb the society ladder beside him when she didn't desire to climb?

He liked the idea that she had a career; it would give her something to do during the day while he was at work. But he loathed her career choice. Whatever had happened in her life to make her choose social work? Somehow, someway he would have to make her see the error of her ways. There were plenty of other careers she could choose from. He would gladly pay for any further education she might need to change careers.

A faint sound at the doorway caused him to jerk around. All thoughts of careers and social climbing fled his mind. Gillian was standing in the doorway looking both breathtakingly beautiful and unsure of herself. The white lace of her negligee was as transparent as a light summer mist. Every delectable detail of her body was his to look at. And look he did.

Firm, lush breasts were capped with dusty pink nipples puckered sweetly against the translucent material. He could span her waist with his hands, and the gentle flaring of her hips lengthened into luxurious thighs made to cradle a man's body. The golden thatch of curls at the apex of those thighs captured his attention and his willingness to breathe. Who needed oxygen when he was about to enter heaven?

"H—" He cleared his throat and tried again. "Hi."

Gillian shifted her bare feet against the carpet and gave him a ghost of a smile. "Hi, yourself."

He waved his hand toward the tray. "I brought up something to drink and eat." He couldn't believe this. He was as nervous as a schoolboy on his first date. Even his palms were beginning to sweat. He took a deep breath to calm his nerves and promised himself everything was going to be okay as soon as he kissed her. When they kissed, there was no hesitancy, no shyness, no awkwardness. He still remembered her thank-you kiss for her birthday present, given to him Thursday after Chico and his friends departed. That kiss had been keeping him warm for the past two days. He fought his desire-primed body and moved toward the tray.

"I couldn't eat another thing, but a glass of ice-cold

water would be great.'' She took a couple of hesitant steps into the room.

Mason quickly filled two glasses and met her near the foot of the bed. He handed her a glass. ''How about a toast?''

''To what?''

He noticed how her gaze seemed riveted to his chest and wondered if she was observing how fast his heart was racing. Lord knew, he could hear the damn organ thundering away like a racehorse. He raised his glass to hers and said, ''To us.''

Gillian shot a quick glance at the bed behind him before lightly tapping her glass against his. ''To us.''

Mason watched as her lips closed on the crystal brim. A shudder of desire departed his stomach and traveled southward. It ended in the base of his manhood, where it flared to life. His mouth suddenly felt as dry as the Mojave Desert. He took a deep gulp of the sparkling water and silently cursed the Council and their rules. What he needed now was a drink. A stiff drink, to match the part of his anatomy howling for relief.

Gillian replaced her glass on the tray and looked somewhere over his left shoulder. ''This is a little awkward, isn't it?''

''I've been in more comfortable situations in my life.'' It was the understatement of the year. He couldn't remember ever being so tense in his life. One part of him wanted to assuage the fear he saw in Gillian's eyes and tell her he'd sleep on the couch until she was ready. The *howling* part wanted to haul her into his bed and not let her up until the howling stopped.

She clasped her hands together in front of her and nervously worried her lower lip with her teeth. ''Maybe if we kissed, it would get better.''

Was she crazy! If they kissed now it would be all over before it began. He'd never last, and the one thing he was bound and determined to do tonight was satisfy Gillian. He gave a casual shrug and placed his empty glass next to hers. "We could."

He studied her face, partly because he was trying to figure out what to do next, but mostly because he was petrified to look below her chin. His control was unraveling faster than the plot of a B movie. He took a step closer and lightly drew the back of his fingertips down her jaw to the provocative curve of her chin. The pad of his thumb stroked her moist lower lip. He wondered if she felt the heat of his kisses, or was it only on his end? The last thing he wanted was to appear a fool. "What happens to you when we kiss?"

Gillian parted her lips against his fingers. Her gaze was now riveted to his mouth. "I can't think when you kiss me."

"Is that good or bad?" He couldn't think when he kissed her, either. He tilted his head to the side and stroked the soft, dewy inside of her lip. Would she be this moist when he sank himself deep within her?

"Good—" she nipped his thumb "—very, very good." She brought her hand up and captured his fingers. "Kiss me, Mason," she begged.

He didn't need another invitation. His mouth slanted down on hers with desire born of frustration. Ever since she waltzed into the society party months ago wearing nothing but sequins and a light, flowery scented perfume, he had wanted her. Lord, how he wanted her!

Gillian sighed softly into his mouth and wrapped her arms around his neck. The soft diaphanous material of her gown brushed the dark curls covering his chest, which then arrowed down before disappearing beneath the black drawstring tie of his pajama bottoms.

Mason pulled her closer and heatedly stroked the length of her back, crushing the sheer material beneath his fingers. He cupped her curved bottom and lifted her off the carpet. He groaned softly before leaving her mouth to trail a string of heated kisses down her throat to the white satin bow tied between her breasts. His teeth took one end of the bow and pulled. The gossamer gown parted, revealing Gillian's hidden treasures.

Her hot fingers toured his back and shoulders as he captured first one nipple then the other between his lips. The sweet, soft purrs coming from Gillian's throat drove him on. He took a step backward and brought them closer to the bed. With a deft movement he removed her gown with a gentle brush. It pooled at her feet like a liquid puddle of melted snow.

In one swift movement he picked her up and gently deposited her in the center of his bed. He untied his pajama bottoms and allowed them to join her gown on the carpet before lowering his body next to hers.

Her graceful arms reaching for him was his ruin. How could he not respond to such a sweet request? His mouth captured hers once more, and with her hands urging him on, he made Gillian his wife.

Mason's eye slowly peeked open and stared at the clock on the bedside table. It was after ten in the morning! He never slept past eight, but then again, he had never slept with Gillian before. After he recovered from the shock of learning his wife had been a virgin he had tenderly made love to her all over again. Gillian had dated a lot of different men before their wedding. Considering today's standards, virginity wasn't as highly prized as it once was. He hadn't expected her gift of innocence. The second time they made love he had regained his control and demonstrated to Gillian that speed wasn't a requirement. As dawn had stolen into the room he awakened to find Gillian's inquisitive hands tentatively exploring his body. He had allowed her a moment's curiosity before pushing her over onto her back and playfully showing her what her wandering fingers had started. The morning light had brightened the room as they had fallen asleep in each other's arms.

Mason smiled into his pillow as he contemplated how to greet his bride. Maybe being married wasn't as bad as he first thought. His blushing bride had shown amazing willingness to learn. He could no longer feel her soft, sweet body up against his and he missed its warmth. He could become quite used to sleeping with Gillian.

He turned his head toward her side of the bed and opened his eyes. She was gone! With a jerk he sat up in bed and glanced wildly around the room. Where did she go? He hadn't heard her get up, but then again, he wouldn't have noticed if thieves had pulled a moving van up to the house and stolen every piece of furniture, including the bed.

Mason got out of bed, pulled on his discarded pajama bottoms, and frowned at the empty bathroom. Maybe she was hungry? Hell, he was starving after all they had done between the sheets. Gillian was probably downstairs in the kitchen whipping up a fancy breakfast to impress him with. Maybe he should climb back into bed so her surprise wouldn't be ruined. It wasn't every morning that he received breakfast in bed. Then again, it wasn't every morning he woke up married.

He paced the room for a full minute before heading for the stairs. She was taking too long, and he missed her.

Chapter 6

Mason parked his car behind Gillian's well-used hatchback and glanced up and down the street. It was barely the lunch hour and already the strip joints were open, loud music pouring from their yawning doorways and tainting what should have been a peaceful Sunday morning. A Sunday morning when he should have been lying in bed with his bride of less than twenty-four hours instead of tracking her down to one of the roughest streets within The Blades.

What in the world possessed her to leave his bed, hop into her car and go chasing down deadbeat fathers the first day of her married life? Did she prefer these streets to his touch? That was an unsettling thought. By her response and her willingness to participate in their lovemaking, he had thought everything went well. Extremely well. What they had shared was not an act of duty to consummate their marriage. It had been mind-shattering and body-satisfying. Gillian Barnett Blacksword in his bed had been worth the price of his freedom. Now if he could only find her.

Mason surveyed the gaudy neon lights, black-painted windows and life-size posters—slapped onto every available wall—of nude women with black boxes strategically placed over their most private parts. Tough-looking men leaned against the walls and tougher-looking women strutted their wares. This was the bowels of the city and his Gillian was around here somewhere. Her office was six blocks over. When he had arrived there, he'd found it empty, but he sensed her presence nearby.

When he had entered the kitchen expecting to find his wife preparing breakfast the only thing he had found was a note: Mason, went to work, be back in time to start dinner. Gillian.

What the hell kind of note was that? Went to work! Not only was it the morning after their wedding vows, but it was a Sunday. Gillian had no business working on a Sunday. He had crumpled up the note, tossed it into the trash and had been tempted to head for the country club to play a couple of holes of golf. The thought of some of the members of the Council spotting him on the green was enough to squash the temptation. But his real worry had come from Gillian herself. What could be that important for her to leave the warmth of their bed and head for this hellhole?

Something wasn't right. He had noticed it before, but didn't push the issue. Something or someone was frightening Gillian, and it wasn't him or the wedding. He had sensed it weeks ago on the day she was in his courtroom. Before she had raised her shields, her fear had been palpable. He should have made her confide in him.

How could he help her if he didn't know what was going on?

Mason got out of his car and scanned the area for traces of his wife. His senses told him she was close. Real close. He walked past a hooker who looked sixteen—and stoned—and sadly shook his head at her offer. He stopped at the doorway of a bar and tried to glance inside. A curtain of three-inch red plastic strips blocked his view. His instincts were screaming at him that Gillian was inside.

He glanced up at the red neon light above the door and frowned. What would his wife be doing in a place called Tasty Squeeze? By the thunderous music blasting through the doorway he could well imagine what he would find inside. This, or any other bar, wasn't any place for his wife. He knew Gillian could take care of herself. But there always was a chance she wouldn't sense danger coming. A bullet or a knife could kill her just as easily as any other mortal. Witch or not, she shouldn't be courting danger.

Mason pushed aside the plastic strips obstructing the view of the dancers and entered the bar. He allowed a moment for his eyes to adjust to the dimness before moving to his right. Two female dancers were doing an enthusiastic rendition of a sexual act to the beat of an old Beatles' tune. A half-dozen patrons were cheering them on and waving dollar bills in the air. A bartender was behind the bar flirting with a waitress who had disregarded the city code and removed her top. His frown deepened. He didn't see Gillian.

He was almost to the bar when his senses alerted him to danger. Gillian's danger. Within a heartbeat he raced for the door at the back of the room. The door banged against the wall as he raced down the narrow hall and heard voices raised in an argument. Gillian's voice was one of them.

Gillian stood her ground and shouted down Ray Carnes, better known as Vice to his associates. "I don't take kindly to threats, Carnes."

"Listen, you little bitch. Because of you I now have to pay that slut I was married to part of my hard-earned money."

She jammed her fists onto her hips and raised her chin a notch. Every nerve was on full alert, sensing danger. She had barged into Ray Carnes's office and demanded to know if he was the one threatening her, and he wasn't taking it calmly. She had gone through her computer records and Carnes's name was at the top of her list. She figured if she cornered him, she could get a better read on him. So far his response had been predictable. He was furious with her for tracking him down nearly a year ago, but he wasn't the letter sender.

"You're not supporting your ex-wife, Carnes. Your hard-earned money is supporting those two little boys you fathered." She glanced around the office and cringed. She knew exactly how Carnes was earning his money and it sickened her. But it didn't change a thing. Carnes's ex-wife might have been a dancer at a different establishment when they had been married, but she was now a dental assistant who needed the child-support money to make ends meet.

Carnes moved from behind his desk and took a threatening step closer. "I'm not paying a single dime more. Do you hear me?" His voice shook the walls. "Not one more dime!"

Gillian held her ground and didn't back away. Men like Carnes loved to see fear. The hair on the back of her neck stood up as pounding footsteps raced down the hall toward her. She threw up a shield to guard her back and glared at Carnes. "Who asked you to?" She had the answer she had come searching for. Carnes wasn't the danger.

The door was kicked open with enough force to shatter part of the doorframe. Mason followed the splintering wood into the office.

Carnes took a staggering step back. "Who are you?"

Gillian glanced over her shoulder and groaned. Now she had done it. Mason looked ready to tear someone apart. And that somebody was probably her.

"He's my husband." She gave Carnes a small smile. It felt funny to refer to Mason as her husband. She didn't know if it was a good funny or a strange funny, but now was not the time to examine her feelings. "He gets a little cranky if I keep him waiting too long in the car."

Mason glared at the man standing a few feet away from his wife, but didn't say a word.

Carnes backed up a couple more feet and put the desk between himself and the man who had just kicked his way into his office.

Gillian lowered the shield and gave Mason a small shrug. "Sorry to have kept you waiting, Sugar Bear." She walked over to him and gave his forearm a little pat. She was going to pay for this later, but she wanted Carnes to remember her visit, and especially remember her husband. Mason looked infuriated enough to rip the Tasty Squeeze apart with his bare hands.

"I'll be seeing you around, Carnes," she said as she steered Mason toward the door hanging crookedly from its hinges. She eyed the door and the splintered jamb with a weird sense of amusement. What in the world did Mason think he was doing busting into Carnes's office like some avenging hero? More important, what did Mason think she was doing in the office?

She allowed Mason to lead her through the hallway, out into the bar area and then out onto the sidewalk. He was boiling mad and ready to snap at any moment. She wasn't ready to push any more of his buttons. Maybe tracking down whoever was sending her the threatening letters had been a bad idea. But this morning, when she woke to find herself plastered to Mason's chest, it had seemed like an excellent idea.

Mason stopped at her car. "Get in and drive directly home." His mouth barely moved and his words sounded strained, as if his jaws were clamped together. "We will discuss this there."

Gillian glanced at the people on the sidewalk and noticed their curious expressions. She and Mason appeared to be the center of attention. So much for discretion. "Can we stop for breakfast on the way?" She hadn't eaten anything before running from Mason this morning, and she wasn't really hungry now, but she knew Mason well enough to know he wouldn't cause a scene in a restaurant.

"No." He opened her car door and she got in behind the wheel. "We have plenty of food at *our* house." He closed the door without another word and walked to his car, parked directly behind hers.

Gillian pulled her keys from the pocket of her jeans and groaned. She was in for it now. This was one hell of a way to start off a marriage. She started the car and headed for Mason's house. It wasn't *their* house, not yet.

When she had slipped from his bed around nine o'clock she thought she'd take a shower, fix some breakfast and spend the day unpacking her stuff. One look at the guest room piled with all her things made her realize how unsettled she was. She skipped the shower, but it had taken her ten minutes to find the box containing her underwear. After pulling on jeans and a faded T-shirt she had headed downstairs looking for coffee. Within five minutes she was out of the house and dangerously close to tears. She couldn't find where Mason kept his coffee. His coffeemaker looked like something out of a sci-fi movie. And her favorite mug was packed somewhere over the garage.

She had driven to her office, where she drank three cups of coffee and contemplated the real reason behind her frazzled state. Mason. It wasn't his kitchen or the lack of her smiley-face mug that had caused her to run. It was Mason and what they had shared last night in his bed. Not only had she lost her virginity, but she was scared to death she had also lost her heart. What they had shared went way beyond sex. The mechanics of great sex had been present and accounted for, but there had been an added element she hadn't expected. There had been magic.

Gillian glanced in the rearview mirror and bit her lower lip as she spotted Mason's car directly behind hers. What in the world was she going to tell Mason? The man deserved to know why she had felt compelled to leave his arms and go visit Carnes in his sleazy establishment. A missing coffee mug wasn't going to cut it. And somehow she didn't think Mason believed in magic.

She parked carefully at the side of the garage so Mason would have plenty of room to park his car inside. Her old car was used to the elements. The only times it had ever seen the inside of a garage were when she'd appeared in court and had to use one of the parking structures dotting Center City.

She slowly got out of her car and watched as Mason drove up the brick driveway, parked and then joined her. He looked devastatingly handsome, dressed once again almost entirely in black. His pants were black cotton twill and his pullover shirt was black with a narrow pinstripe of emerald green running through it. A small insignia of a roaring leopard was stitched over the left side of his chest. The leopard appeared more civilized than Mason. Where was the attentive lover from last night?

She gave a heavy sigh and headed for the kitchen.

Mason watched as Gillian walked away from him and entered the house. She appeared defeated. Defeated from what, he hadn't a clue. What did she have to be so downtrodden about? Wasn't he the one who had woken up alone in bed wondering where his wife had gone? He still couldn't believe where he had finally located her. The Tasty Squeeze was located in the worst part of the city. What business did she have with that Carnes fellow? Was he one of the unsupporting fathers she was tracking down? That could explain the only remark he had heard, the one about not paying one dime more.

He had felt Gillian's fear and Carnes's rage before he kicked in the door. Gillian's shield nearly cost him his balance. He should have been prepared for her shield. Gillian wasn't naive enough not to have thrown up a couple of good shields before entering the bar.

With a weary sigh he rubbed his fingers against his pounding temples, where a headache was forming. What in the hell was he going to do? He couldn't very well allow Gillian to continue along her chosen career path. Maybe it would have been better if she had stayed a social worker. Visions of the grainy newspaper photo of the dead social worker who had taken Gillian's place changed his mind.

The easy way out of this situation would be to scan Gillian's feelings. He could find out what had motivated her this morning without even asking. Hell, he could probably pick up an idea on how to get her to change careers. But it would be wrong. Gillian would know what he had done. It was impossible to read her without her knowing it. What little trust they had between them would be shattered, and along with it, any hope of making this marriage work.

What they needed was a good long talk. He followed her into the kitchen and hesitated for a fraction of a second before closing the door. Instead of finding a defeated, subdued Gillian awaiting him, he found a frustrated wife slamming a cabinet door.

"Where in the world do you keep your coffee?" she demanded.

Mason frowned. So much for calmness. He glanced at his coffeemaker. The filter basket was removed and Gillian had managed to locate the filters. But not the coffee. His wife seemed desperate to have a cup of coffee and he could use one himself. "Sit down and I'll make it."

"I can manage to brew a pot of coffee, Mason."

"I'm sure you can." He walked over to the refrigerator and pulled out an airtight container full of coffee beans and set it on the counter. He then reached into one of the bottom cabinets and pulled out a coffee bean grinder.

"You grind your own beans?"

"It tastes better." He went about ignoring her and

making the pot of coffee while meticulously cleaning up after himself.

Gillian followed every move he made while perched on one of the bar stools. "How about if I make us some breakfast?"

He glanced at the clock on the wall. "How about if we make lunch instead?" Without waiting for her response he pulled a loaf of bread from a bread box and started to unload a couple of containers from the refrigerator. "I have some chicken salad and ham and cheese. Or would you prefer a salad?" A ripe tomato joined the assortment on the counter. He ignored the rumbling in his stomach and casually reached for two plates. A nice sensible lunch seemed like a reasonable, calm approach. After all, he was a reasonable man, or so he kept telling himself. His bride was giving him plenty of ammunition to doubt himself on that score.

Gillian slid off the stool and unwrapped the loaf of bread. "Chicken salad sounds great."

Twenty minutes later they were on their second cup of coffee and the sandwiches were gone. Mason set his cup down and casually asked, "Want to explain to me why you left?"

She shrugged. "Business."

Mason shook his head. "Wrong answer, try again."

"I had to ask Carnes a few questions and this morning seemed like a good opportunity. The Tasty Squeeze is jammed seven nights a week and I like to avoid crowds whenever possible." She took a sip of her coffee and lowered the cup. "Besides, he has a bouncer at night that would make Arnold Schwarzenegger look like a midget."

"Do I want to hear how you know all that?"

"No. Besides, I won't be making that mistake twice."

Mason wasn't positive but he thought he felt one of the hairs on his head turn gray. "What mistake?"

Gillian glanced around the kitchen. "Did I tell you what a lovely home you have?"

"It's *our* home now, and stop stalling."

"I'm not stalling." Gillian rose and carried her coffee cup over to the dishwasher.

"I don't want you going there again." He might as well lay his cards out on the table.

Gillian found a bag of chips and popped one into her mouth. "Don't worry. I don't need to see Carnes again."

"I was referring to that entire district down there, not just Carnes's place." He stood up and placed his cup next to hers in the dishwasher. It seemed funny to see the two cups side by side along with their plates. They seemed to be paired.

"No can do, Mason. A lot of my clients' unsupporting fathers hang out in that area. It's one of the first places I look."

"Then start chasing a better class of deadbeat fathers."

Gillian chuckled and shook her head. "A better class of deadbeat fathers? Is there such a thing? The women I represent can't afford fancy lawyers and private detectives to hunt down the fathers of their children. The system is so backed up, these kids would graduate from high school before the state had time to track down their fathers. It's me or nobody."

"Then maybe you should look into a career change." He hadn't wanted to bring up this argument so soon in their marriage. He would have preferred to wait a couple of weeks so he could learn more about his bride and possibly have a few suggestions to offer. But she was the one to push the issue with her crazy stunt this morning.

"A career change?" Gillian's expression turned hard and her back looked as if it would snap at any moment.

Mason wondered how much he really wanted this marriage to work. If he pushed the issue, there appeared to be a great possibility that it would be over before it began. But if he sat back and allowed Gillian to repeat her performance of this morning, there was no telling what kind of trouble she could wind up in.

"It was just a suggestion," Mason said. He'd worry about pushing the issue some other time. For now he wanted the marriage to last at least twenty-four hours, so when the Council cornered him later he could say he tried.

"A suggestion, huh?"

He watched as she popped another chip into her mouth and then slowly licked the salt off her lower lip. Heat streaked through his body as memories of last night came flooding back. What that sharp little tongue had done to his body should have been illegal.

"What was so important that you had to talk to Carnes this morning? Couldn't it have waited until tomorrow?"

Gillian munched on another chip while contemplating the foil bag in her hand. After a moment she seemed to come to some sort of decision. "I—" The ringing of the front doorbell stopped her explanation.

"I'll get it," Mason muttered as he walked out of the room. Just when he was finally going to get to the bottom of things, someone had the gall to interrupt. Who would be insensitive enough to bother the newlyweds? Whoever it was, he just might take all this bottled frustration out on him.

He opened the door and glanced around. No one was there. Strange. He was about to close the door when he noticed the elegantly wrapped box sitting on the door-mat. He picked it up and carried it inside. Someone probably forgot to leave it at the reception yesterday and had dropped it off. There wasn't a card on top. It must be inside the box.

Mason carried the lightweight six-inch-square box back to the kitchen and Gillian. "Someone must have forgotten…"

Gillian took one look at the box in Mason's hands and lost all the color in her face. "Get rid of it, Mason. Quick!"

Mason frowned at the box. "What are you talking about?"

"The box." The bag of chips slipped from her fingers and potato chips sprayed across the floor. "Take it back outside."

"Why?"

He started to shake the box but halted the second Gillian screamed, "Don't!" She reached out and gently took the box from his fingers. "Did you see who left it?"

"Gillian, what in the hell is going on?" He didn't like the fear that had sprung into her eyes. She looked ready to faint.

"Can't you feel it?"

Mason scanned the box and took an involuntary step back from the rage and hatred radiating from it. "What in the hell?" He snatched the box back out of Gillian's hands. He didn't want her near the thing.

"Careful!"

He gave her a curious look before setting the box on the corner of the table and quietly asked, "Do you want to tell me how you knew to scan this box?" Scanning wasn't something warlocks and witches did constantly. Not only was it a drain on their powers, but it bordered on being paranoid.

"I scan everything now." She kept her gaze glued to the box and its silver bow.

"Why?"

Gillian's gaze shot up to his. "One of the deadbeat fathers that I tracked didn't appreciate it. He's been sending me some threatening letters."

"How many?"

"I received the fifth one three days before the wedding." She shrugged before giving him a small, crooked smile. "The first four came to my office, the fifth to my apartment."

"Any reason why you didn't tell me, or was this the 'business' you were handling when I questioned you in my chambers?"

"This is the business that had me rattled for the past couple of weeks."

"Along with the wedding?"

"Yes, along with our wedding." She placed both hands onto the box and concentrated for a full minute. "Nothing but hatred." She lowered her hands. "Each time I only pick up the malice and the burning need for revenge. I can't picture the face."

"Want me to try?" He thought he was handling this very calmly, considering his gut was on fire. Someone was threatening his wife and she never bothered to mention it.

"Would you? Maybe you can see something I can't."

Mason gave her a strange look before placing both his hands on the box and closing his eyes. His fingers trembled with the hatred emanating from the box. Dark, twisted thoughts of retaliation were the only thing he could detect. Revenge against his wife. He dropped his hands. "Sorry. I can't see a face."

"Thanks for trying."

He gave her a hard glare. Didn't she realize he would have read the box no matter what? She was his wife now, and he protected what was his. "Do you want to open it, or should I?"

"I will." She removed the bow and carefully peeled off each piece of tape. "It's expensive paper."

Mason continued to glare at the box, ready to raise any shield necessary to protect his wife. He watched as Gillian's fingers shook against the white-and-silver paper. The white cardboard box looked innocent, but he knew it wasn't.

Gillian set the paper aside. She took a deep breath and carefully started to remove the lid. She glanced inside and quickly dropped the lid back onto the box. "Yuck!"

Mason reached for the lid and slowly removed it. He stared down at the box and cringed. Five three-inch-long black leeches were wiggling around on the white tissue paper covering the bottom of the box. They appeared to be searching for food. "Lovely." His fingers reached into the box and pulled out the card tucked into the corner. He read the neatly typed card and then passed it to Gillian.

Does the word BLOODSUCKER sound familiar? Maybe one night you'll wake up with these in your bed and get an idea what it feels like.

Gillian read the card with silver bells imprinted on its corner and shivered. "He doesn't sound too happy, does he?"

Mason noticed how she kept her gaze away from the box and couldn't blame her. Leeches weren't the most attractive creatures. "Does this have anything to do with Carnes?"

"I ran a list of all the men I helped get court orders against. Carnes was one, and he struck me as the type of guy who would pull a number like this."

"Is he the one doing it?" If so, Mason would personally see that Carnes never saw daylight without the benefit of steels bars for the next twenty years.

"No." Gillian frowned at the potato chips scattered across the floor as if she just noticed them for the first time. "He's still sore and mad at me, but he isn't the sender. Where do you keep your broom?"

Mason walked over to the small closet where his cleaning lady kept all the cleaning supplies. He handed Gillian the broom before picking up the box and its wrapping. "I'll get rid of this."

She bent down and picked up the foil bag and tossed it into the garbage can. "I'd appreciate that."

Mason carefully carried the box, the wrapping paper and the bow out the door. He glanced over his shoulder to make sure Gillian wasn't looking out the window, then opened the trunk of his car and placed the box inside. Later he would take it to a police detective he knew, to see if they could get a fingerprint and a name to match. Now he needed to continue this talk with Gillian. She might have explained why she tracked down Carnes this morning. But she hadn't explained why she felt compelled to leave his bed to do it.

He entered the kitchen and glanced around. Gillian

and the spilled chips were no longer in sight. Couldn't she stay put for more than two minutes? He headed for the hallway wondering where she had disappeared.

Gillian stood in the middle of the guest bedroom and wondered where to start. All her clothes on hangers were already hanging next to Mason's in his closet, but everything else was packed away or scattered throughout the room or the attached bathroom. The first thing she needed to do was unpack so she would feel more settled, and so that the next time she went looking for underwear, it wouldn't take ten minutes to find it. She also wanted to avoid Mason for a while. She had a feeling he wasn't done questioning her on her behavior this morning and she wasn't in the mood.

Her nerves were frayed. What she needed now was some down time. Everything was happening too fast: the threatening letters, the wedding, Mason's lovemaking, her confrontation with Carnes, and now a box full of leeches.

She shivered, forcing the vision of bloodsucking leeches from her mind, and reached for the first cardboard box to unpack.

"So this is where you're hiding," Mason said.

Gillian glanced up from the box she had dug into. "I'm not hiding." She waved a fistful of socks at him. "I'm unpacking."

"Need any help?"

She looked at the boxes in front of her, then at Mason. "You could carry these into our bedroom." *Our bedroom!* It sounded so intimate. So loving. "You said I could use the other bureau in there, right?"

"It's all yours." He picked up the first box. "It's been empty since the day I purchased the set." He headed out the door.

Gillian frowned as she pulled another box closer and unfolded the flaps to peer inside. What kind of man left a bureau empty for years? He had known they were getting married for thirteen years now, but still, it seemed a little odd that he would have left the triple dresser with the huge mirror attached to it empty all these years. She watched as Mason returned for the second box and wondered if the half of his closet that had been empty last Thursday night had also been unused for years.

When Mason returned for the third box, she picked up the fourth and followed him into their bedroom. "Thanks." She started to unpack the boxes and neatly place everything into the bureau. Out of the corner of her eye she kept a watch on Mason, who was sitting on the bed observing every move she made, as if fascinated by her choice of clothes.

Mason's voice broke the strained silence. "What made you decide to go into social work?"

She fumbled a sweater she was holding and had to refold the garment before placing it into the bottom drawer. "I like helping people." She gave him an amused glance before stacking the carton she just emptied onto another empty box. "The sight of blood makes me sick, so that left out medicine. I'm not talented with my hands, so building homes to house the poor was out. I don't like cooking enough to do it eight hours a day, so I couldn't feed the poor." She started in on the next box. "So that left our social system. I'm great at paperwork."

"Why did you leave it then?"

Gillian blushed. Mason's gaze seemed riveted to the stack of colorful panties in her hands. She dropped the silky garments into the drawer and then chastised herself for the act. Mason was now her husband, and after last night there wasn't an inch of her body the man hadn't seen, touched or kissed. What was a dozen silk panties to that?

"I left because I was tired of butting my head up against a wall of red tape. There were forms for this, applications for that and waiting lists that nearly broke my heart." She placed a pile of bras next to the panties. "One day I ran across one of the mothers who I had helped get training and a job. She worked herself off welfare and had every right to be proud of that fact. I was so proud of her."

"What happened?"

"She told me she was going to quit her job and go back on welfare. It seems she could make more money being on welfare than working a forty-hour week and paying a baby-sitter for her three children. Her ex-husband had left his job with no forwarding address and his child support had stopped. She could no longer make ends meet without that support check."

"So that's how you started chasing down deadbeat fathers."

She closed the drawer and looked at Mason. "You've seen the women and children I help. I'm their last hope. They put in applications for child-support enforcement services and have been relegated to someone's back burner. The fathers aren't white-collar workers who pick the kids up every other weekend. They're pond scum who hide from their children and their responsibilities."

"The *law* should be tracking down these men, Gillian. Not you."

The way he said the word *law,* one would think it was a godsend instead of being a backed-up, red-taped bunch of bureaucrats usually chasing their tails around in circles. "The law can't do it all, Mason. The numbers are just too overwhelming."

He stood up and walked toward her. "But why you?"

"Why not me?"

Mason's fingers reached out and tenderly brushed a strand of her hair away from her cheek. "Is it worth the threats and the possibility of danger? Is it worth constantly looking over your shoulder and scanning everything that comes into your life?" His finger traced her lower lip. "Is it worth gift-wrapped leeches?"

Gillian shuddered. Whoever was threatening her had been following her. That was the scary part—not a bunch of fat, ugly worms. How else could he have known about the wedding yesterday? Their engagement hadn't been publicized in the newspaper. It was one thing to have letters mailed to her office or apartment, where anyone with a phone book could have gotten the addresses. But it was entirely a different feeling to know that the man had walked up to the front door of her new home, set the box down and then brazenly rang the doorbell. If this madman was that daring, what else would he risk?

Chapter 7

Gillian paced the only room in the house she felt comfortable in, the family room. She had spent an hour this afternoon rummaging through her boxes stored above the garage, selecting a few items and scattering them throughout the room. Her ferns were placed strategically both to catch some sunlight and to add a little color. Simon, her porcelain dragon, stood guard by a set of French doors. An assortment of framed photos were now displayed on a side table, where before had sat a black hunk of what appeared to be iron, molded into some senseless configuration. She had studied the object for a full three minutes before placing it in a new, more fitting location: the top shelf of the closet where Mason kept his golf clubs. A couple dozen of her favorite books were now crammed onto the built-in shelves, which had contained nothing but an assortment of carved wooden ducks.

She hadn't realized it during her tour Thursday night,

but there seemed to be a multitude of ducks spread throughout Mason's home. Her husband must have a thing for ducks. Not the cute, fuzzy yellow ones, but wild ones. Mallards, pintails, mandarins and many she couldn't identify were placed in nearly every room. She had kept a couple of the exquisitely carved and hand-painted ducks on the shelves, but placed a few of the more colorful ones throughout the room. She didn't have a problem with sharing her room with her fine feathered friends, just hunks of iron that represented Lord only knew what.

The room was beginning to resemble a space she could feel comfortable in. Someplace where she could kick off her shoes, put her feet up and enjoy a cup of tea and a good book. In the winter a crackling fire would be an added bonus. The room still had a long way to go before it felt lived-in, but it would do for now. The same thing could be said for Mason. He had a long way to go before he felt like a husband, but she didn't have any major complaints, at least not yet.

She had expected more of an argument from him this afternoon about finding her in Carnes's place and about the threats she had been receiving. But Mason had been strangely quiet about both incidents. One part of her wanted to breathe a sigh of relief. The other part knew it wasn't over yet. Mason was trying to figure out the best way to handle his new wife. She didn't need to read Mason to know what he had been thinking; it had been in his eyes.

Mason didn't like the fact that she had gone waltzing into a strip joint in The Blades. He also didn't appreciate it that she left his bed while he was sleeping. He didn't like her job. He didn't like her prior job as a social worker. He glared at poor Simon every time he entered this room and he had frowned at the three blenders she had received as shower presents. What she was going to do with three blenders, especially since Mason already had one, was a mystery to her.

The only thing Mason seemed to enjoy was the dinner she had cooked and their lovemaking last night. She didn't have any frame of reference, but he must have enjoyed making love—why else would he want to repeat it twice more during the night?

She walked over to the French doors and stared out into the night. A thick row of trees and bushes marked the end of Mason's property, effectively acting as both a fence and a cover of privacy. The backyard was enormous. There was enough room for a pool and tennis court with an acre to spare. Neither had been added, and thinking of the barren patio, she wondered if Mason ever went out back to enjoy his little piece of paradise.

The one thing they had going in this marriage was great sex. She had sat at the kitchen table an hour ago and been fascinated by his hands. Those same hands holding a fork had taken her to heaven. Of course, there had been a number of other parts of his body that had helped her journey. She wondered if Mason felt the same way, or was it merely satisfying to him? She had not only been satisfied, she had splintered into a million pieces. His strength, his control, had held her together. She wanted to see Mason shatter within her arms. She wanted him to feel the same things she felt when they made love. She wanted Mason to lose his highly prized control.

The sheer curtain fell back into place as she turned her back on the night. Mason was in his office reviewing the cases he had scheduled tomorrow. With nervous fingers, she smoothed the silky flowing skirt she had put on after taking a shower. If Mason wasn't going to come to her, maybe it was time she confronted the lion within his own den.

Mason leaned back in his chair and frowned at the mass of folders scattered across his desk. How was he supposed to concentrate on tomorrow's cases when his wife was in the next room looking like a lost puppy? A beautiful lost puppy that was slowly making him lose his mind as well as his control.

Before dinner she had taken a shower and changed her faded jeans and T-shirt for a sleeveless pale blue blouse with a dozen tiny buttons and a flowing skirt done in a multitude of blues that ended below her calves and gave him an enticing view of her ankles. Snappy white sandals graced her feet and highlighted the pearly pink toenail polish she wore. All through dinner he had been fascinated by the tiny buttons streaking down her chest and the alluring fragrance of her seductive perfume. It had taken every ounce of his control to eat his meal and help clean up afterward. All his body wanted to do was to lay her down in the middle of the kitchen floor and sink into heaven.

Memories of last night hardened his body but he refused to become a slave to his hormones. Every Sunday night, since he became a judge, he had retired to his office to look over his upcoming cases and make some final preparations for the coming week. He wasn't about to change his schedule now that he had gotten married. He liked his life organized and well planned. Having a seductive wife wasn't part of his game plan.

For years he had never considered Gillian provocative. In his mind he had still pictured her as the lanky twelve-year-old who was all skinny legs and arms and had a bad overbite. Over the years he had seen her at a lot of the society's functions, but she always managed to arrive late, leave early and never once draw attention to herself. Then came the night of the society party at the country club when she strolled in through the doorway wearing the sequined dress that raised more than his blood pressure. It was the first time he had noticed Gillian as a woman, a sexy, desirable woman. He would have preferred a plain wife who would play by his rules. Better yet, he would have preferred no wife at all.

Now he was stuck with a wife who not only frequented strip joints and courted danger needlessly, but was also the object of some twisted individual's sick plan for revenge. If all that wasn't enough to make him turn gray overnight, she also could turn him on without even realizing it. The way her lips wrapped around a fork should be illegal. When she bit into her first piece of steak she had moaned the same sweet little sound she made when making love. He had to gulp down his entire glass of water before he could continue eating his meal. Even the way she said his name excited him.

How was he supposed to get any work done after she had looked so damn sad walking around the house as if wondering why she was there? Maybe he should have consulted with her two years ago when he bought the house. Had he been wrong to select a nice, big stately house that the real estate woman assured him any woman would be thrilled to call home? He had picked the nicest and safest neighborhood and had hired one of Philadelphia's top interior decorators to furnish the house. He had been satisfied with the results, but Gillian didn't look too pleased. In fact, she ignored the majority of the house and seemed to have claimed the family room as her own.

Her massive ferns added a nice touch of color to the room, but Simon, her inane dragon, looked out of place. The books she crammed onto the shelves were not only disorganized and placed helter-skelter, but the majority of them were paperbacks. Nothing at all like the leather-bound collection he had in his office. He appreciated the fact that she seemed to like his duck collection and displayed them in more prominent positions throughout the room. But he couldn't help but wonder what had happened to the ridiculously expensive sculpture the de-signer insisted went so well with the room.

Besides all that, Gillian seemed to be adjusting to her new home. It was a shame the same couldn't be said about him adjusting to Gillian. He'd think about purple dragons and missing artwork later. Right now he had a more pressing issue to worry about. Gillian's safety.

Whoever sent the leeches wasn't joking around. The person was serious. Dead serious. The little he could get from Gillian concerning the letters she had been receiving only confirmed his opinion. His wife had made an enemy and her safety was in jeopardy. The maniac also knew where she lived.

"Are you busy?" Gillian said.

Mason glanced up to see his wife standing in the doorway. "No, come on in."

She nodded at the folders spread across his desk as she stepped into the room. "What are you working on?"

"Just getting a feel as to what kind of cases I'll be working on this week."

"Which one has you so perplexed?" She stood next to the desk and scanned the folders.

Mason gathered up the papers into one neat pile. "What do you mean?" He hadn't been working on any of the cases. In fact, he hadn't even started to review them.

"You looked like the weight of the world was resting on your shoulders when I walked in."

He placed the folders into his open briefcase and sat back. "I was thinking about you." He refused to glance at the row of buttons trailing between her breasts.

"Me?" She gave him a soft smile and leaned her hip against the desk. "What were you thinking?"

She didn't have to look so damn satisfied. "I was reflecting on the fact that someone wants to harm you."

Gillian's smile slipped. "Oh, that."

"Don't you understand how serious this is?" He stood up and walked from behind the desk to stand in front of her. "The authorities have to be notified."

"I already talked to someone and there's nothing they can do until this person makes a move."

"Who did you speak to, and why didn't you tell me earlier?"

"You didn't give me a chance. I talked to one of the local police who patrolled by my apartment."

"Why didn't you go to one of the seven society members who are on the force? Maybe one of them could have traced a fingerprint."

"First off, if I went to one of the society members they would have felt obliged to notify the Council. Secondly, the Council would not only tell you, but they would have informed my parents. Six months ago my father was diagnosed with heart disease. They're pretty sure it can be treated with medication but he shouldn't be subjected to unnecessary stress."

"Why didn't you tell me about your father?"

She shrugged. "There hasn't been a whole lot of

communication between us, Mason. I couldn't see burdening you with my problems.''

"I'm your husband."

"You weren't six months ago."

Mason walked away from her and paced to the other side of the room. The temptation to shake some sense into her was too inviting. She didn't want to burden him with her problems! It was the most ridiculous thing he had ever heard, and in his profession he had heard some extravagant excuses. "I'm your husband now, Gillian."

"So now I'm telling you." She perched herself up on the corner of his desk and lightly swung her feet. "My father has a weak heart so go easy on him. My mother's a nervous wreck as a result of my father's condition, our wedding and my sixteen-year-old sister. The only time I think she relaxes is at work and then she's usually elbow deep into someone's insides." She gave a small grimace. "Isn't it strange what soothes some people?"

"From what I hear, your mother is a very talented surgeon."

"She is, but she knows all the talent in the world won't save my father if his heart stops." She smoothed her skirt over her knees. "My parents love each other very much."

"They had an arranged marriage, too, didn't they?" He had seen her parents together and knew Gillian was speaking the truth. Patricia and Luther Barnett appeared to have found not only contentment, but happiness as well. He wondered how they had done it.

"Yes." Gillian tilted her head to one side. "Not all arranged marriages work out like your parents, Mason.

The Council has an amazing track record when it comes to matchmaking.''

"Do you think ours will make it, or is it destined to crash and burn?'' He cringed at his own question. Talk about being pessimistic! Their marriage was barely twenty-four hours old and already he was looking for the crash.

She gave a shrug. "As they say down at the courthouse, 'the jury's still out on that one.''' She slid off the desk and examined a couple of books on a shelf. "I think if we are going to make it, we need to talk.''

"About?''

"Whatever is bothering you.'' She picked up an exquisite carved duck and inspected it.

Mason watched the way her fingers trailed over the delicately carved feathers of one of his favorite pieces. He could almost sense those roaming fingers on his own heated flesh. Gillian was doing it again. Here they were having a very serious conversation about their future and all he could think about was carrying her upstairs and tasting her sweetness once again.

"I don't like the fact that some madman is threatening you,'' he said.

"Neither do I.'' She gave him a slow smile and placed the duck back onto the shelf. "See, we can agree on some things, Mason.''

"I bet we won't agree on how to handle it.''

"How would you handle it?''

"First thing tomorrow morning we go downtown and pay a visit to someone I know and trust. He's a detective named Jon Hall at the fifteenth precinct. We'll turn over all the letters and the box of worms to see if they can get a print. The second thing we'll do is make sure

The Silhouette Reader Service™ — Here's how it works:

Accepting your 2 free books and gift places you under no obligation to buy anything. You may keep the books and gift and return the shipping statement marked "cancel." If you do not cancel, about a month later we'll send you 6 additional books and bill you just $3.80 each in the U.S., or $4.21 each in Canada, plus 25¢ shipping & handling per book and applicable taxes if any.* That's the complete price and — compared to cover prices of $4.50 each in the U.S. and $5.25 each in Canada — it's quite a bargain! You may cancel at any time, but if you choose to continue, every month we'll send you 6 more books, which you may either purchase at the discount price or return to us and cancel your subscription.

*Terms and prices subject to change without notice. Sales tax applicable in N.Y. Canadian residents will be charged applicable provincial taxes and GST.

If offer card is missing write to: Silhouette Reader Service, 3010 Walden Ave., P.O. Box 1867, Buffalo NY 14240-1867

NO POSTAGE
NECESSARY
IF MAILED
IN THE
UNITED STATES

BUSINESS REPLY MAIL

FIRST-CLASS MAIL   PERMIT NO. 717-003   BUFFALO, NY

POSTAGE WILL BE PAID BY ADDRESSEE

SILHOUETTE READER SERVICE
3010 WALDEN AVE
PO BOX 1867
BUFFALO NY 14240-9952

Play The Lucky Hearts Game

and get...
FREE BOOKS & a FREE GIFT...
YOURS to KEEP!

yes! I have scratched off the silver card. Please send me my **2 FREE BOOKS** and **FREE GIFT**. I understand that I am under no obligation to purchase any books as explained on the back of this card.

Scratch Here!
then look below to see
what your cards get you...

345 SDL DH5J   **245 SDL DH5H**

NAME   (PLEASE PRINT CLEARLY)

ADDRESS

APT.#   CITY

STATE/PROV.   ZIP/POSTAL CODE

Twenty-one gets you
2 FREE BOOKS and
a FREE GIFT!

Twenty gets you
2 FREE BOOKS!

Nineteen gets you
1 FREE BOOK!

TRY AGAIN!

Offer limited to one per household and not valid to current Silhouette Intimate Moments® subscribers. All orders subject to approval.

Visit us online at
www.eHarlequin.com

you're never left alone and that you refrain from going to your office or any other part of the city.''

Gillian chuckled and slowly shook her head. ''It's a good thing this is my problem and not yours.'' She glanced with great interest at the computer sitting on his desk. ''If you had your way I wouldn't be working, would I?''

''Not in your current profession. I don't have anything against my wife working. In fact, I would probably encourage it.''

''But not as a child-support recovery investigator?''

Mason gave a weary sigh. ''No.''

''I bet not as a social worker, either.''

''No.'' He locked gazes with Gillian and waited for the explosion that never came. She looked confused and hurt, but not angry. Any other woman in America would have tried ripping his head off for making such a statement. It was both chauvinistic and barbaric to suggest to your wife that she change her career, especially one she loved. And Gillian really loved working with and helping the poor.

''I'm not going to quit, Mason. The women who come to me need me. I not only love what I'm doing, but I'm making a difference.'' She gave the computer another glance before saying, ''But I'm willing to compromise.''

It was more than he expected. Visions of sleeping on the couch for life had filtered through his mind. ''What kind of compromises?''

''I'll allow you to take the box to Detective Hall in the morning on the condition he doesn't make it public. I don't want my parents to get wind of this. All the letters have been looked at and there weren't any prints.''

"Seems reasonable to me."

"My brother Cullen and my sister are coming here tomorrow around lunchtime to drop off the wedding gifts from the reception. I'll have them come with me to my office so I can pick up the mail and check on things."

"I don't want you going to the office. If you give me your keys, I'll stop by on my way home from work to pick up your mail."

She shook her head. "No can do, Mason. I'm not going to hide from this jerk, and you know as well as I do that I can protect myself. But I will try to do most of my work here at home until this guy is caught."

"You can do that?"

"On one condition."

"Which is?"

"That I borrow your computer. Mine's at my office and I'm not about to lug it here for a day or two."

"My computer?" He glanced at the machine sitting on his desk. Everything concerning his life was in that computer. It was the heart behind his organizing. His planner. His calendar. No one but him had ever used the thing. But if it would keep Gillian at home, then he really didn't have any other choice. "Don't go into any of my files and you may use it."

"Great."

"And you'll promise to stay out of The Blades?" It was dangerous just to walk down the streets in that part of the city on a good day. Never mind what could happen to her now that a psychopath was after her.

"I promise to avoid the area as much as possible, but I still have to drop in at my office for mail and to meet a client or two. I'll see about locating a couple of fathers who aren't in that general area."

It wasn't what he wanted, but it was an arrangement he could live with, for the time being. Maybe that was the secret behind a successful marriage—compromise. From what he remembered of his father, the man never compromised. It had to be Clint Blacksword's way or no way. "What about having someone stay here during the day while I'm at work?"

"Do you really want a wife who has to be baby-sat?"

"Not really, but I prefer my wife to be alive when we celebrate our first anniversary."

"Careful, Mason," Gillian said as she took a step closer to him. "Someone would think you might actually like me."

A seductive gleam seemed to have entered her eyes. He was all for seduction or any other game Gillian was willing to play. Last night he was unsure of what pleased him more—finding out Gillian was a virgin, or the way she responded to his every touch.

"Who said I didn't like you?" He took a step and closed the distance between them. There were many things he was beginning to like about his wife. He might not agree on her career, but he had to respect her fortitude against his opposition. He liked the way she refused to cower to a madman, but he still feared for her safety. Gillian was the kind of woman you could depend upon during a crisis. She would keep her head and not go screaming off into the night. He admired her strength, even when it was pitted against his own. There was more to his wife than just a beautiful face and body.

He liked the way her hair caught the sun, turning the golden tresses into streaks of shimmering light. The way her pale blue eyes changed into turbulent pools whenever he kissed her. He especially prized the way she shattered in his arms when they made love.

Mason reached out and tenderly stroked her cheek. "There are many things about you, wife, that I'm beginning to like."

She turned her head and placed a kiss in the center of his palm. "Such as?"

His fingers trailed down her throat, ending where the deep V of her blouse began. "The provocative little moan you make in the back of your throat when I'm deep inside you."

"I moan?"

Mason chuckled softly at the flush of red sweeping up her cheeks. "There's nothing to be embarrassed about." He worked the first tiny button through its hole. "I happen to like that moan." The second button came undone.

Gillian's hands came around his neck and she placed a kiss on his jaw.

Mason felt her cool lips against his rough jaw. "I should shave."

Her arms tightened. "Don't you dare. I happen to like the dark shadow. It makes you look a little bit wild."

"Wild?" No one had ever called him wild before. It was an interesting observation, considering Gillian herself made him feel slightly uncivilized. "I don't want to scratch you." The next two buttons came undone.

Her fingers caressed his jaw. "I'll take my chances."

Mason noticed that her eyes were turning a stormy blue, and they hadn't even kissed yet. Her lips looked sweet and ripe, ready for his loving. Several more buttons found themselves undone. "You might change your mind once you know where I'm planning on kissing you."

Gillian smiled, stood on her toes, and with her lips

gave one of his earlobes a playful tug. "Promises, promises."

He gave a low growl, just to show her how wild he was feeling at the moment, and finished unbuttoning her blouse. With a quick brush of his hands, the silky garment landed near her feet. With the tip of his finger he traced the edge of the ice blue lace cupping her breasts. Dark, rosy nipples budded beneath the lace. "Do you have any idea what you do to me?"

She placed one of her hands upon his chest, and with the other she flattened his hand over the curve of her left breast. "I would say it's the same as you do to me."

Mason could feel the pounding of her heart beneath his hand. The thunderous rhythm matched his own beat for beat. He wrapped his other arm around her waist and pulled her against his body so that she would have no doubt what she was doing to him. The semi-arousal he had walked around with all day had turned into an aching mass of need screaming for relief. Screaming for Gillian. "I'd say it's harder."

Gillian closed her eyes and wiggled her hips against him. "I'd say you were right."

With every sway of her hips her lace-covered breasts teased his shirt and his control. His arousal thickened behind the barrier of his pants. Heat fired his blood as her fingers pulled the hem of his shirt out of the waistband of his pants and expertly undid the two buttons at the base of his throat. With a flick of his fingers he undid her bra and pushed it off her shoulders. With a twist of her hands she had his shirt off and sent it flying across the room.

He bent his head and placed openmouthed kisses down her throat to the seductive nubs pleading for his attention. He was more than willing to give them his

attention, along with every other part of her body. They
had all night, all week, all year. Hell, they might even
have a lifetime to tease, taste and satisfy each other.

He captured her wandering fingers as they reached
for his belt. He raised his mouth from the moist nub he
had suckled and tried to calm his breathing with a deep
breath. "We have to slow down."

"Why?"

"Because if we don't, I'm afraid we'll be making
love on the floor in a minute." He brought her hand up
to his lips and kissed the tip of each finger.

Gillian glanced down and eyed the thick carpet with
great interest. "I've never made love on the floor before."

"I know." She had only made love in a bed. His
bed.

"Is it truly uncomfortable?" Her hand trailed down
his chest, teasing his dark nipples beneath their covering
of curls.

"Gillian," Mason growled in desperation as her hand
went lower. He couldn't bring himself to stop its descent. When her fingers pressed against his hardness he
knew he had lost. "You're about to find out."

Gillian opened her eyes a half hour later and tried to
stifle the giggle threatening to erupt. Of all the scenarios
she could picture her new husband in, this wasn't one
of them. They were both totally naked, lying on a bed
of discarded clothes on Mason's office floor. Well, she
had her answer. The thick hunter green carpeting covering the floor was both soft and comfortable, but she
was afraid she was going to have a couple of rug burns
in some very interesting places. The giggle she'd been
trying to control escaped.

"What's so funny?" Mason leaned up on one elbow and stared down at his wife.

"Uh, nothing." Mason seemed unamused by the situation, but she thought she could detect a slight twitch at the corner of his mouth. "You really ought to give your cleaning woman a raise."

"Why's that?"

She glanced back under the desk less than a foot away from her head. "Not a dust bunny in sight."

"And how do you suppose I go about telling her how we know there aren't any?"

This time she was positive the corner of his mouth twitched. "I'll explain it to her if you want," she replied impishly.

Mason stood up in one swift movement with her in his arms. "You, dear wife, will not say a word to Lottie."

Gillian wrapped her arms around his neck and snuggled deeper into his arms. She glanced at the room as he carried her out the door and into the hallway. "I don't think I'll have to."

"Why's that?" He took the steps two at a time.

"Not only will our clothes scattered throughout the room give us away—" She paused to place a kiss on his collarbone and admire the way the muscles in his arms bunched and swelled as he carried her weight.

"I'll pick them up later." He carried her into the master bedroom and deposited her in the middle of the bed. "What else was there?"

"Next time you're in there, check out the interesting imprints our bodies made on the piling of the carpet." She chuckled at the flush sweeping up Mason's cheeks. "Anyone who isn't half-blind will know these marks didn't come from a shoe."

Mason's deep chuckle joined hers as he lowered himself onto the bed and into her arms. "Woman, you are a menace to my peace of mind."

Gillian felt his warmth cover her and smiled.

The leeches were everywhere. Their gaping mouths were wide open and searching for blood. Dozens of slimy black bodies covered the bed in their pursuit for food. They were creeping their way up legs, over arms and across Gillian's face. The more Mason pulled them off her, the more there were. Dozens, hundreds, maybe even thousands of bloodsucking leeches were trying to drain the very life out of his wife!

Mason jerked up in bed and wildly looked around. The faint glow from the hallway was the only light in the room. He glanced down beside him. Gillian was peacefully sleeping, oblivious to the terror he was feeling. His gaze skimmed the bed looking for any signs of what he had just witnessed. Nothing. Nothing but wrinkled sheets and the soft sound of his wife's breathing.

What in the hell had happened? One minute he had been cradling his sleeping wife's satisfied body and slowly allowing sleep to claim him, and the next there were leeches everywhere. It had been so real, he could still feel their squishy bodies between his fingers and see the marks they left behind as he pulled them off Gillian. She hadn't cried out; in fact, not one sound had escaped her throat. But her eyes had spoken of her terror, of the pain, pleading with him to help her. The more he tried to help, the worse it became.

Mason slowly slipped out of the bed and glanced around the floor, the walls, the furniture. Not a single thing was out of place. His hands were trembling and the sweat of fear coated his body. He reached for his robe hanging on the back of the bathroom door and pulled it on before softly closing the door and turning on the light.

He grimaced at his own reflection in the mirror. His face was chalky white and his dark eyes held a wild look. With an unsteady hand he turned on the cold water and splashed his face. He yanked the thick white towel from the rack and buried his dripping face into its softness and groaned. What he had just experienced was either a dream or a premonition.

He'd never experienced foresight before and honestly believed he didn't possess that particular power. A few members of the society had been gifted with clairvoyance, but he wasn't one of them. As for dreaming, he didn't know. He'd never dreamed before, and if this was a normal dream, he never wanted to again. What he had experienced must be what people called a nightmare. It was the only explanation he could think of. He had just weathered his first nightmare, and he was afraid it had won.

He draped the towel back onto the rack and left the bathroom. Gillian was still sleeping deeply, as if she hadn't a care in the world. The glow from the hallway illuminated the fiery chain of rubies surrounding her delicate neck. Last night he had realized that he'd forgotten to give her her wedding present. He remembered the gift earlier, after they had made love at a more leisurely pace in the comfort of their bed. She had had tears in her eyes as he fastened the necklace for her.

The rubies burned with their fire against her exquisite throat. It was the only thing she was wearing. That and the fragrance of their love.

Mason ran his fingers through his hair and read the house. Nothing and no one was there. Everything was

as it should be. No intruder, no leeches and no danger.
He hung the robe back up on its hook and slipped back
into bed.

He gently pulled Gillian back into his arms and held
her tight. Sleep wasn't going to come easily. The nightmare had stolen his peace as easily as Gillian had stolen
his heart.

Chapter 8

Mason stared at Detective Jon Hall and the forensics expert.

"Nothing?"

"Sorry, Mason, but the box, paper and bow are clean. The only prints we picked up are yours and Gillian's," Jon said before he turned to the other man. "Thanks for rushing this, Pete. I really appreciate it."

"No problem, Jon." Pete, the forensics expert, ground out his cigarette and stood up. "Sorry I couldn't be of more help."

With a sense of hopelessness, Mason watched Pete leave. Finding a print was his only chance to identify the culprit and to put an end to the threats before they became actions. "Well, Jon, what do you suggest?" He was fresh out of ideas and had no problem with seeking advice from someone with more experience in these matters. He had met Jon a couple years back while presiding over a case. Not only had they respected each other's work, but a friendship had developed between them. Jon was a cop Mason trusted, but more important, he wasn't a member of the society. The Council would never hear about the threats made to Gillian. He had dropped the box off to Jon on his way to work. Now, on his way home, he had stopped to hear the results. They weren't what he had been hoping for.

"There's nothing much you can do legally without knowing who's making the threats. You said Gillian has a list of all the men she tracked who've had child support withheld from their wages?"

"Yes, and she has already eliminated two of the men."

"If you can get me a copy of the list I could run it through our records. Maybe I can come up with something."

"Gillian's already done that." Mason gave Jon an amused glance. "Don't ask how she tapped into the police files. You don't want to know."

Jon chuckled. "No one can say you married a boring woman." He gave Mason a light slap on the back. "You're a better man than I am."

Mason refused to smile at Jon's comments regarding his wife. Gillian and the word *boring* didn't belong in the same sentence. "What else do you suggest?"

"I had the box examined, but there's nothing special about it or the wrapping paper. Anyone could have purchased it in about a thousand different stores."

Mason glanced at the box sitting on Jon's desk. Thankfully Jon had disposed of the leeches that had been inside. After the nightmare he had had last night he didn't think he could stomach seeing the creatures again. Jon was a good friend and an excellent police detective.

"I do have one other suggestion, but you might not want to use it."

"What's that?"

"Tabitha Tateman." Jon appeared to be studying a dried coffee ring on his blotter as if his life depended upon it.

"She's Gillian's closest friend."

Mason knew how much that suggestion had cost Jon. Mason knew the two of them had worked together on a rape case some time ago but he didn't know the whole story. All he knew was that the rapist had been killed by Jon in a shoot-out, and neither of them had ever spoken of it again.

It wasn't as if the idea of asking Tabitha for help hadn't crossed his mind. It had, and just as fast as he'd thought of it, he'd discounted it. Gillian would never even consent to approaching Tabitha with such a simple request as doing a reading on the letters or the box. He couldn't blame her. Tabitha deserved her peace.

"I can't do that, Jon."

"Good." Jon gave him a ghost of a smile. "I felt it was my duty to point out all your options, no matter if I agree with them or not."

"I know. That's why I came to you." Mason gave a weary sigh and stood up. "I guess that means I'm back to square one."

"If you get me a copy of Gillian's list I'll see what I can dig up. I might have a couple tricks up my sleeve that your wife doesn't know about." Jon carefully picked up the box, tissue paper, wrapping paper and bow and placed them in a clear plastic bag and sealed it. "I'll keep this here in case we need it later."

"Fine. I'll fax you the list tonight." Mason reached across the desk and shook Jon's hand. "Thanks for everything, Jon. And I'd appreciate this not being leaked to the press.''

"I understand.'' Jon stood up. "You keep a close eye on your wife until this guy is caught.''

Mason met Jon's gaze. "I will.''

Mason pulled his car into the garage thirty minutes later and glanced at Gillian's car parked outside. He still hadn't figured out why his wife refused to park her car in the garage. She definitely needed a newer mode of transportation, but he couldn't see buying her one until she changed careers. A new car didn't stand a chance being parked in The Blades.

Maybe a new car would entice Gillian to change careers, but he doubted it. His wife didn't seem impressed with material possessions or expensive things. This morning he had spotted a bright yellow coffee mug with a smiley face in the kitchen cabinet with the rest of his dishes. *His dishes.* Gillian had to go out of her way to locate that mug from the pile of boxes stored above the garage. It symbolized something more than what it was. It was something of hers. Something she could look at and think, *mine.*

He closed the garage door and looked at his house as if for the first time. It was *his* house, *his* dishes, *his* furniture. What he had thought to be so simple wasn't. Gillian wasn't just going to hang her clothes in the closet, fill the empty bureau with a kaleidoscope of silky panties, hang her toothbrush next to his and call it home. Maybe instead of everything being his or hers, he should concentrate on making everything *theirs*.

For better or worse, she was in his life and in his bed. For the first time in his life he hadn't wanted to leave his bed that morning and go to work. He would have given anything to pull his bride back into his arms and make sweet love to her for the next week or so. Now was a hell of a time to appreciate what the honeymoon was designed for. His two-week vacation wasn't scheduled until late December, five months away.

Mason opened the kitchen door and immediately wanted to close it again. The entire kitchen appeared to be trashed. He slowly set his briefcase by the door and glanced around the room in amazement. Bowls, pots and nearly every spice known to man were scattered across the counter. A cookbook was propped open with a butcher knife and flour coated every available surface. It appeared his wife was cooking. Lord save him if her cooking reflected her method. He took a hesitant step closer and sniffed. He could detect the aroma of cherry pie, possibly meat loaf and a wet dog. *A wet dog!* He sniffed again. Definitely a wet dog.

The faint sound of Gillian's laughter reached him. He followed that sound to the laundry room tucked off the kitchen and slowly opened its door. If he thought the sight of the kitchen shocked him, he had been wrong. This was shock.

Gillian heard the door open and glanced over her shoulder. "Oh, good, you're home." She tightened her grip on the wiggling bundle of towels in her arms and whispered, "Behave."

"Who, me?" Mason's gazed skimmed the small room.

"No, Fred." Gillian glanced at the room and felt her confidence slip a notch. A half-dozen dripping-wet towels were lying on the floor. They had only managed to absorb half the water.

"Who's Fred?" His gazed landed on the squirming bundle of towels his wife was clutching to her chest.

"Our new watchdog."

"*Our* new watchdog?"

A black shiny nose, a tuft of black hair and one deep brown eye escaped the bundle. She straightened her shoulders and raised her chin a notch. "I figured we could use the added protection." A high-pitched bark seconded her statement.

"Where did you purchase this vicious attack dog?"

A pink tongue snaked out of the terry cloth and licked her fingers. "I didn't purchase him. I found him."

"Where?"

"Near my office, and before you say a word, you knew I was going there today. Cullen and Raine were with me the entire time." Fred's head broke all the way out and she scratched the dog behind one of his floppy ears. "In fact, without their help I would never have been able to catch him. I think he must have been beaten."

"You brought an abused stray home with you?" He eyed the dog with great distrust. "Don't you realize what kind of diseases he could have? What if he bit you? I won't even mention parasites and fleas."

"He didn't have parasites and I didn't just take him home. I stopped at a vet, who examined him, gave him all his shots and a clean bill of health. Except for being slightly undernourished and a bad case of fleas, Fred is in excellent health."

Fred glanced between Mason and Gillian, gave another high-pitched yap and proceeded to happily pant.

Gillian rubbed the puppy briskly with the towel and placed him on the floor. Maybe once Mason saw how adorable Fred was, he'd stop harping. She had just spent the last hour scrubbing, soaking and shampooing the dog within an inch of his life. She used half a bottle of doggy shampoo and an entire one of flea dip to disinfect the poor thing. If she was ever going to convince Mason to allow the dog to stay, it would be easier if his house wasn't infested with fleas.

Mason glanced down at the animal and burst out laughing. "That's an attack dog? What's he going to attack? Killer caterpillars?"

Gillian reached back down and scooped up Fred. "I didn't say he was an attack dog. I said he was a watchdog." Fred looked pitifully skinny with his black hair plastered to his sides. During his bath she had been appalled by the way she could feel his ribs beneath her fingers. And that had been after he polished off a cream-filled donut on the drive to the vet and two whole cans of dog food after they had gotten home.

"What's he going to watch," Mason asked, chuckling, "television?"

"No, he's going to watch me throw your dinner into the trash in a minute." She had married an insensitive jerk. How could he say such a thing about a poor little puppy? Fred had integrity. She had felt it the instant she spotted him hiding in an alley behind a trash bin. Fred was going to make a wonderful watchdog.

Mason stopped laughing. "You're serious. You want to keep *this* dog as a watchdog?"

Gillian tightened her hold on the squirming puppy, who was busily trying to lick her shirt where a glob of donut cream had been smeared during his earlier snack. She could see the argument forming in Mason's eyes. He didn't want the dog in his house. Then again, he hadn't been real happy with getting her, either. "Yes." She held her breath and waited.

Mason glanced at the damp puppy licking his wife's chest and sighed. "Is he housebroken?"

Gillian grinned. "He seems to be."

"Seems to be?"

"I'll clean up any accidents he might have." She held the puppy up and rubbed his nose with her own. She had finally gotten a dog. It had only taken her twenty-five years and one husband, but she had done it. Fred licked her cheek and she laughed as she set him back down on the floor. The puppy made a beeline for one of the squeaky toys she had purchased at the pet store, which also sold her the shampoo, the leash, a set of bowls and food. "I'll also replace anything he might chew up."

Mason shook his head and eyed the animal gnawing on a pink squeaky toy. "What have I done?"

Gillian stepped as close to Mason as she could without touching him. He looked so handsome and stuffy in his suit. Here it was after six and his tie hadn't even been loosened. She reached up and placed a quick kiss on his cheek. "You made me very happy. Thank you."

Mason captured her mouth in a slow kiss. "You're welcome."

He tried to pull her closer but she backed away. "I need a shower." Her shirt and jeans were drenched with the smell of wet dog and flea dip.

He eyed the dog gnawing contentedly on his toy. "I'll join you." He stepped closer and backed her against the washing machine. "Will dinner hold?"

The heat of his gaze melted all her resistance. She had no idea if dinner would hold or not, nor did she care. "Will you?"

Mason growled and rubbed up against her. "No."

Gillian grinned, wrapped her arms around his neck and plastered herself to his hard body. The hell with the suit. That's what the cleaners were for.

* * *

An hour and a half later Mason met the pizza deliveryman at the front door and paid him. So much for Gillian's meat loaf. They had been so carried away as they left the laundry room that Gillian had forgotten to shut off the oven. By the time they had showered, made love on the bathroom floor, showered again and then got dressed, the meat loaf had been burnt to the consistency of tree bark.

He had been ordered to call for pizza and to take Fred out back while Gillian cleaned up the laundry room and started in on the kitchen. He had gladly taken the easier end of the deal. Tossing an old tennis ball to a puppy beat tackling the mess she had made in the kitchen.

How Gillian had talked him into letting her keep the dog was still a mystery. He didn't like animals. Didn't understand animals. And never had any desire to own one. Within the past forty-eight hours he not only obtained a wife, had a psychopath delivering leeches to his door and experienced his first nightmare, but now he had a dog. A vicious watchdog that barely came up to his calves and that had a bark the Tabernacle Choir would envy. Even when Fred became full grown he still wouldn't reach his knee. The burglars must be shaking in terror by now, knowing what a ferocious dog guarded *their* house. And what in the hell kind of name was Fred for a dog?

Mason carried the flat white box into the kitchen. "Pizza's here."

Gillian finished wiping egg yolk from the cookbook and carefully closed the book. "Great, I'm starved." The laundry room was clean and dry. A load of towels was already in the washer and the window had been opened to air the room out. The kitchen was almost back to normal and the meat loaf was in the trash. Even Fred had turned up his nose at the burnt offering. It was the first tidbit of food the puppy ignored. So much for impressing Mason with her wifely skills. It was a good thing he didn't marry her for her culinary talents.

She joined him at the kitchen table and swiped the first piece of pizza. She took a bite and sat at one of the places she had set earlier. "It's all your fault."

"What is?" He took a bite out of his slice.

"That dinner got ruined." The tip of her tongue licked a drop of tomato sauce from the corner of her mouth. "I'll have you know that I make a very good meat loaf."

Mason grinned. "So you tell me."

The slice of pizza Gillian was raising toward her mouth stopped in midair. Mason had smiled! Hell, it wasn't even a smile, it was a grin. That flash of white teeth and the sparkle that had gleamed in his eye did the most amazing thing to her heart. If she thought Mason was handsome when he was all dark and moody, it was nothing compared to when he smiled. She continued to stare at him as the grin slowly disappeared.

"What's the matter?" Mason reached for a napkin and wiped his mouth.

"You should do that more often."

"What?"

"Smile." She took another bite of her pizza and was fascinated by the flush stealing up Mason's face. He was embarrassed! "I always knew you were handsome, but I never realized just how handsome until now." Gillian grinned as his flush deepened to a dull red.

He muttered, "Thanks," as he got up and headed for the refrigerator and pulled out two cans of soda.

She glanced over at Fred, sleeping on the rug in front

of the sink with his pink squeaky toy between his paws. Maybe she should bring a dog home every day. She liked Mason when he was like this, all relaxed and casual. There was a distinct possibility that their marriage might work out after all. He wasn't nearly as oppressive as she first thought he would be, and the sex… What could she say about their lovemaking besides that it was perfection in the highest form? Mason touched more than her body when they came together. He touched her heart. Her soul. But was it love?

Could she love a man who didn't believe in it? Who didn't love her back? Her mind cried no, but her heart wasn't so sure. She had to try to discover what was in his heart. She had to get through Mason's iron control before she could touch his heart.

The only time his control threatened to slip was when they made love. It wasn't enough. She didn't want to find a heart filled only with lust, desire and physical need. She wanted more. Needed more.

Mason's gift was his control. She understood that, accepted that. But it didn't mean he had to control everything that touched his life. He didn't have to control her or their marriage. She was gifted with love and compassion, but it didn't mean she loved everyone and everything. Lord knew she tried. People who didn't pull at her heartstrings were few and far between. But they were out there.

To see what was truly in Mason's heart, she had to get past the iron gate of his control. She had to understand her husband. To know what his hopes and dreams were. For that she had to comprehend his past. She knew just about what everyone else in the society knew about Mason and his family. Maybe a little more. His parents were pledged in one of the few marriages that never worked. He had two younger sisters, and by the time he was twelve he was truly the man of the house. From all accounts Mason was a somber young man who took his role in his family very seriously. His mother refused help from the Council and raised her family the best she could. The key to who Mason really was lay in his past.

"Penny for your thoughts," Mason said as he handed Gillian a glass of soda.

"Oh, sorry." She took the glass. "My mind was wandering."

"It looked serious." He took a second slice of pizza. "Anything I can help you with?"

Gillian shook her head as she polished off her slice. She took her time slowly chewing the crust. In her mind, it was the best part of the meal. "Can I ask you a question?"

"If you can't, who could?"

"Why do you hate social workers?" The question had been bugging her for a long time. Mason didn't seem to mind a working wife. Just one that worked in her field of expertise, social services.

Mason stared at her for a long time before answering. "My contact with one of them, years ago, wasn't a pleasant experience."

Mason had had contact with a social worker! When? Who? But more important, why? Was there an old girlfriend who worked in social services who broke his heart? As calmly as she could, she asked, "Care to explain?"

"Must I?"

"I can't force you to tell me." She could tell he really didn't want to discuss the subject. "But if you don't I'll be forced to seek the answer elsewhere. Or worse—'' she gave him a big smile, hoping to sway him ''—I'll use my own imagination to think up a scenario to go with that statement.''

''I shudder to think what your mind could come up with.''

''Just look at it this way. If you answer one of my questions, I'll have to answer one of yours.''

One of his black eyebrows shot up to the middle of his forehead. ''Any question?''

She had to think about that one. *Any question?* Would she answer any question Mason might pose? Maybe not willingly, but she'd answer. ''Sure, why not? You're my husband now and there shouldn't be any secrets between us.'' She gave him an impish grin. ''But then again, you might wish you had left my secrets buried.''

''I'll take my chances.'' He toyed with the moisture that had built on the outside of his glass. ''My mom had a hard time raising us kids after my father walked out. When you get to know my mom better, you'll realize her 'gift' must be stubbornness. She blamed the Council for her disastrous marriage and refused all offers of help from the society. The only time she accepted their help was for my education. She was putting in ten hour days, six days a week, at what was a sweatshop a couple blocks over from our apartment. She sewed for sixty hours a week and still couldn't make ends met. The rent was always due and Kara wasn't the healthiest of kids. She had asthma, constant ear infections, and her appendix and tonsils were both taken out before her tenth birthday. Mom missed a lot of work because of Kara.''

Gillian could hear the love in his voice when he talked about his sisters and mother. Would it one day be there when he talked about her?

"Anyway, to make a long, boring story short, occasionally, when things got too tight, Mom applied for public assistance. Nothing much, just a helping hand so Kara could get the proper medicine and some food for the table."

She cringed. She knew all the parts Mason was leaving out of his story. Over the years she had seen families like his, felt their pain, and each and every time it saddened her heart. Mason was a proud man whose childhood must have torn at his soul. "Was she denied?" She had heard stories before about families who had been denied. That would explain his dislike for the system.

"No, she got a few crumbs here and there. But it cost."

"What did it cost?" Gillian knew he wasn't referring to money.

"Our self-respect." Mason gave a shrug and continued to streak the condensation on his glass with the tip of his finger. "A nasty, uppity social worker snooped around the apartment and asked insulting and private questions. Just the way she walked around and inspected everything let you know what she thought. We might have been poor, but we weren't filthy. Once, when we kids should have been in the bedroom being quiet, we snuck out into the hallway and listened. My mother was in tears, crying as if her heart would break. Do you know what this moral, respectable soul of the social system suggested?"

"No." But she could imagine. Lord, could she imagine.

"She wanted my mother to place us in a foster home." He glanced up and locked gazes with her. "Do you have any idea what that did to my mother? This woman walked into our home and practically told my mother she was an unfit parent.''

Gillian broke eye contact first. She felt nauseated. One within her own ranks had betrayed the system. To insinuate that Nadine Blacksword was an unfit mother was preposterous. "She was wrong, Mason." It was a sad, simple response, but it was the best she could do. There were good social workers, and there were bad. Mason's mother got one of the bad ones.

Her arms ached to hold the hurting boy that was still buried inside him. But she didn't reach out. Mason, the man, wouldn't appreciate what he would see as pity, though it was really compassion.

Mason stared at her for a long time before shrugging. "Can we change the subject now?"

"Sure." Gillian stood up and started to clean off the table. "I know what we can do."

Mason gave her a wicked grin.

"Not that," Gillian said, chuckling. The man was shameless. Ego-boosting, but shameless nevertheless. Lord, they had practically killed themselves in the shower an hour ago. No matter what books said or movies showed, doing the "wild thing" in the shower was dangerous. More people had to have shown up in emergency rooms throughout the country having sex in the shower than for bike accidents. They probably hauled their broken bodies out of the tub, pulled on some clothes and strapped on a pair of in-line skates before calling the ambulance.

She and Mason had barely made it out of the slippery death trap in one piece. Of course they had only made it as far as the soft throw rug covering the bathroom floor.

Gillian grinned at the memories and tugged on Mason's hand. "We can do *that* later." She pulled him out of the room and into the hall. "I want you to see our booty."

Mason glanced behind her at her backside. "I'd like to look at your bootie."

"Not that bootie." She pulled him into the dining room, where Cullen, Raine and she had stacked the wedding presents earlier. "This booty." The entire table and buffet were covered in shimmering presents. She picked up the nearest present, wrapped in white paper with silver bells, and placed it in his hands. "You start."

Mason looked at the present in his hand and the rest of the mountain of boxes piled throughout the room and groaned.

They were back! Hundreds, possibly thousands of leeches squirmed their way across his bed to Gillian. This time, instead of trying to pull the creatures off his wife, he tried to pick up Gillian. Every time his hands reached out they encountered another bloodsucker. He couldn't get a grip on Gillian. Her pale blue eyes were wide with terror and silently begging him to help. He tried desperately and failed miserably. With unblinking eyes, she watched him fail.

With a roar of frustration Mason jerked awake.

Gillian sat up and placed her hand on her husband's shoulder. "Mason?"

At her touch Mason snapped his head around and stared at her. In the dimness he could make out her worried expression. There were no leeches, no judgmental looks. Only concern for him. He turned away and dragged his hand down his face. A curse tumbled from his mouth. His body trembled and he wanted to scream. What in the hell was going on?

Gillian reached for the light on the nightstand and clicked it on. "What's wrong?" She pulled the blanket up to cover her nakedness and moved closer to him.

"Wrong?" Mason opened his eyes after the initial flare of light. He studied the anxiety pulling at Gillian's mouth. Her mouth was designed for loving, not worrying.

"You yelled."

"What did I yell?" He did a scanning of the house, but could only pick up the presence of Fred snoring away on the kitchen rug he had adopted as a bed. No one was there. Gillian was safe.

"I don't know. I woke at the sound." She brushed a lock of his dark hair off his forehead. "Was it a dream?"

"A dream?" Lord, no one would class the horrifying scene he just experienced as a dream. It was so real! He could feel their soft bodies, smell their odor and see Gillian's fear. The taste of his own fear was still in his mouth.

"You told me you didn't dream." She pushed him gently back down and snuggled against him.

Mason's arms wrapped around her like a vise. He never wanted to let her go. He heard somewhere that dreams had a meaning. He wondered if nightmares did, too. He raised his head and placed a tender kiss on the top of Gillian's head. "I've never dreamed before."

Her hand flattened against his chest as if listening to his heart pound.

"You're dreaming now?" she asked.

"If you want to call it dreaming. Then yes, I'm starting to dream."

Gillian raised her head and studied his face. "What do you call it?"

"A nightmare." He pushed her head back to his chest.

"Want to tell me about it?"

"No." Lord, was she crazy? How could he tell her what his nightmares were about?

"I used to have nightmares as a child."

"You did? What were they about?"

"I could never remember." He felt her smile against his chest. "I used to wake everyone in the house with my screaming, but I could never remember what had frightened me so."

"Maybe it's better if you don't remember." He would rather have not remembered this dream. He would pay anything to forget.

"I don't think so." Her fingers tugged at a dark curl. "I was afraid of everything for nearly two years. I was scared of the dark thinking maybe that was what caused my nightmares. I was terrified of the neighbor's dog, loud noises and even bubbles."

"Bubbles?"

"Don't ask." She chuckled. "To a child's mind the world could be a frightening place and I tended to have a vivid imagination."

"What caused the nightmares to stop?"

"I don't know. One day I realized it was a week since I had one, then a month, and next thing I knew they were gone. Now when I dream, I remember them. They're a little foggy and hazy, but that's okay. They're mine."

Mason lay there and listened to Gillian's soft breathing. His heart rate was slowly dropping back to normal and the trembling in his fingers was barely noticeable. Why were dreams foggy and hazy when nightmares were graphic and intense? Why was he having the bad dreams about leeches when logic told him Gillian was the one who should be experiencing the anxiety? She was the one being threatened, not he. So why was his sleep being tortured?

"Gillian?"

"Yes."

"I finally figured out what I want to ask you." He wrapped a silken strand of hair around a finger. He answered her questions concerning social workers, now it was his turn. "Tell me one of your dreams."

Gillian's fingers stilled from their roving. "One of my dreams?"

"Pick one, any one."

"Dreams are strange, Mason. They don't make a lot of sense. Sometimes they aren't even about you." Her fingers continued their journey. "I'll tell you about a dream I have quite often. It's one of my favorite dreams, but I don't know why. I'm not even in it."

This dreaming business sounded strange to him. How could you dream and not even be in it? "Okay, let's hear it."

"There's this little boy, I guess around three or four years old. The whole dream takes place on a beach. A tropical beach, because there are palm trees in the dream. I can see the ocean and hear the birds. Most of the time I can actually smell the salt air and a faint hint of flowers. I don't know what kind of flowers, because I never see them. Only the child. Anyway, this boy is the cutest little kid I've ever seen. He has a bucket and a shovel and he builds sand castle after sand castle."

"Go on."

"That's it. The entire dream is about this boy on a crowded beach who builds sand castles."

"That's your favorite dream?"

"Sounds stupid, huh? I don't know why, but there's something special about that little boy and his sand castles. Whenever I have that dream, I feel invincible. Like I'm on top of the world. That everything in my life is going to work out perfectly."

Gillian dreamed of a little boy and felt exhilarated. If he dreamed of a child he would have felt nothing but panic. Fred, the soprano watchdog, was one thing, but a child was something totally different. He didn't want a child. Even though Gillian and he weren't using protection, he prayed that she wouldn't conceive. He didn't want to be a father. He had firsthand knowledge of what a father who didn't want to be a father became. It wasn't a pretty sight. How did a person know he would be a good father or a bad father without having the child first? He never wanted to risk having a child and then discover he had inherited not only his dark hair and eyes from his father, but his selfishness and irresponsibility too.

Did Gillian's dream of a child mean she wanted children? He knew their marriage was arranged so that they could have children and keep the society growing. But it didn't mean Gillian wanted children. Maybe she was just as trapped as he felt. It was one thing to want children, quite another to be forced to produce them.

Mason reached over and turned off the light. He kept Gillian in his arms and kissed her. If her dreams of a boy and his sand castles made her feel good, then who was he to argue? "It sounds like a wonderful dream."

Chapter 9

Mason entered his chambers with a weary set to his shoulders and glanced at the pile of mail. He was tired. For the past week he had been buried in work at the courthouse, and buried in Gillian at night. He played with Fred for endless hours and was even starting to enjoy the playful pup. He still had his doubts about Fred being a watchdog. The only thing the pup watched was food. Fred's stomach was an endless pit. And he had the energy to match.

He wished he could say the same about himself. The only kind of energy he had was nervous energy—caffeine-induced energy. When he was at work his mind was on Gillian and what she might be doing. So far she had heeded his advice and stayed out of The Blades, only visiting her office when someone was with her. Usually he accompanied her after he got home from work. They stayed long enough to pick up the mail and listen to the answering machine. Her office remained neat and untouched. He wished he could say the same about his office at home. Gillian had taken over the room with the same gusto she had applied to their home.

Her folders and papers were scattered throughout what was once his office. It was now theirs. Sometimes at night they both retired to the room and worked side by side. Of course, he had to admit, not a whole lot of work got done. Who could concentrate with the enticing scent of Gillian's perfume teasing the air?

The family room was almost unrecognizable. He classed the room into two categories. Before Gillian and After Gillian. He preferred the After Gillian look. There was something about the room that was warm and inviting. His new bride was having that effect on the entire house. He actually looked forward to going home each night.

The only darkness in their lives came whenever he or Gillian thought about the lunatic who had been threatening her or when he awoke in the middle of the night suffering from the same recurring nightmare. It was getting to the point where he didn't want to sleep for fear of the terrifying dreams. They were getting worse and becoming more vivid. Only the gentle soothing of Gillian's hands and her sweet whispers calmed him enough to relax—but not sleep—through the remainder of the night.

Since the delivery of the leeches over a week ago, there had been no further contact. No letters, no presents, nothing. And that frightened him. Nothing had happened to make the sender nervous, so why had he backed off?

Jon Hall had come up with nothing from the list of possible suspects. Every man on that list probably hated Gillian for tracking him down, but no one had a criminal record that would red-flag him as being the culprit. As a favor to Mason, Jon was paying a visit to every man on the list. So far he was three-quarters of the way down, and nothing. Either the guy was a convincing liar, hadn't been contacted yet or he wasn't on the list.

Hell, they were so in the dark concerning his identity it would take a lighthouse sitting in the guy's yard to identify him. So why hadn't they heard from him? The only explanation Mason could come up with was terrifying. The psychopath was planning something. Something big.

Mason hung up his robe and poured himself a cup of coffee. The sooner he got through his mail, the sooner he could go home and see what type of mischief Gillian had been up to today. A slow smile curved his lips as he reached for the stack of mail.

The top letter caught his attention. His secretary usually opened every letter and handled what she could. This letter was in a plain white envelope and marked Private. Mason picked up a letter opener and slit it open. Half a dozen pictures of Gillian toppled to his desk. His shields came up and he scanned the envelope. The same twisted hatred that surrounded the box full of leeches radiated from the envelope. Using two pencils, he carefully pulled the sheet of paper from the envelope and spread it onto the desk. The words, cut out of magazines and pasted on, sent cold terror shuddering up his spine. He blindly reached for the phone and punched in the numbers for his house. As the first ring sounded in his ear, his gaze returned to the letter: *Have you seen your wife today?*

Using the top of a pen, he slowly separated the photos. Each one contained Gillian, but all were taken at different locations, on different days. One was taken in

front of her office. She was with her sister and Cullen.
Another was taken at the local food store. Gillian was
pushing a shopping cart and eyeing the cookie aisle with
what appeared to be glee. There was even one with him
standing beside her picking out patio furniture.

The phone was in the middle of the third ring when
it was picked up.

"Hello, Blacksword residence," a woman's voice responded.

"Who's this? Where's Gillian?" Mason demanded
as his heart dropped to his knees. That wasn't Gillian's
voice.

"This is Birdie, sir. Can I ask who is calling?"

"This is Mr. Blacksword. Where's my wife?"

"On the back patio, trying to get the new grill to
work. Would you like me to get her, sir?"

"Yes, please," was grated out through his teeth. He
concentrated on his wife and knew she wasn't hurt in
any way. With each passing day he could pick up more
of Gillian's emotions. He wondered if that happened to
every married couple, or if they were unique. Right now
his concern for his wife was satisfied, but he wondered
who in the hell Birdie was. He couldn't remember any
of Gillian's relatives having that name, and it surely
wasn't a Blacksword relation.

"Hello, Mason?"

"Gillian?"

"Who else were you expecting?"

"Obviously not Birdie. Who is she?" Before she
could reply, he asked, "Are you all right?"

"I'm fine, why?" There was a quick catch in her
voice. "What happened?"

He didn't have to tell her what prompted his phone
call. He could tell by her voice she knew. "I'll tell you

when I get home. I'm leaving right away, and I'll be calling Jon Hall to meet me there.''

"Tell Jon I'll be throwing on an extra steak for him."

No questions, no hysterics, just tell the police detective she'd be throwing on an extra steak. Either Gillian was very brave and unflappable in the face of danger, or she was extremely gullible. He didn't know which. "Put up your shields."

"They've been up since I heard your voice."

Mason could picture her wrapping her finger around the cord and worrying her lower lip with her teeth. He wanted to pull her into his arms and have his shields protect her, but he was a good twenty-five minutes away. "Who's Birdie?"

"We'll talk about her when you get home, okay?"

"Gillian?"

"Mason, please. Birdie isn't involved in this other thing. She's a sweet lady who's down on her luck."

"Gillian…"

"Mason, please. Just hurry home. You're scaring me."

Scaring *you!* He glanced down at the pictures of his wife and knew what real fear was. Whoever had snapped the pictures had been close enough to Gillian to touch her. To harm her. "I'll be there in half an hour. Don't answer the door or the phone until I get there." Mason replaced the receiver without saying goodbye. For some reason the word stuck in his throat and refused to emerge.

He flipped through his phone number file and punched in Jon's number.

Gillian heard Mason pull up and hurried around the side of the house. He hadn't even bothered to pull the car into the garage, but stepped out of the car and came straight for her. She was wrapped in his arms as if he hadn't seen her in a year instead of that morning, when they shared a loving goodbye that nearly made him late for court.

She pressed her face into his shirt and smiled. He smelled of lemon fabric softener, a hint of soap from his morning shower and just a faint whiff of his spicy after-shave. He not only smelled good, he felt good. She missed him terribly when he was at work and she was left alone to fill the hours. Her work had kept her busy, along with settling into the house, meeting Lottie, the cleaning lady who came every Tuesday and Friday, and playing with Fred. But she still missed Mason.

Mason stepped back and raised her face for a brief kiss.

Gillian melted into the kiss and cursed its briefness. "Hi."

"Are you all right?"

"Don't I look all right?" She smoothed back a lock of his hair that her fingers had mussed during their kiss.

"Want to tell me what's going on?"

"Jon should be here any minute. I'll tell you then." He glanced around the yard. "Now who is this Birdie?"

"Shh...keep your voice down. She's in the kitchen putting the finishing touches to our dinner."

"She's a cook?"

"Kind of." Gillian glanced at the house behind her, where she knew Birdie was contentedly cooking up a storm. What had seemed so simple this morning was now difficult.

"Gillian?"

"This morning I went to visit Tabitha at her shop. I was hoping to pick up one of those huge palm plants she had used for our wedding. The master bathroom could use something to brighten it up. I thought a palm in front of the window up there would add some life into the room.'' The entire room was done in white and black tile. It needed something.

"Fine, buy a plant for the bathroom. Buy two. Hell, buy a dozen if it makes you happy. Just continue.''

She smiled briefly. "Thanks. Anyway, when I got there Tabitha was all upset. It seems a homeless person had taken up residence in the alley behind her shop.''

"Tell her to call the police.''

"Mason—'' she lightly punched him in the arm "—that's not very charitable of you.''

"The police wouldn't harm him. They'd make sure he got to a shelter and had a meal or two.''

"It wasn't a he.'' Gillian glanced once again at the house.

Mason followed her gaze and groaned. "You didn't?''

"She's such a nice lady, Mason. Wait till you meet her.''

His gaze stayed riveted to the kitchen window. "We have a homeless person in our house cooking our dinner?''

"She's an excellent cook and she knows the difference between a petunia and a geranium.'' Gillian kept her gaze fixed on the knot in Mason's tie. "I kind of told her she could stay in the apartment above the garage in return for some cooking and gardening.''

"You what?''

Gillian cringed at the softness in Mason's question. "I also made sure she understood that it was contingent on your approval. I know I shouldn't have invited her home without talking to you first, but she looked so scared and alone.''

"Gillian…'' He ran his fingers through his hair. "You just can't invite homeless people to come live above the garage.''

"I didn't invite her to live here. I offered her a job.'' Gillian risked a quick glance at Mason's face and then immediately dropped it back down to his tie. He didn't look too pleased. "She's a good woman, Mason. I scanned her thoroughly, and the only malice she holds is for the company her now-dead husband used to work for. Seems they bet the pension fund on a high-risk market and lost it all. Her social security is a mere pittance, there are no benefits from her husband's old job and she's sixty-five. Too young and healthy for a state-run nursing home, but too old for anyone to hire. She lost her apartment three weeks ago and she had no one to turn to. She's been on the streets since then.''

"What about her family?''

"There isn't any. She never had children and her only sister passed away last year.''

"Gillian, don't you see…''

"Why don't you meet her first, Mason.'' Gillian grabbed his hand and started to pull him toward the house. If she couldn't talk him into allowing Birdie to stay, maybe once he met her he would change his mind. The woman looked like she walked out of a Norman Rockwell picture. She reminded Gillian of an all-American grandmother—rosewater perfume and fresh-baked cookies. That was after an hour-long bath and the washing of every article of clothing she possessed. It had taken Gillian and Birdie the better part of the afternoon to make her presentable. Birdie was nervous about meeting Mason, but not half as anxious as Gillian.

A stray dog was one thing, but a person was an entirely different matter.

Mason allowed Gillian to pull him into the kitchen. He wasn't looking forward to meeting Birdie. Once again his wife's heart acted before her brain. What in the world was she thinking, to bring a vagrant home with her? With all the danger hanging over her head, the last thing he needed was an unknown factor thrown into the equation.

The first thing he noticed was how neat and orderly the kitchen was. With Gillian preparing their meals for the past week, the kitchen had looked like a cyclone hit. The delicious smell wafting through the room was the second thing he noticed. The third was the older woman standing by the sink looking scared but proud. Birdie didn't look like any of the homeless people he saw sleeping on benches, in doorways or over the exhaust grates dotting the downtown area.

Birdie looked like a grandmother. Her hair was short, mostly gray, and had the remnants of a long-ago perm. Her dress was neat and clean and boasted violets, lots of violets. A pair of sturdy white shoes graced her feet, and a string of fake pearls adorned her throat. Birdie's cheeks held the healthy glow of sunshine and a pair of silver-framed glasses were perched on her nose. The thought of this gentle woman searching through garbage bins for her next meal sickened him.

"Hello, I'm Mason Blacksword."

She placed the tray of deviled eggs she had been holding onto the counter and wiped her hands on the apron tied around her waist. "Hello, Mr. Blacksword. I'm Bertha Cummings." She reached out her hand. "My friends call me Birdie."

Mason shook her hand and knew instantly what Gillian had meant. There wasn't a nasty bone in Birdie's body. "My friends call me Mason."

One of Gillian's eyebrows rose, but she didn't say a word.

"I know your wife said I could stay in the apartment above the garage, but I won't hold her to it if you decide otherwise. I'll go right now if you like."

Mason didn't like the feeling of being put on the spot, but he admired Birdie's integrity. He glanced at the array of food sitting on the counter and frowned. He could tell his wife hadn't made a single dish. None of them was in her repertoire. He had seen her short list. Hell, he had tasted every item on that list at least once already. "How about if we have a two-week trial period?" He gave her a friendly smile and tried not to drool over the bowl of potato salad and the strawberry shortcake sitting on the counter. "You might discover you don't like working for us."

Birdie blinked rapidly and returned his smile. "Thank you, sir."

"It's Mason, Birdie." He had seen the tears forming behind her glasses and was relieved none had fallen. He didn't want her gratitude, he wanted dinner. "How soon before dinner is ready?"

"It's all done, except for the grilling of the steaks." Gillian picked up the tray holding three thick porterhouse steaks. "I'll go put them on the grill."

Mason glanced at the steaks. "We need another one. Jon's coming."

"I know." Gillian headed for the door leading to the back patio.

"What about Birdie?" He glanced at the older woman and then back at the steaks his wife was holding.

"Don't worry, Mason. I won't starve. I have a nice fresh spinach salad in the refrigerator for me."

Mason looked appalled. "Spinach salad?"

Birdie chuckled. "I guess I should mention that I'm a vegetarian. I don't mind cooking meat, but I draw the line at eating it."

"Oh." It was the only response Mason could think of. He just employed a cook who was a vegetarian. It sounded like hiring a pilot who was afraid to fly. He followed Gillian out to the patio. He loved thick, juicy steaks and wasn't about to give them up. If he hadn't given them up after all the medical reports on cholesterol and fats, he wasn't giving them up to please Birdie.

Mason glanced around the brick patio. "I see that the furniture we ordered was delivered." A round table with four chairs sat beneath a flowered umbrella. All the chairs and the two chaises were padded with the same pink-and-green floral print. Their new grill sat to the side. "They set up the grill?"

"No, I put it together while Birdie was making dinner." Gillian turned a couple of knobs, smiled and placed the steaks on the rack.

"You put it together?" He backed up a step and eyed the propane gas tank sitting below the grill.

"I'm not stupid, Mason. I do know how to work a screwdriver and read directions."

Mason glanced at the sizzling steaks. His wife obviously knew what she was doing. The sound of a car pulling up caught their attention. "That must be Jon. I'll go meet him." He walked away from Gillian and around the side of the house.

Forty minutes later four adults sat under the umbrella and groaned. Correction, three of them groaned. Birdie looked like an indulgent grandmother and a woman who had found something very precious to her. Dinner had been wonderful, as well as entertaining. Fred was contentedly rolling around in the grass, munching on a thick steak bone.

Jon, whom Gillian had only met at their wedding, turned out to be the center of the conversation. He enlightened them with some amusing tales from his years on the force and seemed totally enslaved by Birdie's cooking. Gillian was in danger of losing her cook before she even had a chance to unpack.

"So this is how married people eat." Jon patted his flat stomach in an extravagant gesture. "Maybe I should try it."

"What, get married?" Mason questioned.

"No." Jon grinned at Birdie. "Visit married couples more often."

Gillian laughed and started to pile the dirty dishes onto a tray. "If you ate like that at every meal, no one would ask you."

"What, to come on over for dinner?" Jon stood up and picked up the near-empty bowl of potato salad and the plate holding the remaining deviled eggs.

"No—" Gillian grinned, "—to get married."

It was Jon's turn to laugh. "No woman in her right mind would want me."

Mason frowned at the easy banter between Jon and his wife. "I think it's time we got down to some business."

Jon's smile vanished. "I'm sorry, Mason. We were having such a good time I nearly forgot what I came for." Jon headed for the kitchen.

Mason nodded and helped by carrying in the tray of dirty dishes Gillian had piled up.

Gillian didn't like the seriousness in Mason's eyes. Whatever had happened to him today really must have shaken him.

"We'll be in Mason's office," Gillian said to Birdie, jerking her head in the direction of the room. "We'll be out in time for dessert." She glanced at the dishes and food littering the counter. "Don't you dare bother with this mess. I'll take care of it when we're done."

Birdie retied the apron around her waist. "I'll put on a pot of coffee." She shooed them from the kitchen. "My cake tastes best with a fresh cup of coffee.

Mason led the way to his office. Gillian closed the door behind them before saying, "I'm not going to like this, am I?"

Jon stood there and glanced between the two.

"No, you're not, Gillian, and I'm sorry." Mason took a deep breath and said, "From now on, you can't go anywhere without a bodyguard."

Gillian looked at Mason and slowly shook her head. "I don't believe I heard you correctly."

Mason opened the top desk drawer and pulled out the envelope he had placed there before dinner. "I received this at my office today." He held the envelope out to Jon.

Jon read the envelope and studied the postmark before carefully shaking the contents onto the desk. Gillian gasped as she recognized the photos. They were all of her. Jon muttered an expletive that should have earned him a reprimand from Gillian. Instead she felt like muttering one or two of her own. How dare this person follow her around and invade her privacy!

Jon carefully spread open the letter and read the pasted message. He glanced across the desk at Mason. "My guess is, it caused more than a few gray hairs."

Mason continued to stare at his wife. "Something like that."

Gillian read the words and wanted to weep. It was one thing to try to scare her, it was another thing altogether to frighten her husband. No wonder Mason called home in such a state. She glanced up at her husband and met his worried gaze. "Sorry."

"What the hell do you have to be sorry for?" Mason ran his fingers through his hair and looked away.

"He's playing with your mind now instead of mine."

"She could have a point there, Mason," Jon said. He studied the assorted photos. "Each picture shows Gillian in a vulnerable position. If this guy had been shooting a rifle instead of a camera, you'd be a widower by now." He picked up a snapshot of Gillian standing outside of their home talking to the man from the lawn service and handed it to Mason. "This guy wants to play with you for a while. If he wanted to harm Gillian, he's had plenty of opportunity, and he wants you to know that."

"Wonderful," growled Mason as he started to pace. "What's our next step, Jon?"

"I can take this stuff back to the office and have it tested for prints, but I doubt if there are any."

"What else?"

"That's about it, legally. Without knowing who is sending the stuff there's not much the police can do."

"What about illegally?" Mason asked after a moment's thought.

Gillian stared at her husband in disbelief. The Honorable Judge Blacksword was contemplating doing something from the wrong side of the law. As far as she knew, Mason considered the law to have only one side. The right side. His side. "Mason, I don't think—"

"Dammit, Gillian, this guy is serious!"

Gillian gave Mason a slow smile. He was worried about her! Her husband actually cared what happened to her. She knew Mason cared about people and what happened to them, because of his profession. You didn't go into the judicial system without caring. But this was personal—really personal.

She walked around to the back of the desk where Mason was standing and brushed a soft kiss across his cheek. "Thank you." It wasn't the declaration of undying love she had been hoping for, but it was a beginning. Caring was a nice, firm foundation to build the rest of their lives on. It was more than what a lot of marriages had. She gave him another smile as confusion flashed in his eyes. The poor man had no idea what she had just thanked him for.

She placed her hand inside his and gave it a light squeeze. "We won't be doing anything illegal, Mason." She turned and faced Jon.

"So, Jon, you're the expert. What can we do?" she asked.

Jon carefully gathered up the photos. "I think we should notify some higher authority."

"No." Mason and Gillian answered at the same time.

Jon raised an eyebrow and waited for a further explanation.

"I can protect my own wife," Mason growled.

Gillian glanced at Mason as his fingers tightened around hers. He was serious! Just the way he spoke, she knew he was referring to his powers. A warlock very rarely used his powers, and she had never known Mason to use his. That was what made him so revered within the circles of the society, because that was the key element in a great warlock. To have the powers and never

use them. Throwing up the occasional shield or scanning was nothing. It came as naturally as breathing to
a warlock or witch. The powers Mason possessed were
phenomenal. A member of the society couldn't help but
notice the force that surrounded him. Now, after all
these years, he wanted to use that force to protect her.
She could think of no finer gift from her husband. But
it was a gift she must refuse.

"I can protect myself, Mason." She could not allow
him to jeopardize his position in the society by possibly
calling attention to himself. In all probability, one day
he would sit on the Council, and she would not like to
see a black mark against his name because of her. The
Council frowned upon using one's powers unless it was
absolutely necessary. To use one's powers was to call
attention to oneself. Witches and warlocks were never
to call attention to themselves. There had to be other
options.

Jon glanced curiously between Mason and Gillian but
didn't comment on their strange conversation.

Gillian noticed Jon's expression and wondered what
he must be thinking. Mason trusted Jon, or he would
never have asked for his help. Jon and Mason's friendship went back years and she was positive that Jon suspected something was unusual about Mason.

Mason glared at Gillian. "I can protect you better."

She knew the Council allowed the use of powers for
the preservation of life. There were too few members
in the society as it was. He probably could protect her
better than the police or a bodyguard, but he didn't have
to go around banging his chest. Few could compete with
his strength, including her, but it hurt that he had to
bring up who was stronger, who was bigger and who
was the male. Here she had been looking at their mar-

riage as an equal partnership, not who was more powerful. She dropped his hand and moved away from his warmth.

She looked at Jon, who was trying very discreetly to disappear into the woodwork. "Jon, since it's my life which seems to be in jeopardy, I will be calling all the shots. Mason is my husband, not my lord and master." She gave a heavy sigh. "I don't want this to go any farther than you in the department. I don't want this leaked to the media. Mason's well-known throughout the city and I'm sure the papers would have a field day with this."

She ignored Mason, who was standing beside her looking like he wanted to explode. "My father has just been diagnosed with a heart condition. With proper medication and my mother's care he should be fine, but the doctor warned against added stress. I believe having a psychopath after his eldest daughter constitutes stress."

"Sorry about your Dad," Jon said. "I understand your concern, but I think Mason may be right in insisting on you having some sort of bodyguard whenever you go out."

"Are you volunteering your services?" she asked. Jon seemed like a reasonable person. She wouldn't mind so much being stuck in his company. Hell, with an actual police detective watching over her, maybe Mason would allow her to go back into The Blades.

Mason took a step closer to Gillian and said, "I think I can take my wife wherever she has to go."

She glanced at Mason in confusion. "You work all day."

"Plan wherever you have to go for the evening."

"What if I can't?" She had two interviews scheduled

this week with women who were interested in obtaining her services. She was due in court before Judge Cronan on Tuesday morning, and she had a list of twenty-eight unsupporting fathers she was trying to locate. How was she supposed to do all that at night?

"May I make a suggestion?" Jon asked.

Mason glared across the desk. "What?"

"Gillian, how about you try to do all your errands, work or whatever at night so your husband can accompany you. If there's someplace you have to go during the day, and there's no one around equipped to protect you, you may call me. I'm scheduled for the four-till-twelve shift next week so I'll be free most days."

"That sounds reasonable." Gillian gave Jon a smile of gratitude. "I don't like the idea of having someone with me every time I leave the house, but I understand the precaution."

"Good," snapped Mason. "If your brothers can't make it, call me before disturbing Jon. I'll see if I can't rearrange my schedule."

Gillian forced her mouth not to fall open. Mason was willing to rearrange his schedule because of her. She closed her eyes and waited for the miracle to occur. Nothing. No flashes of lightning, no blaring trumpets, not even a mild earthquake. She opened her eyes and glanced at Jon. He appeared to be shocked, too. Mason's reputation had preceded him throughout the court system and the police force. Everyone knew about Mason's notorious schedules. They might as well have been carved into two tablets and delivered from Mount Sinai by Moses himself.

"Thank you, Mason," she said softly. "I'll try not to disturb your schedule too much." She took his hint that he wanted her brothers to escort her before she called Jon. The detective might carry a gun, but her brothers had their powers. Mason didn't want her chancing her safety to a mere human.

"Don't worry about it." He glanced at Jon and asked, "That's it?"

"I'm still running down the remaining names on the list you faxed me." He glanced at Gillian. "Try to stay out of the front yard. From what I've seen, the backyard looks pretty secure."

"Okay, I can live with that."

"Also, don't let anyone in the house unless you know them personally. No delivery boys, nothing."

"Anything else?" It was beginning to sound like a prison sentence to her. She could almost feel the walls start to close in around her. Don't do that, don't do this. Call this person. Call that person. Don't breathe. Don't walk. Don't think!

"No, I think that should do it."

All three looked at one another for a moment before both men turned and looked at Gillian. Mason reached out and brushed her cheek with the back of his fingers. "Are you going to be okay with this?"

"Sure, why wouldn't I be?" They didn't have too many choices. Run-and-hide had never been her style. Hopefully this idiot would make his move and be caught, then she could get on with the rest of her life. She also knew her safety would be jeopardized if she didn't follow Jon's advice. "I just want it over with."

"So do I." Mason stepped closer and pulled her into his arms.

She felt safe wrapped in Mason's arms. For the past week she had acted as if nothing was out of the ordinary. She hadn't let Mason know how nervous she was. The box of leeches had really thrown her for a loop.

This joker meant to scare her, and he had. She enjoyed
the comfort of his arms for a moment longer before
backing away and plastering a huge grin on her face.
"I don't know about you two, but I'm in the mood for
some of Birdie's strawberry shortcake and a hot cup of
coffee."

Chapter 10

The unfamiliar sound jolted Gillian from her sleep. She sat up as Fred's frantic barking echoed throughout the house. She scanned the house and came up empty. No one was in the house besides her husband and their dog. She concentrated on the apartment above the garage and could only pick up the peacefulness of Birdie's slumber.

Mason woke up a second later. "What is it?" he mumbled as he shook the sleep from his head. "Why is Fred barking?"

"I don't know." Gillian started to slide out of bed to go investigate. Mason's hand stopped her.

"Stay right here." Mason slipped from bed and reached for his robe hanging on the back of the bathroom door.

Gillian could tell he was scanning. She was going to tell him it was clear, that she had already searched, but it probably wouldn't do any good. In the past three days since the photos of her arrived at his office, Mason had been so protective she was beginning to feel suffocated. She went nowhere without her husband by her side. She couldn't ask her brothers to accompany her on trips outside the house. Cullen and Kent would demand to know why she needed protection, and then they would probably tell her parents. And besides, Cullen and Kent as bodyguards would probably be more suffocating than Mason.

She got out of bed and ignored Mason's glare. "I'm coming with you." She grabbed her robe, which had been hanging next to his. "There's no way you can stop me."

"There's plenty of ways I can stop you, Gillian." He reached for her hand and pulled her closer. "But you're right, you'll be safer with me."

Gillian slowly shook her head as she followed her husband out into the hall and down the dimly lit steps. She wasn't afraid. With her shields up there wasn't anything to be afraid of. Mason had misunderstood her curiosity as fear. Fred was downstairs by the front door barking his head off and growling. Something had upset the dog. Her gut instinct was telling her she wasn't going to like what disturbed the dog at one-thirty in the morning.

Mason reached the bottom of the stairs and flipped on the light switch. Light flooded the hall, living room and dining room. He bent down and stroked the top of Fred's head. "What is it, boy?"

The dog tried to bury his nose in the crack beneath the front door. A low, dangerous growl rumbled throughout Fred's quivering body. His tail was stiff and practically standing straight up.

"Is something out there, boy?" Gillian questioned. Her scanning couldn't detect a human presence outside the house, but she did perceive an evil force. She backed away from the door the same instant Mason's shields surrounded them all. "He was here again."

Mason studied the oak door as if he was seeing through it. "I know." He glanced over his shoulder at her and softly said, "He's sent something else."

She studied the strain and anger etched into her husband's face. This psychopath was tormenting Mason more than her. Mason was the one suffering through nightmares nearly every night while she slept like a baby. She wondered if tormenting Mason was his intent or if she was his main victim and Mason was just an innocent bystander.

Either way it made no difference. Mason didn't look like he could handle too much more. The only way she knew how to figure out which deadbeat father was doing this was to confront them all. Which was impossible. Mason wouldn't let her leave the house without a bodyguard. She couldn't endanger another member of the society or her family. Calling Jon Hall was an option, but for some reason Mason didn't like the idea of her spending too much time in the detective's company. She would have loved to chalk it up to jealousy on Mason's part, but that would be wishful thinking.

The only option was for them to work together to locate this madman. Her husband wasn't the type of man who would meekly follow her lead and allow her to investigate the way she thought best. Mason would want control. Mason always wanted control. It was who he was.

Right now Mason didn't have control of the situation and it was tearing him apart. But she was drawing a blank as to how to end this predicament. Maybe whatever was outside the door would give her a clue. Maybe this time the psycho had gotten careless and left a lead.

"Would you like me to open the door?" she asked.

"No, you stay back." He turned to the door and opened it.

Gillian could see a cardboard box sitting on the stoop. Evil surrounded the box, but not danger. She knew the surrounding area would be empty, but she scanned it anyway.

Fred took a step closer to the box and growled menacingly.

Mason looked at Gillian. "Hold the dog so I can see what's inside."

She picked up Fred and lovingly scratched behind his ears. His whole body was trembling and he looked ready to rip the box open. "It's okay, boy." She hugged him closer to her chest. "You're a good watchdog, aren't you?"

Mason flipped on the outside lights and flooded the yard and stoop with brightness. Gillian stood behind him and glanced away from the box. She didn't want to see what twisted sick thing her tormentor had come up with this time. Her gaze stayed on one of the two concrete urns sitting on either side of the door, filled with red and white geraniums that Birdie had planted. She glanced down when Mason muttered a disgusted curse.

The top of the box was clutched in Mason's hands. In the bottom of the box was a wooden rat trap, complete with a dead rat. The rodent's sightless eyes were staring straight at her. Fred started to growl and squirm in her arms. She took a step back.

Mason stood up and showed Gillian the message pasted to the inside of the lid. It was just like all the letters they had received. Each word was cut out of a magazine or the headline of a newspaper: *Feel like a trapped rat yet?* He dropped the lid back onto the box and closed the door.

"I'll drop it off with Jon tomorrow morning on my way in to work." He walked into the kitchen and yanked his car keys off the peg by the back door. "There has to be something they can do."

Gillian knew Mason was fighting a battle with himself. The law was not doing enough; in fact, they weren't doing anything. The sad part was, there was nothing they could do besides file a report. "It's harassment, Mason. He hasn't threatened my life. He's playing mind games with me. The most the police could do, once we discover who it is, is give him a slap on the hand and possibly issue a restraining order against him."

"They should lock him in jail and throw away the keys."

She wholeheartedly agreed with that. She would love to see this sicko locked up for a real long time, but she knew it wouldn't come to that. "Even our laws have limits, Mason."

"You don't think I know that?"

"You may know it, but now you have to accept it."

Mason glared at her for a moment before storming back to the front door and slamming it behind him.

Gillian sighed and gave Fred a doggie treat from the box sitting on the laundry room shelf. "You're the best watchdog in the world, Fred." She placed him on the rug in front of the kitchen sink, next to his plastic squeeze toy. "Thank you for the alarm. I'll have Birdie cook something tomorrow with a big fat juicy bone in it for you."

Fred wagged his tail, as if he knew what she was talking about, before lying back down. The danger had passed.

Gillian walked out of the kitchen and headed for the stairs. Mason saw to it that the house was locked back up. The man was becoming obsessed with checking the locks. He was doing it twice, if not three times nightly.

Twenty minutes later Mason joined Gillian in their bedroom. She was standing by the window searching the night. Her long blond hair was tousled and tangled from their lovemaking. He couldn't get enough of the silken strands. He couldn't get enough of his wife. The light by the bed illuminated the room with a soft glow.

By the stiffness of her shoulders he could tell she was still upset. He wondered if she was upset with him for being so protective or at finding this madman's latest keepsake. Somehow, he thought it was him.

He knew she was champing at the bit to go out and locate this psycho. But he couldn't allow her to go alone, and for some reason she seemed reluctant to ask him to join her. His wife was a very independent woman, while he, contrary to modern-day thinking, was a very old-fashioned man. He wanted to fight her battles for her. It was a very sobering thought, considering that when he married her he had thought to merely suffer through quietly and tolerate her existence. Now he wanted to slay dragons for her. When had it all changed?

The only other woman he ever wanted to slay dragons for was his mother. She, too, wouldn't let him. He had only been twelve, too young and full of hatred for a father who had abandoned them. Nadine Blacksword was a proud woman who was determined to make it on her own, without the help of the society or her headstrong son. And she had. The years were rough and long, but they all managed to make it through them. But he still remembered the feeling of uselessness, watching his mother work from morning to night, every day, year after year, and never get ahead.

He had stood by and watched the work, the years and the worry take its toll on the mother he loved. His mother was now fifty-one years old and no longer working ten-hour days bent over a sewing machine. She was now the assistant buyer of infant clothes for a fancy department store in Center City. Her hair was stylish, her clothes fashionable, and since she met and married Walt Martin, she looked years younger and happier than he ever remembered seeing her. But it was her hands that twisted the guilt deep within his soul. Years of demanding work had taken their toll on her hands. They were slightly bent and more often than not the joints were painfully swollen with arthritis. Every time he saw her hands he remembered what she had endured for him and his two younger sisters.

His mother had forbidden him to use his powers to help their situation. Nadine had insisted that her children learn to survive just like other human children. And they had, but it had been so hard for him to watch powerlessly.

He couldn't stand by and watch helplessly again. His youth had used up all his patience, if he ever had any. Gillian needed help and it was his job, as her husband, to give it to her. But was that the only reason he wanted to fight her battles, because it was his duty as her husband? Or was there something more?

He stood in the doorway and silently watched her stare out into the darkness as if the night held the answers she was seeking. His feelings for Gillian confused him. He knew he cared for her, really cared. He had hoped for compatibility in their marriage bed at the very least, and was granted burning hot passion. His body hardened at the mere thought of her, and by her response night after night he had to say honestly that she, too, was consumed by the fire.

From the moment he pledged his life to this woman in Senator Targett's garden, his entire world had been turned upside down. His once neat and orderly home was filled with statues of purple dragons, huge plants, a frisky pup and a formerly homeless vagrant who created tantalizing aromas in the kitchen.

Fred was a good pup and had only managed to chew on one old pair of sneakers and one brand-new golf shoe. Tonight Fred had earned his keep. He'd had doubts about Fred being a watchdog, but the spirited pup had proved his worth.

Birdie was a dream. He would never admit to Gillian her cooking was bland at best, undigestible at worst. He had been trying to figure out a way to kindly suggest to his wife that he would gladly do some of the cooking at night, without hurting her feelings.

In the past three days he had been subjected to a virtual smorgasbord of meals prepared by their new cook and gardener. Birdie loved to cook and he loved to eat her cooking. Her services were well worth the cost of feeding her and the utilities for the garage apartment. If the next week and a half turned out as good as the first three days, Birdie not only had a permanent job but a raise.

Gillian's compassionate heart had done remarkably well. A watchdog and a cook all within the first month of marriage. He shuddered to think what the first year would bring. Lord help him, but there were still three empty bedrooms in the house. If he didn't find a way to control Gillian's charitable heart, he was going to end up with a house filled with homeless people and an endless stream of pets.

He'd worry about his wife's compassionate heart later. Now he had more important things to do. Like hold her.

Mason quietly walked over to Gillian and wrapped his arms around her. He pulled her close and rested his cheek against the top of her head. His gaze followed hers out into the night. He could see the outline of the trees that bordered the western portion of their property and the distant glow of a neighbor's porch light. Their neighborhood was a safe sanctuary from the slums of the inner city. A sanctuary some madman had violated.

"Don't worry, we'll find him," Mason said.

She leaned back into him. "I'm not worried about that."

"What are you worried about, then?"

Gillian turned slightly in his arms and looked up at him. "I'm concerned about you."

"Me?"

Her fingers reached up and caressed his jaw. "You're not sleeping well at night. You have a nightmare almost every night and you won't talk to me about it." Mason watched as she worried her lower lip between her teeth. "You told me you never dreamed."

"It's not a dream, Gillian. It's a nightmare."

"One you won't share with me?"

There was no way he could share this horrifying dream with her. And it came every night. Some nights he could hide it from her, most nights he couldn't. "I much prefer your dream." When he woke up trembling and covered in sweat, Gillian would cuddle up close and tell him about her favorite dream. The one with the little boy on the beach building sand castles. For some reason, her dream calmed him and filled him with hope—the same emotions she swore she felt every time she dreamed that one particular dream. At first he couldn't figure out why, but the more he thought about it, the easier it was to explain. The calmness came from Gillian's sweet voice whispering in the dark, and the sense of hope he felt probably had something to do with the sweetness of the dream. If he could have nightmares, surely he would dream about a peaceful beach one night.

She gave him a soft smile and buried herself against his chest. "I know you like that dream. That's why I keep telling you about it."

Mason couldn't prevent his arms from tightening. He could feel the slight trembling of her body beneath her satiny robe. "It's okay, Gillian." His voice grated with strength and fear as he hugged her harder. "I'll protect you."

Gillian glanced up but he couldn't read the emotions shimmering in her pale blue eyes. "But who's going to protect me from you?"

He pushed her away so he could see her face more clearly. The trembling of her lower lip tore at his heart. "Protect you from me?" He would die before he would harm a hair on her head. Was this psychopath doing more damage than he had imagined? Was Gillian now frightened of everyone, including her own husband?

Gillian studied the concern etched into her husband's face. He thought she was afraid of him, and she was in a way. But not for the reason he was assuming. She didn't fear for her physical well-being, she feared for her heart. During the past ten minutes she had been staring at the darkness wondering how to tell her husband she loved him. It was a strange phenomenon. Here they were, married, sharing every conceivable intimacy two lovers could share, and yet neither one had spoken the words. She feared Mason would never utter those words.

She knew Mason cared for her. When they were downstairs he had wrapped his shields around her and Fred without a conscious thought of doing it. It came naturally to him to protect her when danger was at hand. It was one of the most exquisite gifts Mason had ever given her. The rubies he had given her were a sign of possession, but his shield was an act of love. Problem was, Mason didn't believe in love.

Gathering her courage, she gave her husband the gift of her love. "You're holding my heart, dear husband." She brushed a kiss across his surprised mouth. "Be gentle with it."

Mason cupped her chin and gazed into her eyes. Gillian shivered at his intensity, but she bared her soul for him to see. He could have easily scanned her feelings and discovered her love, but instead he wanted to read it in her eyes. She allowed him to and prayed that one day he would allow her to search his soul in return.

Whatever he saw there caused him to frown quietly for a moment. His fingers released her chin and slowly stroked her lower lip. "I'll treat it as if it was made out of the finest crystal."

Gillian glanced at his chest. The robe he was wearing gaped at the front, giving her an enticing view of the midnight curls that swirled across his chest. It wasn't the response she had wanted, but it was better than having him hand her heart back to her. At least he wanted to keep it safe. But she wanted to exchange it for his. An even exchange.

"Gillian?"

She forced the sadness from her eyes and glanced up. "Yes?"

"I don't know what you want from me."

Your love! Only your love. She couldn't tell him that. "I only want what you're willing to give." It was a partial truth. She did want his love when he was willing to give it.

His fingers trailed down her throat, leaving a trail of heat in their wake. The lapels of her robe parted, revealing the same thing she wore every night since their wedding. Nothing. She did try to wear a couple of the lacy diaphanous gowns she had received as shower gifts, but it took longer to get them on than for Mason to get them off. She wasn't complaining though. There was something sinfully delicious about sleeping naked in your lover's arms.

She could feel her nipples tighten and her breasts swell in anticipation of his touch. The warm liquid feeling pulsed through her veins to pool at the junction of her thighs. Mason's slightest touch could make her want.

He bent his head and followed the path his fingers had taken with his mouth. He placed a moist kiss between the curvaceous mounds of her breasts before glancing up. "I could give you this."

She knew what he was referring to. He could give her pleasure, unlike any she had ever dreamed about. The fire was already started. She could feel it burning. It snatched her breath and stole her strength. The flames scorched her skin and caused her fingers to tremble as she reached for the sash of Mason's robe. "It will do."

She tugged the sash and pushed the thick navy robe off his shoulders. The terry robe landed at his feet. Breathless at the sight of his readiness, she added, "For now."

Within a blink of an eye her robe joined his on the floor and he swept her up into his arms. Her breasts were crushed against his chest as her tightly budded nipples buried themselves beneath his black curls. His mouth was hungry when it captured hers, and she fed his hunger with everything she had. Breaths mingled, tongues danced and fingers searched for all the hidden places of pleasure.

She knew what Mason liked. She knew where to touch and where to caress with her mouth. She also knew Mason liked to be in control in bed, as well as out of bed. Tonight he wouldn't give her his heart, so she wasn't going to give him his control. The instant Mason placed her on the wrinkled sheets and followed her down, she rolled.

With a smile of triumph she straddled Mason's hips and captured his hands. She wasn't fool enough to believe she was actually holding him down. He could have easily reversed their position, but she had surprise on her side. Mason had curiosity on his.

"Gillian, what do you think you're doing?" He turned his head from side to side, gazing at his captured hands on either side of his head.

She bent down and gently circled one of his dark brown nipples with her tongue. "Enjoying myself." She repeated the action on the other hard nub. "Any complaints?"

His hands clenched into fists but he didn't move. "Not a one."

She could feel his arousal tremble with anticipation and she wiggled her hips. She bit down on her smile as

Mason groaned. "You've always been on top and seemed to enjoy it." She wiggled her hips again and playfully nipped at his lower lip. "Tonight, I think I'll take a turn."

Mason swallowed hard. "I don't think this is a very good idea, Gillian."

She captured his lip between her teeth and stroked it with her tongue. She released his mouth and glanced up. "Why?"

"If it's power you want, you already have it." His hips arched off the bed.

"It's more than power." She released his one hand and trailed her fingers down his chest. She circled his navel before threading her fingers into the thatch of thick curls surrounding his straining staff. Her fingers lightly stroked the length of his arousal. His hips arched off the bed with every stroke, but his hands stayed where she had put them. "It's control, Mason."

Her fingers wrapped around his warmth and tenderly pumped. "Every night, you're the one in control. Let it be me, just this once." She looked into the heat of his gaze and knew he was listening very carefully to every word she said. "Trust me, Mason." She gave him a wide smile. "It won't hurt—" she tightened her grip just a fraction "—much."

Mason groaned and cupped her bottom. He raised her up so she was positioned directly on top of him. "You may have your control tonight, just hurry."

Gillian felt his shaft nudge her wet opening and slowly shook her head. "Control can't be hurried, Mason. You should know that." Very slowly she lowered herself and brought him deep inside. She could feel Mason's fingers pressing into her buttocks but didn't move. She wanted to set the pace.

"Gillian, you're killing me," Mason grated through clenched teeth.

"No, I'm not." She slowly started to move. It felt strange to be the one setting the tempo. Strange but wonderful. Mason's hips matched her rhythm. She bent down and tenderly kissed his mouth. "I'm making love to you."

Mason stood at the end of the shopping aisle and gazed at his wife. How had she ever talked him into taking her and Birdie food shopping? He had a stack of paperwork waiting for him at home, yet the promise of Birdie's fresh-baked oatmeal cookies had him reaching for his keys. Last week, Lottie, his cleaning lady, had driven Birdie to the food store. Lottie and Birdie had become fast friends. Tonight Gillian wanted to help with the shopping, and he had no option but to go with her. He really didn't mind accompanying his wife. Gillian in a food store was just as fascinating as Gillian in his home.

She was handling her virtual imprisonment extremely well, considering her independent nature. Last night he had found in his office a list she had started of all the things she wanted to do as soon as the culprit was apprehended. The first thing on the list was "Make love to my husband on a beach under the stars." He wondered if she already had a specific place in mind. He was more than willing to make her list a reality, and that particular item, especially.

He pushed the nearly filled cart down the aisle and watched as Gillian leaned over the freezer to reach for something in the bottom. The sweet curve of her denim clad derriere captured his attention. Oh, sweet marital bliss, why had he fought it so long? If it wasn't for the dozen or so people shopping in this aisle, he would have loved to show his wife what the view of her bottom did to his anatomy.

Instead he joined her and asked, "Need any help?" The freezer she was bending over contained ice cream and she was shuffling cartons around in search of something.

"I'm looking to see if they have any pistachio ice cream." She handed him containers of Rocky Road and Double Dip Fudge Brownie. "Could you put these in the cart for me?"

He took the ice cream and placed it in the cart. "Planning a party?" He knew for a fact that there were already two or three containers of ice cream in the freezer at home.

"Nope, just want something to pick on at night." She continued her search.

Mason shook his head in confusion. Obviously she wasn't leaving without pistachio ice cream or until she checked every container in the freezer. He leaned over and started to search the other end. "Do they even make pistachio ice cream?"

"Someone has to make it, Mason. I remember seeing it once." She picked up a container, grinned and placed it in the cart.

"You found it?"

"Not yet. That was Watermelon Supreme." She bent back over and continued searching.

Mason frowned. What was with the ice cream? He never noticed Gillian's apparent love for the stuff before. He glanced at the cart. The way it was going, his wife was either going to end up with freezer burn or enough ice cream to build Frosty the Snowman.

Five minutes later he briskly rubbed his frozen fingers

together. "I'm sorry, Gillian, but there isn't a container of pistachio ice cream anywhere in the store." Of course he now had five containers of strange ice cream in their cart. Whatever happened to vanilla and chocolate?

Gillian stared at the ransacked freezer and pouted.

He pulled her away before she picked up another carton of ice cream and kissed the enticing pout. "There's an ice-cream specialty shop right around the corner from the courthouse. If you behave yourself tonight I'll stop by on my way home from work tomorrow and see if they have pistachio."

A mischievous sparkle leaped into her eyes. She dropped her voice and seductively whispered, "What do you class as behaving myself?" Her gaze dropped to the front of his jeans.

"Keep that up and I'll buy you a gallon of the stuff." He brushed her mouth with a promise and captured one of her hands. He pushed the cart, and pulled his wife down the aisle in his search for Birdie. He had to locate the cook before he could take Gillian home and see exactly what she would do for pistachio ice cream.

The dawn had barely lightened the bedroom when Mason felt Gillian jump out of bed and run for the bathroom. Concerned, he followed her to the door, which, in her rush, she hadn't closed all the way. He stared at the door, wondering what to do. Their marriage was indeed extremely intimate, but not so intimate that he would barge in on her while she was in the bathroom.

The sound that greeted his ears had him pushing open the door. Privacy be damned, his wife was sick. He watched as Gillian reached for a washcloth, soaked it with cold water and pressed it to her pale face.

"Gillian, are you all right?"

She lowered the cloth, giving him a small, sickly-looking smile before losing the rest of her stomach's contents into the toilet.

Mason took a step into the room and glanced around frantically for something to do. He didn't know what to do. All he knew was that he wanted Gillian well.

She straightened back up, rinsed her mouth out and reached for the washcloth again.

"Gil?"

She lowered the cloth and tried desperately to give her husband a smile. "I believe we're pregnant."

Chapter 11

Gillian watched Mason's face as her stomach cramped once more. She willed the nausea down and blinked rapidly, trying to clear the moisture from her eyes. She wanted to see her husband's face as she shared the exciting news she'd been suspecting for the past week. They were going to have a baby!

The look on Mason's face wasn't what she had been envisioning. He not only appeared to be in shock—that she had been expecting—but he looked disappointed, even angry. Didn't he want the baby? Her hand instinctively covered her abdomen, where she was positive their child lay. "Mason?"

His gaze was riveted to her hand covering her abdomen. "You're pregnant?"

"No." She shook her head and offered up another smile of hope. "We're pregnant." She hadn't done anything on her own. They had created this life together. Wasn't this child, and hopefully others, the main reason behind their marriage? Wasn't this the reason the Council matched them up in the first place, so they could create life?

By Mason's expression someone would gather it was the last thing he wanted. Lord, what if it *was* the last thing he wanted! Her stomach twisted and rolled with that distressing thought. Mason didn't want their child. How could that be? She must be misreading the expression on his face. Tossing up what felt like everything she ate this week must be affecting her vision. How could her husband, the man she loved, not want their child?

"Mason," she asked softly, "don't you want children?" She held her breath and waited for his laughter. Of course he wanted children. She was working herself up over nothing. Pregnant women were notorious for that, weren't they?

Mason slowly looked up from where her hand sheltered the life that was possibly growing within her. He saw the concern and the hope pooling in her eyes. Eyes the color of the morning sky when she was happy. Eyes that turned a turbulent shade of bluish gray when the heat of passion burnt between them. Eyes he couldn't lie to. He took a deep breath and gave Gillian the truth. "No."

Gillian felt that single word pierce her heart. Mason didn't want their child! She closed her eyes against the anguish storming in her heart. Softly, she asked, "Do you hear that sound?"

Mason stiffened and cocked his head toward the doorway. "What sound?"

She knew he was scanning the house for the slightest sound that might mean an intruder. "It's the sound of crystal breaking."

Mason jerked around and stared at her.

She saw the color seep from his face and hardened what was left of her heart. Her voice trembled, but it was strong and clear. "Get out of here."

"Gillian..."

She took a step closer and physically pushed him toward the door. She wanted to cry and she was about to heave whatever was left in her stomach. She'd be damned if she'd do it in front of a man who didn't love her or their child. Her second push was more forceful. Mason stumbled backward into the doorway.

"Damn your black heart, Mason Blacksword!" she shouted as she clutched the door. Screaming relieved the tension threatening to swamp her and it helped hold the tears at bay. She refused to buckle under the strain. "Damn your selfish, pigheaded control, and damn the Council!" Her voice echoed off the walls and bounced from mirror to mirror.

Mason backed up another step as the door started to close in his face.

She took one last look at Mason's pale face and felt herself start to crumble. "And damn my foolish heart for caring." The door closed softly, but the loud click of the lock was final.

Gillian wrapped her robe more tightly around her and slowly sank to the floor. Mason didn't want their child. How could that be? It didn't make sense. All week long she had been anticipating his reaction when she told him. She had envisioned a candlelight dinner and soft romantic music playing in the background when she told him they were going to become parents. Instead she had broken the news by tossing up her cookies at five o'clock in the morning.

It shouldn't have mattered. Mason had no right to tell

her he didn't want their child. He should have kept his
mouth shut, grinned like an idiot and helped her back
to bed while lovingly patting her stomach. That was
how it happened in the movies. Why couldn't it have
happened like that in real life?

She wiped at the tears slowly rolling down her face
with the sleeve of the robe. In real life Mason never
lied. He always spoke the truth no matter what. He had
never given her false words of love, but she had thought
he was content in their marriage and had cared. Now
she knew the truth. Mason would never love her.

The cold tiles surrounding the whirlpool bath chilled
her back through the robe. She didn't care. It felt good
to feel something besides the ache in her chest where
her heart used to be. Her hand dropped protectively to
her still-flat stomach. No, that wasn't right. She did feel
something. She felt love for their child. No matter how
things worked out between Mason and her, she would
always love this child they had managed to create.

If there was a child. She hadn't seen a doctor, or even
taken one of those pregnancy tests you did at home.
Her body had been giving her the signals. She was two
weeks late for her normally regular period, eating ice
cream as if someone was giving it away, and this morning she heaved while the sun was rising. She and Mason
made love every night since their wedding, and they
had never once used birth control. She was no obstetri-
cian, but it spelled pregnancy to her.

She had planned on calling the doctor this morning,
after Mason left for work, to make an appointment.
Now she didn't want to. It would feel funny having the
doctor know she was pregnant without telling her parents, or Mason's mom. Once the parents knew, her sister and brothers would know and Mason's sisters, too.

Her grandmother would have to be told, and then the society. She didn't want the society to know, at least not yet.

The society had been known to throw huge celebrations when a prominent member was expecting. She wasn't the special member, Mason was. In time, Mason would, in all likelihood, sit on the Council. The Council surely would want to throw a gala celebration to announce the pending birth of Mason's child. The whole thing would be a farce, one she wasn't up to attending. Not until she had some answers.

Why had Mason married her, if he was so opposed to children? He knew that was the reason behind the match in the first place. Why hadn't he stopped it?

Didn't Mason want any children? Or just hers? Her mind racked itself looking for the answers. She remembered seeing Mason with his two new nephews from Russia, Alex and Nick, at the wedding. Mason had seemed both patient and indulgent with the rambunctious four-year-old twins. Not the sign of a man who hated children. He had even volunteered to hold her three-year-old nephew, Turner, their ring bearer, during one of the endless photo sessions in the senator's garden. Celeste, her six-year-old niece, had even gotten a dance out of him. Mason wasn't an ogre when it came to children.

Why hadn't they discussed children before they had gotten married? All couples surely talked about something as important as children. But not in their case. Their marriage was specifically arranged so they could have children, hopefully a lot of children. It had never crossed her mind that Mason might be opposed to the idea.

The one thing she had looked so forward to in this

marriage was the one thing her husband didn't want. What an ironic twist of fate. Her dream of a large, happy family with a loving husband and a house full of children had been smashed with one simple word—no. *Do you want children, Mason?* He didn't even hesitate in his response. *No.*

Her hands protectively covered her abdomen as tears ran unchecked down her face. It didn't matter that Mason didn't want children. It didn't matter that she did. The fact remained that they were going to have one, and somehow, someway, they were going to have to work something out.

A faint knock interrupted her musing. "Gillian," Mason called softly, "are you all right?"

No! screamed her mind, *I'm not all right. You just shattered my heart and my life.* She swiped at the tears and sniffed. "Go away!"

"I think we should talk."

She glared at the door, where his robe was still hanging. The last thing she wanted to do now was talk. Maybe later when her stomach calmed down and the tears dried. But not now. "We'll talk later."

There was a long pause before he answered. "I have to be in court later this morning."

Gillian glared harder. Lord save anyone who would dare mess with Mason's schedule. Not even the disastrous announcement of his pending fatherhood could interfere with his career. His Honor would be in court on time or heads would roll. She didn't care about his court or his precious schedule. For weeks her career was put on hold while some madman threatened her. Sympathy for his nine-o'clock court date wasn't forthcoming. "So what's stopping you?" He was free to go where he pleased.

"You're in our bathroom."

Gillian glanced around the room as if seeing it for the first time. The once-stark black-and-white room had changed dramatically since her arrival. Two huge plants now sat in front of the double windows overlooking the backyard. The plants gave the feel of the jungle when lounging in the whirlpool tub. She had relegated Mason's black and white towels to the other bathrooms and had gone out and bought huge thick towels and rugs in apricot. The double-sink counter, which had been barren, was now littered with her hairbrush, a couple of barrettes, her blow-dryer and a bottle of her favorite perfume. The eight-inch-wide rim behind the tub was now crammed with baskets of washcloths and soaps, crystal containers holding bath salts and bubble bath and two ceramic statues of brightly colored parrots.

Who was she kidding? This wasn't their bathroom; it appeared to be hers. Everything of Mason's was meticulously placed in the cabinet above his sink, just like always. Except for his robe, no one would guess he shared this bath with her. It was like their lives. If it wasn't for the gold band encircling his finger and the life growing deep within her, no one would guess they shared a life together.

"Gillian?"

She looked at the windows with the morning sun streaking in through the glass and the sheer white curtains. She couldn't face Mason right now. She needed more time. A lot more time. "Not now, Mason."

"But we need to talk."

"I only have two words for you—Go away!" She honestly didn't want to discuss anything with Mason. Right now she had a problem of her own. Should she stay, or should she go?

* * *

Mason drove up his driveway and immediately let out a sigh of relief. Gillian's car was still there. He glanced at the house and felt her presence. She hadn't left him, at least not yet. All day long, during endless court sessions, he thought of nothing but Gillian and the child she claimed she was carrying. Their child!

He had called home six times. Each time Birdie had answered the phone. Never Gillian. His wife had refused to come to the phone. Who could blame her, though. If the situation was reversed, he wouldn't talk to him, either. How could he have been so callous as to tell her he didn't want their child? Especially while she was physically ill and trying to be so cheerful at the same time.

He parked the car in the garage and stared at the back wall through the windshield. Assorted rakes, shovels and yard tools hung neatly on hooks but he didn't see them. He was seeing his past. His heritage.

He remembered being six and sneaking down the hall to listen to the latest quarrel. Arguments between his parents weren't anything new, but something told him that night's fight was different. His mother's sobs and his father's shouts filled the small kitchen. Every neighbor on their block probably had heard his father. He wished like hell *he* hadn't.

"What in the hell do you mean, you're pregnant? I thought I told you to use something." His mother's reply was lost in her sobs. "Well, the Council's not the one busting their ass trying to support a bunch of runny-nosed brats. I told you I didn't want the two we have, I'm sure as hell not going to be stuck with another one. Get rid of it!"

Even though he was only six years old, he knew what they were fighting about. He was going to become a brother again, and his father didn't want the new baby. But how did one get rid of a baby? By his mother's sobs and his father's renewed shouting, he knew his mother didn't want to get rid of the baby. He also knew what he had suspected for a long time. His father hadn't wanted him or his baby sister, Amy.

"I'll leave you, Nadine, if you keep this baby. I should have been more of a man and defied the Council. I should be married to the woman I love instead of being stuck with you and a bunch of crying babies that suck the life out of you. Do you think one of them is fertile, Nadine? How are you going to like it when one of them tests fertile and has to marry someone they despise? What if your precious Amy has to marry a man who makes her frigid like you? What if little mamma's boy Mason marries a woman he doesn't love and is forced to produce baby after baby after baby? He'll end up hating you, his wife and all your snot-nosed grandchildren. A man can only take so much, and Mason is my son. He'll grow up just like me, no matter what you or the Council do!''

Mason cringed and forced his mind away from the memories. *He'll grow up just like me!* That simple phrase had haunted him since he was six. He didn't want to be his father. For the past twenty-three years of his life, everything he did, he did to prove to the world he wasn't his father's son.

The startling reality was that their paths were already preordained by the Council. Clint Blacksword had to marry a woman he barely knew and didn't love. Mason Blacksword married a woman he barely knew and didn't love. His mother conceived him within the first month of marriage. Gillian conceived their child within the first month of marriage. Were the coincidences going to stop there, or were there more to come? Would he grow to detest his life, his wife and their children, just like his father?

He never wanted to put a child of his through the pain he had suffered at the hands of his own father. Clint Blacksword hadn't been physically abusive to his family. His father had been an expert at mental and emotional abuse. Four and a half years after his second sister, Kara, was born, Clint Blacksword walked out on his family, never to return. Those four and a half years had been devastating to their family. Clint lost his job, their nice lower-middle-class home and every other possession they had had. Somehow it always managed to be his mother's fault, or his sisters' fault, or his fault. Clint blamed everyone but himself for his problems. And he wasn't afraid to let them know it, either. Mason shielded his sisters and mother as best as he could and tried to carry most of the blame.

Mason knew he was probably just frightened. Who wouldn't be? But the biological fact remained—he was his father's son. Only time would tell how alike they were.

Mason got out of the car and reached for his briefcase.

He had a couple hours' worth of work to get through tonight, but he wanted to talk to Gillian first. He needed to talk to his wife. To make her see it wasn't that he didn't want their child, he was just scared to death to become a father.

He entered the kitchen and gave Birdie a halfhearted smile. "Something smells good." He glanced into the family room hoping to spot Gillian. The room was empty.

"She's upstairs sleeping." Birdie continued to chop

up fresh vegetables and dump them into the salad bowl. "Dinner will be ready in about ten minutes."

Birdie knew there was something going on—who wouldn't after six phone calls, all of which Gillian refused to answer? But she didn't seem to be picking a side. "Do you think I should wake her for dinner?"

"No, let her sleep." Birdie scraped the cucumbers on the cutting board into the bowl. "She looked exhausted."

"What was she doing all day?" Gillian had still been locked in the master bathroom when he left for work. Twice more he had tried to talk her into coming out. Both times she refused. He had been hoping she had calmed down in the past eleven hours so they could talk. Now that he was home she was taking a nap. He guessed their conversation was going to wait a couple more hours.

"I don't know. She spent most of the day upstairs." Birdie set the salad and a bottle of dressing on the table.

Mason frowned at the table set for one. "Did she eat anything?"

"She barely touched anything at all today."

His frown deepened. That didn't sound too good. Weren't pregnant women supposed to eat for two? "Thanks, Birdie, for staying in the house today." He wondered how much he should tell Birdie. Being at work all day, he was glad Birdie was around to keep Gillian company.

"I didn't mind." She pulled a casserole from the oven and put it on the table. "Gillian didn't seem to want company, so I spent most of the day reorganizing your pantry."

Mason yanked at his tie and stared at the table for a

moment. "I think I'll go upstairs and check on her. I'll be right back."

Birdie gave him an encouraging smile. "Dinner will keep."

Mason left the kitchen and climbed the steps to the second floor. He entered their bedroom and felt the loss immediately. He glanced around. Gillian had moved out of their room. He slowly walked down the hall to the guest bedroom and pushed the door open. Gillian was curled up in her old bed, and her possessions, which he had noticed were missing from their room, were now on top of her old bureau.

His wife had left him! He should count his blessings that she hadn't packed up everything and moved out of their house. But the one-room difference spoke volumes. Gillian would not be sharing her bed with a man who claimed not to want their child.

He walked quietly into the room and stared down at his sleeping wife. Even with the dark smudges beneath her eyes and sleep-tousled hair, she was the most beautiful woman he had ever seen. Both inside and out. She was going to be a wonderful mother. Gillian would teach their child how to love and laugh. Laughter was something his own childhood had lacked in abundance.

What did he have to give a child? That question worried him. He could offer the financial security his father never provided, but there was more to raising a child than providing a decent house and three balanced meals a day.

He glanced down at her slim body beneath the light blanket, where their child lay. A sense of pride filled his soul. Gillian was carrying their baby. Was it a boy or a girl? Would it have black hair like him, or pale blue eyes and golden hair like Gillian? So many questions. So many possibilities.

Would his child love him or would he be filled with the same hatred he felt for his father? Hatred he never got to express because Clint Blacksword had run out on his family and had died before he was heard from again. How could his child love him when he was unsure if he, himself, was capable of such an emotion?

Mason shook his head slowly. That wasn't true. He was capable of love. He loved his mother and his sisters. Always had, always would. He watched as Gillian muttered something in her sleep and rolled over. She seemed to be searching for something or someone. Her hand reached out and a tiny frown pulled at the corner of her mouth. Was she searching for him? A moment later she hugged the extra pillow to her chest and slipped back into a restful sleep.

What did he feel for his wife? Desire, definitely, but it went deeper than that. Much deeper. She had handed him her heart and he had promised to keep it safe. This morning he had shattered that precious gift. As he had stood on the other side of their bathroom door he'd had the unsettling thought that her heart wasn't the only one breaking. The sight of her tears, the sound of her crying had ripped his to shreds. Was that love? Was it possible that he was already in love with his own wife?

He glanced around the guest bedroom looking for an answer. It wasn't written on the walls. There was no big red heart with the words Mason Loves Gillian written anywhere inside the room. How did a man know when he loved a woman? There hadn't been any fireworks or rockets exploding to signal the event. The passion that raged between them was hot enough to scorch the sheets, and there were no signs of it diminishing. He wanted to crawl into bed with her and hold her through the night. Every night. He wanted a future with Gillian.

How could he reach for the future when his past was still in control?

Mason pulled the light blanket up higher over Gillian's shoulders. The air-conditioning was cool and he knew how much she loved to snuggle under the blankets. His fingers trembled slightly as he brushed a wayward lock of her hair away from her cheek. Her complexion looked pale and the dark smudges of fatigue stood out clearly. She needed to see a doctor as soon as possible. For her health. For their child's health.

He brushed a tender kiss on her cheek and turned away. Somehow they would work all of this out. For now, she needed her sleep, more than he needed his peace. Mason walked from the room and softly closed the door behind him.

Mason stood by the French doors overlooking the backyard and watched as Gillian tossed a Frisbee to Fred. The frisky pup was loving every minute. His heart contracted as a beautiful smile broke out across Gillian's face. It was the first time he had seen her smile in two days. He missed that smile. He missed her warmth. He missed his wife. Ever since she'd told him she was possibly pregnant she'd been avoiding him. He couldn't blame her.

Every time they were in the same room together he didn't know what to say, where to begin. He'd never had to explain himself to anyone before. He'd brought a dozen red roses home yesterday, hoping to break the ice, and she had barely glanced at them. She napped when he was home, ate dinner before he even got home from work and had a hundred excuses not to talk to him at any particular moment. His patience was wearing thin. He wanted his wife back.

The yellow Frisbee sailed through the air and Fred tripped over his own feet trying to run after it. Gillian's laughter at the dog's antics reached his ears. This afternoon he had rushed through a case so he could arrive home before she headed for the guest bedroom. Justice had been swift, but sure, and a half gallon of pistachio ice cream was sitting in their freezer. Gillian was going to have to talk to him this evening.

He tossed his suit jacket and tie onto the back of the couch and stepped out onto the patio. Fred spotted him, dropped the Frisbee he had been carrying, barked excitedly and ran for the patio. Mason bent and patted the pup without taking his eyes off Gillian. His wife's greeting wasn't anywhere near as enthusiastic as the dog's.

Gillian slowly walked toward the patio. She gave her husband a nod. "I'll go see about dinner."

"Birdie's handling it." He stepped in front of her before she could reach the door. "She said it's going to be about another hour."

She kept her gaze directly on his chest. "Good, I'll have time to take a nap then."

Gillian's naps lasted for hours. If she disappeared into the guest bedroom now, he wouldn't see her again this evening. "I thought we might sit out here and talk." He liked the patio with its bright chaises, tubs filled with a kaleidoscope of flowers and cool breezes. All the years he had lived here he had never used it. Until Gillian came along he'd never noticed how stifling the airconditioning could be compared to cool evening breezes. Twilight was the best time to sit, watch Fred chase lightning bugs and enjoy the peacefulness.

"There's nothing to talk about, Mason."

He felt his heart give a sudden lurch. "You're not pregnant?"

"I believe I am, but it's not official yet."

He gave her a smile and took a step closer. For a minute there she'd scared him to death. Over the last two days their baby had become very real to him. "I think we should talk about the baby."

Gillian glanced up and he noticed the tears pooling in her eyes. "We already talked about the baby, Mason. You don't want it. I do."

"Please, Gillian, let me explain. You caught me by surprise the other morning." His fingers plowed through his hair in frustration. He didn't know where to begin.

"Morning sickness has a way of making everything a surprise." She stepped around him and opened the door. "I need to take a short nap. Jon Hall called and he'll be stopping by around eight. He wants to fill us in on the investigation."

"What else did he say?" It had been almost two weeks since the dead-rat incident. He had been praying the joker had finally given up.

"Nothing much. He wants to run a couple of things by me. But so far nothing." She stepped into the house. "Call me when he arrives."

Mason watched her go with a sense of helplessness. She wouldn't talk about the baby, nor would she give him a chance to explain. He had been tempted to shout that he wanted their child, but knowing Gillian, she would demand to know why. Why the change of heart? Why now? What could he say? That a child they created together meant everything to him. She would want the words and he didn't know how to say them. How could he tell Gillian he loved her when his past and his fears were pulling him away?

He loved Gillian. The past two days had shown him how much. He missed her warmth and her passion in their bed. He missed her laughter ringing throughout their house. He missed her smiles and he missed her sweet kisses. Everywhere he went, he thought of her. They lived in the same house but she might as well have been living on the other side of town. He wanted her, that went without saying. But more important he *needed* her. Gillian was showing him how to live for the first time in his life. Gillian had taught him how to smile and how to laugh.

He couldn't walk into their bathroom and look at the whirlpool tub without thinking of the night she surprised him with a strawberry bubble bath. It had taken two days to get rid of the sweet, fruity scent and the smile that seemed permanently fixed on his face. Was that the night their child had been conceived? Or was it the night she gave him her heart and took control of their loving? He would go to his grave remembering that night.

With a heavy sigh he and Fred entered the house. Tonight, after Jon left, they were going to have a real long talk. Even if he had to tie her to a chair to make her listen.

Gillian entered the kitchen the next morning and cringed. Mason was still there, and he wasn't happy. Well, tough donuts for him, she wasn't jumping for joy, either. Her stomach was still heaving and rolling after the latest bout of sickness. She pulled the sash on her robe tighter and walked to the refrigerator. She popped open a can of soda and took a sip.

"You shouldn't drink soda for breakfast."

She glanced at her husband but didn't respond. He looked worse than she felt. By the fatigue on his face, he obviously wasn't getting any sleep, either. If they continued like this they would both be in the hospital before her first trimester was up. That was if she was pregnant. If she wasn't pregnant, then she would be in the hospital a lot sooner than that. It just wasn't normal to greet the dawn by vomiting and to feel so tired all the time.

Mason fingered the handle on his briefcase and glanced at his watch. A frown pulled at the corner of his mouth. "About last night…"

"Forget it, Mason. I'm not the one you should be explaining anything to. Try calling Jon and apologizing for your bizarre behavior. Here he has been doing us both a favor trying to locate whoever's been sending me the threats, and you practically threw him out of the house." She still couldn't believe her husband's behavior last night. Jon had come all the way to their house, on his own time, and Mason had treated him horribly. He had been like Dr. Jekyll and Mr. Hyde. One minute they were in his office, and the next, Jon had been hustled out the door. "Whatever in the world possessed you to act like that?"

"You." His knuckles turned white from the grip they held on the handle. "You possessed me."

"Me?" What in the world was he talking about? All she had been doing was sorting through some information with Jon. She vaguely remembered some comment Jon said to make her laugh. She couldn't remember now what the comment was. From that moment on the night had changed.

"Yes, you!" He paced to the door and back. "You were sitting there laughing with him."

"He made a funny comment." Her eyes narrowed as she stared at her husband.

"You never laugh with me anymore."

In amazing clarity it finally dawned on her. "You're jealous!" Her husband was jealous of Jon Hall. He had absolutely no reason to be jealous of Jon or any other man. Didn't he realize how much she loved him? She took a step forward and slowly smiled.

"I'm not jealous!" Mason walked back to the door and pulled it open.

"Mason?"

He glanced again at his watch with annoyance. "I'm going to be late. We'll talk tonight."

She gave him her sexiest smile. She knew she looked like something a cat wouldn't even bother to drag in, but she didn't care. Mason was jealous! "I'll be waiting."

He looked like he wanted to say more, but didn't. He glanced once more at his watch, turned and headed out the door.

Chapter 12

Mason replaced the car phone and stared out the windshield at the endless rows of marble gravestones. His secretary would handle everything until he arrived at the courthouse. What he planned on doing wasn't going to take long. He should have done it years ago. He needed to confront his father and release his past. Visiting Clint Blacksword's final resting place was the best he could do.

Leaving Gillian standing in the kitchen this morning was one of the hardest things he'd ever had to do. But she had been right. He was jealous of Jon Hall and the easy banter that had developed between him and his wife. He could lose Gillian to another man. Just because they were married, it didn't mean they couldn't get unmarried. It was an eye-opening, heart-stopping thought. One that had him heading out to the cemetery his father was buried in, instead of Center City and the courthouse.

Tonight when he left work he would be heading for home and his future. Gillian had said she would be waiting for him. He wanted to meet her with an unclouded heart. With a determined look he opened the car door and headed for his father's grave.

The plain gray headstone was in the second row where he looked. He hadn't visited the grave since the day of the funeral, seventeen years ago. But he remembered the general location. He read the marker, Clint Edward Blacksword, and engraved below was the year he was born and the year he died. No words of love or prayer had been added. No "Loving Husband and Father," no "Adored Son." Nothing but the years. It was the sad and sorrowful ending of a man who walked this earth for thirty-six years. The grass was neatly mowed and turning brown under the summer's burning sun. No flowers bloomed or were wilting beneath the marker. In all likelihood no flowers ever graced his grave. Who would bring them? Surely not his mother or sisters. The society had shunned Clint Blacksword years before his death.

He stared at the marker and wondered how to begin. He refused to call the man buried below "Dad." "Dad" was the name you gave the man who raised you, loved you and taught you to be a man. Clint Blacksword had done none of those things. "Father" sounded too damn respectful. "Sir" would have been a joke. He decided to skip the salutation and come straight to the point. In a low whisper he said, "I'm your son, Mason, and I'm nothing like you."

His hands curled into fists as he glared at the dried grass. "You were a selfish, gutless man, a horrible, cruel husband and an abusive father. You had so much in this world, but you refused to see what was in front of you."

Mason glanced at his white-knuckled fists and fought the emotion clogging his throat. Feelings long buried came storming to the surface. The film of moisture coating his eyes distorted his vision. Taking a deep breath, he told his father what the child inside him wanted to say for over twenty years. "I could have been a good son. You never gave me the chance. You never gave any of us a chance. It was always about you, you, and you." A tear rolled down his check, but he ignored it. "We could have been a happy, loving family."

Mason listened for a response, some type of sign to tell him his father had heard his childhood hopes, but there was nothing but the sound of distant traffic and the persistent buzzing of a fly. He sighed heavily and glanced around the empty cemetery. What was he expecting, blaring trumpets and heavenly voices? In all likelihood Clint Blacksword never made it through the Pearly Gates.

"I married a woman the Council selected and she's— I mean, we're pregnant." He could almost hear his father's sarcastic laugh. It had happened just like his father had predicted all those years ago. "Her name is Gillian, and I love her." The laughter halted. "I am going to make this marriage work and I'm going to be the best father I can possibly be."

Mason smiled as peace filled his soul. He felt cleansed. "I used to hate you, Clint Blacksword. I don't anymore. Now I can only pity the man you were. You had no idea what you lost, did you?" Mason turned and started to walk away. He turned back and stared at the grave. For some unknown reason he changed his mind.

"I think in the end you did." Silence greeted his conclusion. Mason gave a slight nod and headed for his car.

Gillian pulled up in front of her office and glanced up and down the street. Everything appeared normal and no strange cars had followed her. She knew Mason would hit the roof if he found out she left the house, but this was important. After he left this morning she had been walking on air. Mason was jealous. He wouldn't be jealous if he didn't care, would he? He said they were going to talk when he came home from work. The hours seemed to stretch endlessly in front of her and one very important question still remained unanswered. Was she truly pregnant? How could they discuss the future when she didn't know what the future held?

There was one easy way to find out. She had quickly gotten dressed in an old pair of jeans and a T-shirt and headed for the nearest pharmacy. A simple pregnancy test would give her the answer. Once she was out, and nothing sinister happened, she had decided to drive to her office and pick up the mail and see if there were any messages. It had been four days since she and Mason had been there last. She wanted nothing to distract them tonight.

Gillian picked up the small paper bag sitting on the seat next to her and headed for her office. Mail was scattered across the rug, where the mail person had crammed it into the slot. She skimmed the envelopes and smiled. It was either all junk mail or envelopes with return addresses she recognized. Jon Hall might be right, after all. The person who had been threatening her might have grown bored with the game or tired of waiting for her to come out alone. Hell, for all she

knew, the man could have gone on vacation to Disney-
land. She closed and locked the door behind her. There
was no sense taking unnecessary risks.

Gillian tossed the mail onto the desk and pulled the
small box out of the paper bag. She didn't want to drive
the twenty-five minutes back home before doing the
test. She wanted to know now.

Two minutes later she came out of the bathroom and
carefully placed the test in the center of her desk and
sat. Within five minutes she would know if a life was
forming inside her. She glanced from her watch to the
test and nervously drummed her fingers. The seconds
seemed to last for minutes, and the minutes for hours.

For the past two days Mason had been acting awfully
unusual. He seemed so unsure of himself, as if he didn't
quite know what to do or say. The Mason she had come
to know didn't have an unsure bone in his body. At
least he never used to, until she had mentioned the *P*
word—pregnant. Maybe he never thought of himself as
a father before and her possible pregnancy came as a
shock to him?

The man had to have some inkling how babies were
made. You just couldn't go at it night after night without increasing the odds. The odds had all been on the
baby's side, so why the shock?

For days she had been avoiding him and any form of
communication. At first it had been because she was
angry and upset with her husband. How could he not
want their child? Then fear started to set in. What if he
wanted to call off the marriage before the baby arrived?
Before he had a chance to fall in love?

She had been tearing herself up inside worrying about
a million and one possible ways for Mason to end their
marriage. Until this morning. When he accused her of

laughing with Jon, and not him, it hit her like a stone wall. Mason was jealous of Jon. That was why he practically threw the poor detective out of their house last night. Mason was jealous of another man. Earlier, when Jon had offered to escort her wherever she had to go during the day, her husband had offered to rearrange his schedule. She was the real reason behind the proposed schedule change, not because he thought Jon would be inconvenienced. Mason didn't want her running all over the place with the handsome detective.

Mason loved her! Of course he hadn't figured that out yet, but she had confidence in his ability to see the truth. The future indeed looked very promising. Now all she had to do was wait another minute to see if the future also included a baby.

She stared at the big hand of her watch and took a deep breath when it finally moved to the appropriate number. It was time to see what the future held. She glanced at the small plastic test and grinned. A big pink plus sign gave her the results. She was pregnant!

Gillian leaned back in her chair and plopped both feet up on the desk and grinned like an idiot. She was going to become a mother. A tiny life—that she and Mason had created—was growing inside her. She wondered if it would be a boy with dark hair and dark eyes, just like Mason. Or a girl with her light hair and blue eyes. It didn't matter to her what combination it came in, as long as it was healthy.

There were a lot of disadvantages to being pregnant. One was her new morning ritual in the bathroom, but that should pass. Her stomach would probably grow to the size of a blimp and she would waddle like a duck. She would have to start eating healthier foods and lower her current intake of ice cream. At about three in the morning she had raided the freezer and noticed Mason had picked up another half gallon of pistachio ice cream. The carton was now nearly empty. She could live with a few extra pounds if the end result was a baby.

The one drawback she hadn't given any thought to was her powers. She shouldn't use them. A pregnant witch had a very high chance of not being able to control her powers. It didn't mean she would lose her powers, she just might not be able to control them. The society forbade any pregnant witch from using her powers. Too many things could go wrong—and had in the past.

Some were tragic events. The great Chicago fire of 1871 was indeed started by Mrs. O'Leary's cow with a little help from a pregnant witch named Molly Grady.

Some events weren't so tragic, but caused a stir nevertheless. A pregnant witch was responsible for having it rain frogs in some tiny little village in England. Scientists blamed it on a weather phenomenon called a waterspout, but the society knew the truth.

Not being able to use her powers wouldn't have bothered her at all if it weren't for the joker leaving dead rodents at her door. She hadn't scanned anything for years, until the letters started to arrive. As for her shields, the only time she used them was when she was out trying to track down unsupporting fathers who didn't want to be found. Some of the places she had visited would have required Arnold Schwarzenegger as a bodyguard if it hadn't been for her shields. That meant she was going to be restricted for the next nine months, but that was okay. There were a lot of places she could still go that didn't require a shield. Once this weirdo was caught she would be free to continue with a lot of her work.

With the impending arrival of the little one, she really should start to consider spending more time behind a computer than on the streets. Her brother Kent had offered in the past to help show her how to travel the Internet and let her fingers do the walking instead of her feet. The idea hadn't held any appeal to her in the past, but now it was awfully tempting. Maybe she could convince Mason to permanently share his office with her.

Visions of Mason behind his desk working at night, her behind another desk speeding through the Internet and the baby playing on a blanket with a rattle filled her senses. They would be a family. She didn't know why Mason had told her he didn't want a child the other morning. He wanted their child, she knew he did. At least she prayed he did.

Hadn't he brought home a dozen red roses for her the other day? She hadn't given them more than a passing glance when he handed them to her. But as soon as he left the room, she sniffed each bloom and smiled. Wasn't he the one who picked up more pistachio ice cream yesterday for her? At night, when he should have been sleeping, she could hear him pacing in the master bedroom. Twice he looked like he was about to yell at her, but he had managed to get himself back under control before the outburst.

She had purposely been pushing every button of his she could think of. She wanted him to lose that damn iron control, at least just once. Being in physical danger around Mason was never the issue. Her instincts were telling her that when Mason finally lost his control she would see a side of him she had only been dreaming about. A side that was capable of being in love. When his control slipped, she would finally be able to see his heart.

Gillian leaned farther back in the chair and stared at the ceiling. She wanted Mason to say three little words—I love you—and make her the happiest woman in the world.

The unexpected sound of splintering wood nearly threw her from her precarious perch on her chair. She stared in horror as her office door was kicked in and a man followed the broken door into her office. A man holding a gun—a very deadly-looking gun. She stared at the metal barrel and swallowed. Now was not the time to lose control of her powers.

She had been a fool. Mason was never going to forgive her if she got herself and their child killed. She slowly raised her gaze from the gun and encountered a pair of gray eyes shrouded in madness. She didn't need her powers to know this was the man who had been threatening her.

His name was Lenny Perate and he was one of the deadbeat fathers she had located. His name was never high on her list of suspects because he didn't seem the type, nor was he associated with the rougher sides of the city. Lenny had walked out on his wife and four kids three years ago. The court had ordered him to pay support, but he never had. He had changed jobs and his ex-wife, Carolyn, had come to Gillian for help nearly a year ago.

Lenny had been one of the easier ones to track down. He had left the small shoe store he had been working in and had migrated to a large department store in a fancy mall on the outskirts of the city. He still sold shoes, only now it was to a better class of people. The interesting part about Lenny was that he left his wife and children mere months before an uncle had died and left him some very interesting assets. Gillian had located him and the court ordered him to sell his fancy new sports car and boat to pay back child support. Lenny had a choice—do as the court ordered, or go to prison for contempt of court. Mason had been the judge to sign the court order. Lenny had sold the assets and was still having child support withheld from his paycheck at the fancy department store.

Gillian remembered Lenny as a quiet, almost meek, sort of guy who hadn't put up a lot of resistance. In fact, he hadn't resisted at all. He submissively sold the assets he had inherited and went on with his life. Or so she had thought. It appeared now that Lenny was indeed infuriated over the lost assets and was blaming her.

The madness in his eyes gave her a moment of fear. Lenny looked like he would love to pull the trigger. She slowly lowered her feet to the floor and stood up. "Hello, Lenny."

"Shut up, bitch." Lenny glanced around the office and grinned menacingly.

So much for pleasantries. Her hand instinctively dropped to her abdomen, where her child lay. She quickly ran through her choices. She could use her powers to protect herself, and suffer whatever consequences developed. There was no guarantee that her powers would save her. She could try to send Mason a message and pray that it reached him. Or she could spinelessly stand by and allow Lenny to end her life. Logic told her to try to reach Mason first. If Lenny started to get violent, she'd try her powers. A shield could beat a bullet, provided she saw the bullet coming.

She kept her gaze on the trigger of Lenny's gun and

sent Mason two words: *help* and *pregnant*. There was no sense going into details and pressing her luck. She had a gut feeling she was going to need every ounce of luck she possessed. Her face was expressionless as she asked, "Can I help you with something?" It was a ridiculous question to ask a man pointing a gun at you, but she'd be damned if she'd cry or beg for her life. She'd do that later, but maybe now she could talk some sense into Lenny.

"You're going to die real slow, bitch." He took a few steps closer.

Okay, that had her heart skipping a few beats. Maybe one little shield wouldn't hurt? She watched the gun with morbid curiosity.

Lenny grabbed her arm and pulled her closer. "I've been waiting a long time for this." He jammed the gun against her side. "Let's go."

Gillian dug her feet into the carpet and prayed she wasn't making a mistake. A small shield went up where the gun pressed into her side. "Where are we going?" She breathed a small sigh of relief when nothing unusual happened.

"To the last place you'll ever see." He pushed her toward the door. "Don't worry, bitch, you'll have a nice view of the river."

His chuckle sent a shiver down her spine. Lenny Perate wasn't wrapped too tight. Her feet stumbled through the door, out into the empty hallway and to the front door. She frantically glanced around, looking for someone to help. No one was there.

The gun dug deeper into her side as his other arm wrapped around her shoulder and maneuvered her toward the alley next to the building. "This way, and don't try to scream." He shoved her into the alley.

A modest late-model car was parked there. Gillian eyed the vehicle and thought about the fancy European model Lenny had needed to sell to pay back support. This model was definitely a step down from what he had been driving, but surely it wasn't worth killing someone over. He pushed her against the rear bumper, dug a set of keys out of his pants pocket and opened the trunk. He glanced around and waved the gun at her chest. "Get in."

Gillian maneuvered the small shield to follow the gun. She didn't want to chance an entire body shield. She glanced at the trunk and grimaced. It looked as if it had never been clean. Something slimy was spilled all over the bottom and a flat spare sat crookedly in the wheel well. Nothing else was in the dark space. No crowbar, no jack, nothing she could use as a weapon.

If she used her powers now to stop Lenny, there was an excellent chance they would backfire and cause some type of cataclysmic event right here. The people of this neighborhood could be in danger. Lenny obviously wanted to take her someplace secluded to finish her off. She'd be better off waiting until they got wherever Lenny wanted to take her. There was less chance of anybody else getting hurt that way. The small shield she had erected seemed to be working, and there hadn't been any unforeseen catastrophe when she sent the message to Mason. But she couldn't press her luck any further. Too many innocent people could be at risk.

The gun pressed into her stomach. "Now!"

Gillian gave him one last look before slowly stepping into the trunk.

"Lay down!"

She bit the inside of her cheek, but did as he asked. The second she was down, the trunk lid slammed down, encasing her in darkness. She heard Lenny's twisted laugh as he walked toward the front of the car. She felt the slight movement of the car as he got in, then the sound of the engine starting captured her attention. She knew she would have only one chance to stop Lenny when they arrived wherever he was taking her. It had better be good.

Her arms wrapped around her waist as she bounced and was tossed with every pothole Lenny hit. He was probably purposely hitting every one for her benefit. The stench of motor oil filled the trunk. She stared into the darkness surrounding her and thought of Mason and their child.

Mason looked at the lawyer standing in front of him droning on about his client's rights and tried not to show any emotion. He was both bored and aggravated and wanted desperately to be home with Gillian. They had so much to discuss. So much to look forward to—their future.

"And," continued the lawyer, "I would also like to point out to this court that my client…"

"*Help!*" Gillian's voice erupted throughout the room. "*Pregnant!*" Mason stood up and glanced frantically around the courtroom. The lawyer's voice seemed to end abruptly and Mason noticed Bill Grayman, the bailiff, come rushing forward. He closed his eyes and concentrated on the voice only he had heard. It had been Gillian crying for help. She was in danger and the second word told him why. If Gillian was really pregnant, as she thought, she couldn't use her powers. She was powerless to stop the madman. Why in the hell hadn't he thought of that before?

He glanced around the courtroom and noticed everyone staring at him as if he was insane. He didn't care. Gillian's life was in danger. He jumped down from behind his bench, pinned his secretary with a frantic glance and said, "Reschedule everything." His black robe bellowed around him as he ran for the door.

By the time he reached his car in the underground parking lot he had the robe off and his keys in his hand. He pulled out from beneath the courthouse while dialing his home number on the car phone.

"Hello?"

"Birdie, where's Gillian?" He joined the midmorning traffic and maneuvered around a brown delivery truck.

"She's not here, Mason. When I got here an hour ago there was a note saying she'd be right back."

"Is her car there?"

"No."

Birdie sounded to be on the verge of tears. "It's okay, Birdie. I'll find her." On instinct, he turned right, in the direction of Gillian's office, instead of going straight to their home. "You have my car-phone number. Call if she returns, okay?" He slammed down the phone and concentrated on arriving at her office in the shortest amount of time. If the police wanted to give him a ticket for speeding, they would have to catch him first.

He spotted her car parked out front and parked behind it. What in the world possessed her to leave the house this morning? She had promised to be waiting for him. He opened the main door to the run-down office building and noticed her kicked-in office door. He scanned the area as he rushed into her office. It was empty, but the culprit had been there. He could feel the twisted evil vibrations still trembling throughout the room.

Gillian's pocketbook sat on her desk, along with a

pile of mail. He ignored the mail and slowly walked over to the desk. A small white plastic pregnancy test sat in the middle of the desk. He picked up the box next to the test and scanned the directions. He glanced back at the test. The pink plus sign told him he was going to be a father.

He closed his eyes and read Gillian's feelings. Joy and happiness surrounded the test, but he picked up on her fear. His wife had been afraid when the intruder broke down the door and entered her office. She had every right to be afraid. While she was pregnant there was no guarantee that her powers would work correctly. She might not be able to defend herself or their child. He had heard stories of pregnant witches who had tried to use their powers and either couldn't or had disturbed the world's order of things. Would Gillian use her powers to save herself, knowing she could cause innocent people to perish?

She had sent him the message, but it didn't even take one hundredth of her powers to send two little words across one city. Ever since their marriage, he had been able to pick up on her feelings without even trying. He had probably exerted more effort picking the words up than she had by sending them.

He closed his eyes and tried to read what Gillian was feeling or seeing. The only thing he could pick up was darkness. Gillian was probably surrounded by darkness and that was all she could see. The other option was too horrifying to consider. Gillian and their unborn child had to be safe. Fate wouldn't be so cruel as to take the woman he loved away just when he found her.

He opened his eyes and glanced frantically around the room. The only chance he had of locating and helping Gillian was to read the room and pick up on some of the thoughts of whoever took her. He walked over to the door, hanging by half of a broken hinge, and touched the wood. The feeling of twisted hatred vibrated from the door. It was the same malice that had accompanied the dead rat and the box of leeches. He was dealing with the same man.

Mason stepped into the room and concentrated on that distorted mind. There had to be a clue somewhere. Beads of sweat gathered and then rolled down his face. He flung out his arms and put everything he had into wading through that twisted mind. His fists clenched and his body trembled but he continued to focus. Gillian had trusted him enough to send the message. He couldn't afford to let her down. He might be the only chance for her survival. He was holding the cards for their future and he was scared to death of playing them wrong.

Dark, sinister vibrations filled with hatred and revenge swirled around him. He fought his way through thick tentacles of evil and became one with the man. The past played before him like a fuzzy video. He could see Gillian standing before him trying so desperately to look nonchalant and brave. He saw how her hands instinctively covered their unborn child. His arm reached out and pulled her closer, jamming the gun into her side.

She was concentrating on the gun he held in his hand. Mason could feel the shield she erected across the barrel of the gun. She had protected herself, for the time being. He had no way of knowing how long the shield would last or if it would even work.

Her voice trembled slightly when she asked where they were going.

The man's response seemed to come from his own lips and fill the room. *"To the last place you'll ever see. Don't worry, bitch, you'll have a nice view of the river.''*

Mason saw exactly what the man had been thinking. The river he had been referring to was the Delaware River and the spot was an old abandoned landfill. Mason knew where the dump was because the Betsy Ross Bridge was in the distance.

Instead of breaking the contact with the past, he continued to act the part. He saw Gillian looking frantically around the front of the building as he forced her to the alley. He shuddered at her fear as she stepped into the trunk, and he heard the unbalanced laughter of her tormentor pour from his own mouth.

Standing in the alley, Mason snapped out of the past. His body trembled and his stomach rolled with nausea. He had witnessed the entire event and seen his wife's fear. Having a glimpse of the psychopath's mind, he now understood the man better. He wanted Gillian to die, and die slowly.

He'd kill the son of a bitch with his bare hands. Mason ran for his car, slammed his foot on the gas and punched in the digits of Jon Hall's phone number. He headed for the river and for his wife and prayed he wasn't too late.

Chapter 13

Mason pulled alongside of a rusty metal fence and stepped out of his car. He scanned the area, trying to decide which way to go. The aroma of decaying food and garbage rotting under the summer sun nearly knocked him to his knees. It took him a moment to block out the stench and concentrate on Gillian. All he could pick up was darkness and the faint sound of a child's lullaby. His heart contracted with the thought of Gillian being locked in that filthy trunk softly singing a lullaby to their unborn child. He was personally going to wrap his hands around the psycho's throat and never let go.

He scanned the area and picked up the demented ravings of the man who took his wife. He quickly got back into his car and drove along the road bordering the fence. Nearly a thousand yards passed before he spotted the opening Gillian had been driven through. He turned in and followed the rutted path between mountains of garbage.

The Betsy Ross Bridge was in the distance and he could feel Gillian's presence close by. He stopped the car and quietly got out and followed the rutted lane on foot. When he rounded the third pile of garbage he quickly hid behind a decrepit recliner. A fat, beady-eyed rat scurried away, giving him pause to wonder if this was the place the psycho had trapped the rodent he delivered to Gillian.

Ahead of him was the same late-model car he had seen in his vision. He watched as a lanky man got out from behind the wheel. The man didn't look like a psycho. He reminded Mason of an office worker or salesman slumming for the day. The gleaming metal of a gun, tucked into the waistband of his jeans, spoke differently.

The clean-cut man glanced around before heading for the trunk. To throw a shield around Gillian, he had to see her. The metal of the car was preventing him from protecting her. He positioned a shield around the gun.

Mason anxiously waited as the man opened the trunk, waved the gun and then stepped back. He couldn't hear the words the man used, but he recognized the tone. Gillian sat up, covered her eyes from the light of the sun and then slowly got out of the trunk. Mason threw a shield around her so thick that if a Sherman tank ran her over, she wouldn't suffer so much as a headache. He could tell she felt the shield go up. She glanced around, as if looking for him, before smiling at the man and the gun pointed at her chest.

Gillian looked at Lenny and his measly little gun and chuckled. Mason was here somewhere, she hadn't spotted him yet, but she could feel his shield surrounding her. He had heard her and had come running to her rescue! She wouldn't have to chance using her powers and hurting any innocent people. She held up one finger to signal Mason to give her some time. There were a lot of questions she wanted to ask Lenny. If things got out of hand, all she had to do was stand back and watch Mason go to work. She softly chuckled and started the show.

Lenny waved his gun threateningly. "Stop that. Are you too stupid to realize you're going to die?"

She shook her head and suppressed the laughter, but she couldn't hide the merriment in her eyes. Mason was going to chew this guy up and spit him out, and all because of her. Mason cared! The shield surrounding her was not only for protection, but it was warm and soft, and made from love. She could practically feel the love.

"Put down the gun, Lenny, before you get hurt," she said. Lenny was playing with a very dangerous stick of dynamite called Mason, and the fuse was burning low. She didn't want to see Lenny or anyone else get physically hurt, but she knew he needed some major help and he had to be put someplace where he wouldn't terrorize anyone else. By the look of madness clouding his eyes, it appeared Lenny still wanted to end her life.

"You're crazy, bitch." He took a step closer. "You and your new husband ruined my life! Do you think I would allow you to get away with that? I thought about killing the judge, too, but I figured it would be harder on him if he lived and you died." He gave her a smile that would have chilled her blood if it weren't for the shield. "Don't worry your pretty little head over Blacksword. I'll make sure he knows exactly how you die, and how long it took."

"Listen, Lenny, I didn't ruin your life. You left your ex-wife and four children without any financial support. Carolyn was so late in the mortgage payments, she was about to lose the house. Didn't you care what happened to your children?"

"No, they were all just like Carolyn, always wanting something. Susan needed braces and Scot was always at the doctors sucking my money away before I even had a chance to earn it. The washer was broke, the bathroom sink leaked and Carol wanted ballet lessons!" Gillian cringed slightly as his voice rose with each sentence. "It was my money! I earned it, it was mine! I put up with an obnoxious boss all day long and then I had to go home to that house and listen to them whine all night long."

Gillian felt compelled to say, "Carolyn worked, too."

"So what? You call waiting tables work?" He snorted at the very idea. "They were her little babies, let her support them. I wanted out and I wanted my life back."

"So you walked?" She knew the heartache and misery Carolyn and the children had suffered. She also knew the receipt of the back child support had relieved most of the pressure.

"Not right away." Lenny chuckled and puffed out his chest. "I needed to make some plans first."

It struck Gillian that something wasn't right. If Lenny had just walked away, he wouldn't have remained a shoe salesman. But when she tracked him down, he had been renting a luxury apartment, had a boat parked at the marina and he had been driving an expensive foreign sports car. The boat, car and Lord only knew what else had come from an uncle's estate. He also had a girlfriend named Charmaine. "How did your uncle die, Lenny?"

He gave a chilling laugh that made her blood freeze, shield or no shield. "So you're not so stupid, after all." He nodded his head as if in approval. "Poor, dear Uncle Ed." He shook his head sadly, but the grin stretching his mouth dispelled the illusion of sadness. "He should have known better than to smoke in bed."

"You set the fire, didn't you?" If he killed once to obtain the boat and car, he'd surely kill again because she took them away from him.

"Bingo!" Lenny grinned. "But first I had to do a little safecracking. I didn't take it all, just a nice, tidy little nest egg to hold me over. I didn't want to make the police suspicious when they investigated after the fire."

"Where's Charmaine?" She wondered how much Lenny managed to steal from his uncle's safe.

His grin disappeared. "She left me about a week after the car and boat did."

Gillian refrained from commenting on Charmaine's loyalty. She also knew from the court records that Lenny had been forced to give up the luxury apartment and move into a more modest dwelling once the child support was taken directly from his pay. She could see where the illusion that she had ruined his life had come from. In Lenny's mind he had lost everything.

"Lenny, do yourself a favor and place the gun in the trunk and back away from the car."

A laugh emerged from his mouth. "You're something, lady. You spend your time destroying my life..."

"I spend my time helping women get support they need from you and men like you."

Lenny shook his head. "Who's going to help you?"

He took another step closer. ''I'll tell you who. Nobody! Your precious husband's in court, probably busy ruining some poor slob's life. You should have minded your own business and stayed out of mine!''

''You should have been more of a man and supported the children you helped to bring into the world.''

She had been watching the trigger of the gun, to see if her comment would push him over the edge. If she had been watching his other hand, she would have seen the hand coming and stepped back. Instead, his left fist swung at her face and crashed into the shield. Gillian, startled by his sudden movement, lost her balance and landed on her backside. It was like falling onto a feather bed. Mason's shield cushioned her all the way down. Not one hair on her head had been mussed.

Lenny howled as he cradled his fist. Gillian glanced up in time to see the change come over him. One minute he was moaning about his hand and the next he was staring in horror at something she couldn't see. His mouth opened in a silent scream and his features contorted grotesquely. The gun dropped from his right hand and he started to brush frantically at his arms and legs.

Gillian had no idea what he was seeing, but she knew who was responsible for his bizarre behavior. The sky turned black as night and lightning streaked down as thunder rolled. The heavens seemed to be opening up and displaying their displeasure at the man standing in front of her.

The wind howled and Lenny finally let out a blood-curdling scream that had been lodged in his throat as he glanced wildly around.

Gillian looked to her left and spotted Mason standing in the middle of the storm that surrounded them. He looked magnificent in his fury. His black hair was wind-tossed and his eyes burned like two pieces of coal. Lightning struck the ground on either side of him, starting small fires. Mason had lost his control!

She grinned as paper and garbage danced upon the wind and the heavens poured down. Not one hair on her head moved, not one drop of rain landed on her. It was an awesome display of Mason's rage. The elements had one target and one target only, and that was Lenny.

Lenny stepped closer to the car and screamed again. It was the sound of a man about to lose what was left of his sanity. He was still staring in horror at things she could only guess at. He didn't seem to realize where he was, or that she was even there. Lenny was gaping at the demons only he could see and pleading for mercy or death—whichever was quicker.

Gillian watched as Mason hurried to her and swept her up into his arms.

His eyes bored into her face. "Did he hurt you?"

"No, he never touched me." She raised her hand and gently caressed his rigid jaw. "I was looking at the gun and I didn't see his hand come up. When I caught sight of it, I lost my balance and fell."

He hugged her closer and she gloried in the strength of his arms around her. She and their child were safe now. Nothing would harm them. Mason seemed to be having difficulty breathing, which was amusing considering it was her chest being squeezed by his arms.

Another one of Lenny's screams split the air. He might deserve everything Mason was doing to him, but it still didn't make it right. "Mason, darling, could you tone it down a bit?" She nodded in the direction of Lenny and the lightning bolt that struck a couple of yards away.

Mason glanced over his shoulder at the terror-stricken

man. "Well, since you called me darling, I guess." With a sweep of his hand he sent Lenny flying backward, straight into the trunk. His arm swept downward and the trunk lid slammed shut. One more wave of his arm and the heavenly display ceased and the sun was again shining back down on them. The dump looked exactly as it had before Mason's display. No puddles were on the ground. No burnt garbage where the lightning had struck and the fire had raged.

Gillian had felt the shield he had erected around her disappear. There was nothing between her and Mason but the clothes on their backs. The danger had passed, and they had their future to look forward to. A future that held a child she still wasn't one hundred percent sure Mason wanted.

Lenny's screams were muffled by the trunk. She cocked one eyebrow. "Mason?"

"It's not me, honest. Whatever he's seeing, he's doing it without my help." The corner of his mouth tilted up. "It serves him right, after what he put me through."

"Ah, the nightmares." She had thought it coincidence that Mason started to dream, and to dream nightmares, the same night he found out about the threats.

"Yes, the nightmares." A slight shudder swept through his body at the memory of his dreams. He hugged her closer.

Gillian brushed a kiss on his jaw and tilted her head. The distant sound of sirens was getting closer. "You called the police?"

"I talked to Jon on my way here. I told him where we'd be and why." Mason started to walk away from the car, where Lenny was still screaming. "Jon seemed anxious to join us."

She snuggled deeper into his arms. "I would imagine."

They arrived at Mason's car the same time Jon and two other police cars came barreling into the dump. Mason gently deposited her in the passenger seat with a quick kiss before talking to Jon and the other officers.

Six hours later Mason tucked Gillian's robe more tightly around her legs and asked, "Are you sure you're okay?" They had just spent three grueling hours at police headquarters answering questions, filing complaints and giving statements. Lenny Perate had been in no condition to answer the police's questions. He was currently sedated, restrained and under guard at a mental ward at one of the city's hospital. After leaving the police station, Mason had insisted they stop to see a doctor, who pronounced Gillian in perfect health and showing no signs of her recent ordeal.

When he thought of how close he had come to losing her, it made his heart fluctuate, and a haze of red distorted his vision. He should have strangled Perate with his bare hands.

Over the past couple of weeks he had learned firsthand how ineffective his once-precious law could be. He had felt the pain and frustration of being a helpless victim, waiting, with his hands tied, for the culprit to strike again. He didn't like that feeling one bit. He now had plans to work with the law to strengthen Pennsylvania's stalking laws. He also understood the fear he and every other victim had to live with. One day Perate might be a free man again.

He had thought, when he picked law as his career, that he would have the control he so desperately wanted to obtain. What higher control was there than the law?

It had been a foolish and youthful visualization of the world. In this crazy world, control was fleeting at best. But he liked being a judge and had plans to continue on his chosen career path. Maybe he had been wrong thinking his gift had been control. Maybe his gift was justice. It was an interesting thought, one he would have to give some serious time to later. But now he needed to make sure Gillian was all right.

He couldn't bring himself to rant or rave at her for disobeying his orders about not going out of the house. He was just too damn thankful she was safe. If the situation had been reversed, he knew he would have gone out. No psycho would have kept him prisoner in his own home.

Gillian glanced up at her husband and placed her empty coffee cup on the end table. "I told you, Mason, I'm fine. The doctor said I was fine. The police said I was fine. Even—" she gave a heavy sigh before shaking her head "—the baffled paramedics that you summoned to the dump said I was fine."

"You should have gone with them to the hospital to be checked out, like I asked. You could have had a miscarriage or something."

Gillian gave him a strange look before settling back into the leather couch. "I gather you saw the pregnancy test in my office."

She looked all warm and comfortable relaxing on what he knew to be her favorite spot in the house—the burgundy leather sofa in the family room. The family room—it had a nice ring to it. They were indeed family now.

Fred was contentedly lying next to the dragon statue, chewing on one of Mason's old sneakers by the French doors. After they arrived home and polished off the meal Birdie had been preparing all day, Gillian had taken a shower and changed into her robe. Birdie had discreetly disappeared, once she was assured of Gillian's health and safety, to her apartment above the garage. They were now alone and he had a lot he wanted to talk about.

He sat down next to her and reached for her hand. "Yes, I saw the test."

"And the results?"

"And the results." He gave her a small smile. "On the way into work this morning I made a stop at someplace I should have gone years ago."

"Where?" Her brows pulled together into a frown.

"I stopped at the cemetery where my father was buried." He glanced out the doors and into the fading light of the evening. "I needed to put my past behind me before I could face the future with you."

"And did you?" She gave his hand a gentle squeeze. "Did you put it behind you?"

"Clint Blacksword was a terrible father and husband." Mason turned and faced Gillian. "I'm nothing like him."

She gave him a tender smile. "I know that."

"He said I was going to be just like him."

Gillian heard the pain and turmoil in Mason's voice and gripped his hand harder. "When did he say that?" As far as she knew, Clint Blacksword died when Mason was around twelve years old.

"Before he left us. He said I was going to marry a woman the Council picked and that I wouldn't love her or our children. He said I would be stuck in the same hell he was, producing snotty-nosed brats for the society."

Gillian cringed but kept her gaze locked on Mason.

He seemed to be baring his soul for her to see. This was what she had been waiting for. "The Council picked your wife and you thought your father's words were coming true." She wished she had known about his fears sooner. They explained a lot about Mason and his resistance to their marriage. They also explained his reaction to her pregnancy.

"When I was sixteen, yes."

"And now?" She held her breath and waited for his answer. Their future rested with his answer.

It took him a while before he replied. "Can I have it back?" he asked softly.

She blinked in surprise. "Have what back?"

"Your heart." He pulled her closer. "This time I promise to take better care of it, Gillian." He tenderly cupped her chin and raised her face to his. His lips were as gentle as a summer's breeze as they brushed across hers.

"It has to be an even exchange, Mason. I want yours in return." She couldn't give her heart again without knowing how he felt.

"Don't you know, you already have it, wife. You stole it when I wasn't even looking."

"I don't want a stolen heart, Mason."

"It was freely given. I love you, Gillian." His sweet kiss showed her how freely it had been given.

Gillian felt herself start to drown in the kiss and in his words. Mason loved her! She slowly backed away and worried her lower lip. "What about our child?"

Mason's hand reached out and gently cupped the flat contour of her stomach. "I lied to you the other morning. I do want this baby and every other baby we might create."

She could feel the trembling in his fingers through

the silk of her robe. "Did you tell me you didn't be-cause of what your father said?"

"Partly." He lowered his hand. "I was having a hard time adjusting to how much I enjoyed being married to you. I had visions of taking our vows and then living in pure hell for the rest of my life. I was wrong."

Gillian let out a sigh of relief. "I know marriage is a big adjustment for us both, especially considering our beginning, but it hasn't been too bad. Has it?"

"No, it wasn't bad at all. I was just getting accustomed to Fred and Birdie and to the fact my wife had a psychopath tormenting her, when out of the blue you start tossing your cookies and tell me *we're* pregnant." He gave her a soft smile. "Let's just say I choked and came up with the wrong answer for all the wrong reasons."

Gillian glanced at the tenderness shining in his eyes. "You're going to be a wonderful daddy." She now understood Mason's reluctance. It wasn't that he didn't want kids, he was scared of turning out like his own father.

"How do you know?"

"I know you, Mason. You're not going to change just because a baby arrives on the scene." She reached up and kissed his cheek. The silly, wonderful man was scared of a little helpless baby. "You're going to be the perfect father—a little controlling, I'm sure, but don't worry, I'm handling that."

"And you'll probably spoil the kid rotten." He hauled her closer and kissed her deeply. "But don't worry, I'm handling that." He kissed her again and they slowly sank into the depths of the couch.

When they both caught their breath, he asked, "You're not afraid I'll turn out like Clint Blacksword?"

"Mason..." She shook her head. She never realized how vulnerable her husband was when it came to his past. It just proved the damage some parents did to their kids. "You might have inherited Clint Blacksword's dark eyes and hair, and even his height." She tapped him on his chest. "But you didn't inherit his heart or soul."

"How can you be sure?" He stood and picked her up into his arms.

"I've seen your heart, darling." She snuggled into his embrace and felt the heat of his hands through the silk. Desire pulsed through her body. Mason loved her and their child. The tip of her finger outlined a big heart against his chest. "There's enough room in it for me and a dozen little babies."

He started to carry her from the room. "A dozen?" Mason sputtered as he came to a complete stop.

"Okay, we'll compromise. Half a dozen." She gave him a seductive smile. Her fingers toyed with the ends of his hair brushing the back of his neck. She knew he liked it when she played with his hair.

"Six kids! Are you crazy?"

"Yes." She reached up and finished wrapping her arms around his neck. "Crazy about you, that is."

Epilogue

Gillian sat down in the lounge chair between Mason's legs and sighed with pleasure as his strong fingers rubbed suntan lotion onto her back. Nearly five years of marriage and Mason's hands never ceased to excite her. She gazed to her right, where their two-year-old daughter, Sonya, lay asleep under an umbrella. Playing the morning away on the beach had tired Sonya out.

Mason followed his wife's glance. "She looks just like you when you sleep." His mouth brushed her shoulder.

"I sleep with my butt up in the air?"

"I wish," Mason said, chuckling. "I was referring to the peaceful expression on her face. Like she doesn't have a care in the world."

Gillian looked at her daughter and smiled. Love filled her heart whenever she looked at her children. Sonya had her light blond hair and pale blue eyes. Tyler, their four-year-old son, had Mason's coloring. "Why shouldn't I sleep like that? I *don't* have a care in the world.''

His hands encircled her waist and came to rest on her stomach. "How are you feeling? The sun isn't too much, is it?''

"I'm fine, Mason. Stop worrying about every little thing." She covered his hands with hers and grinned. "Me and the baby are fine." Her pregnancies were harder on Mason than on her. She was carrying their third child, but the only outward signs so far were her morning visits to the bathroom. Mason had insisted they take a family vacation now, while it was still safe enough for her to travel. They had chosen Maui, the same island they had had a belated honeymoon on nearly five years ago.

Back then they had rented a private villa on a private beach and hadn't seen a soul except for a maid who straightened the house in the morning and left enough food for the day. The first night under the Hawaiian skies, Mason had made love to her on the beach. She still remembered that it was the first thing she had wanted to do as soon as the psycho who had been threatening her was caught. Mason spent the next six months making sure every one of her wishes came true.

This vacation they had chosen a family resort and a bungalow large enough to handle the two children and Birdie. Today, Birdie had the day to herself, but tonight she was going to watch the kids so she and Mason had some private time. By the gleam in Mason's eye this morning, when he told her of the arrangement, she had a feeling they were going to find a secluded beach somewhere and once again she was going to end up with sand in some most unusual places.

Their marriage was wonderful, and she wouldn't

have traded the last five years for anything. Of course it hadn't been all fun and games. They both still had a lot of adjusting to do. She worked at home now, sitting behind a computer hunting down deadbeat dads on the Internet. She also pestered the Council and the society to help set up a support clinic in The Blades for abused and neglected mothers and their children. Mason had been promoted to appellate judge two years ago, and there was talk about him being appointed to the federal court before much longer. They still butted heads when he got too controlling or when she brought home a stray.

She glanced at Tyler sitting by the water's edge building a sand castle and sucked in a quick breath.

"What's wrong?" Mason glanced at her face with concern. "Is it the baby?"

"The baby's fine." She brushed his brow, where worry wrinkles had formed. "Do you remember I used to tell you about a dream I sometimes have?"

"The one about the boy at the beach building sand castles?"

"That's the one." She nodded at Tyler and his assortment of buckets and shovels. "I know you're going to think this is crazy, but that's my dream."

"Tyler's the boy from your dream?"

"Identical, right on down to his bathing suit and the red bucket in his hand. I don't know why I never realized it before. He's been to the New Jersey shore a dozen times or so."

Mason glanced around at the swaying palms that were mere yards away from the water. "When you told me about the dream you always mentioned the palm trees and the scent of flowers. New Jersey doesn't have palm trees or the flowers."

Gillian leaned back into her husband's embrace. "Since when did you become an expert on dreams?"

His lips nuzzled her neck but his gaze stayed on his son. "Since the day I married you." His teeth playfully nipped at the delicate lobe of her ear. "Since the day I married you."

* * * * *

Uncover the truth behind

CODE NAME: DANGER

in **Merline Lovelace's** thrilling duo

DANGEROUS TO HOLD

When tricky situations need a cool head, quick wits and a touch
of ruthlessness, Adam Ridgeway, director of the top secret
OMEGA agency, sends in his team. Lately, though, his agents have
had romantic troubles of their own....

NIGHT OF THE JAGUAR
&
THE COWBOY AND THE COSSACK

And don't miss
HOT AS ICE (IM #1129, 2/02)
which features the newest OMEGA adventure!

DANGEROUS TO HOLD is available this February
at your local retail outlet!

Look for *DANGEROUS TO KNOW*, the second set of
stories in this collection, in July 2002.

magazine

♥──────────────────────────── **quizzes**

Is he the one? What kind of lover are you? Visit the **Quizzes** area to find out!

♥──────────────────── **recipes for romance**

Get scrumptious meal ideas with our **Recipes for Romance**.

♥──────────────────────── **romantic movies**

Peek at the **Romantic Movies** area to find Top 10 Flicks about First Love, ten Supersexy Movies, and more.

♥──────────────────────────── **royal romance**

Get the latest scoop on your favorite royals in **Royal Romance**.

♥──────────────────────────────── **games**

Check out the **Games** pages to find a ton of interactive romantic fun!

♥──────────────────────── **romantic travel**

In need of a romantic rendezvous? Visit the **Romantic Travel** section for articles and guides.

♥──────────────────────────── **lovescopes**

Are you two compatible? Click your way to the **Lovescopes** area to find out now!

Silhouette —
where love comes alive—online...

Visit us online at
www.eHarlequin.com